THE WRITERS' TRADE
& Other Stories

Also by Nicholas Delbanco

Running in Place: Scenes from the South of France
The Beaux Arts Trio: a portrait
About My Table & Other Stories
Group Portrait: Conrad, Crane, Ford, James, and
    Wells
Stillness
Sherbrookes
Possession
Small Rain
Fathering
In the Middle Distance
News
Consider Sappho Burning
Grasse 3/23/66
The Martlet's Tale

THE WRITERS' TRADE

& *Other Stories*

Nicholas Delbanco

William Morrow and Company, Inc. / New York

Copyright © 1988, 1989, 1990 by Nicholas Delbanco

The author wishes to thank the Corporation of Yaddo, for its sheltering support.

The stories originally appeared in the following publications: "The Writers' Trade" in *The Paris Review;* "And with Advantages" in *Michigan Quarterly Review;* "Panic" in *The Southern California Anthology;* "Palinurus" in *Salmagundi;* "The Brass Ring" in *Tikkun;* and "Everything" in *The Kenyon Review.*

Library of Congress Cataloging-in-Publication Data

Delbanco, Nicholas.
   The writers' trade & other stories / Nicholas Delbanco.
      p.   cm.
   Contents: The writers' trade—And with advantages—You can use my name—His masquerade—The day's catch—Panic—Palinurus—The brass ring—Everything.
   ISBN 0-688-04732-7
   1. Authorship—Fiction.   2. Authors—Fiction.   I. Title.
II. Title: Writers' trade, and other stories.
PS3554.E442W75   1990
813'.54—dc20   89-35588
                                                            CIP

Printed in the United States of America

First Edition

1 2 3 4 5 6 7 8 9 10

FOR WILLARD BOEPPLE

CONTENTS

The Writers' Trade............................... 11

And With Advantages 37

You Can Use My Name 65

His Masquerade 91

The Day's Catch 117

Panic 185

Palinurus 211

The Brass Ring 233

Everything 259

THE WRITERS' TRADE

& Other Stories

THE
WRITERS'
TRADE

Mark Fusco sold his novel when he was twenty-two. "You're a very fortunate young man," Bill Winterton proclaimed. They met in the editor's office, on the sixteenth floor. The walls were lined with photographs, book jackets, and caricatures. "You should be pleased with yourself."

He was. He had moved from apprentice to author with scarcely a hitch in his stride. It was 1967, and crucial to be young. One of the caricatures showed Hawthorne on a polo pony, meeting Henry James; their mallets were quill pens. They were swinging with controlled abandon at the letter A.

Bill Winterton took him to lunch. They ate at

L'Armorique. The editor discoursed on luck; the luck
of the draw, he maintained, comes to those who read
their cards. He returned the first bottle of wine, a Pouilly
Fumé. The sommelier deferred, but the second bottle
also tasted faintly of garlic; the sommelier disagreed.
They had words. "There's someone cooking near your
glassware," Winterton declared. "Or you've got your
glasses drying near the garlic pan."

He was proved correct. The maître d'hôtel apologized and congratulated him on his discerning nose. The
meal was on the restaurant; they were grateful for
Winterton's help. This pleased him appreciably; he
preened. He spoke about the care and nurturing of talent, the ability to locate and preserve it. Attention to
detail and standards—these were the tools of his trade.
This was the be-all and end-all, the alpha and omega of
publishing, he said.

Mark began his book in college, in a writing class.
His father came from Florence and told tales about the
family—the Barone P. P. who thought he had swallowed a sofa, the passion for clocks his aunt indulged
obsessively, the apartment in Catania where they sent
the younger sons. Of these characters he made his story,
fashioning a treasure hunt: the grandmother from
Agrigento whom the northern cousins spurned, the
legacy she failed to leave but set her children hunting.
He borrowed his father's inflections; his ear was good,
eye accurate, and the book had pace. He completed a
draft in six months. Then the work of revision began.

Bill Winterton was forty-five and given to hyper-
bole. He had been a black belt in karate in Korea; he
had known Tallulah Bankhead well, and Blossom Dearie;
he had heard Sam Beckett discourse on Jimmy Joyce.

He drank and lived in Rhinecliff and was working on a
novel of his own. Mark's book was slated to appear the
second Sunday of July. "That's the first novelist season," Winterton informed him. "Coming out time for
the debs. We want to get attention while the big boys
are off at the beach. Not to worry . . ." He flourished
his spoon.

Mark worked that summer in Wellfleet, at a bicycle rental garage by the harbor; he also served ice cream.
He spent long hours clamming at low tide. He liked
the brief defined conviviality of work, the casual commerce with strangers. He rented the upstairs apartment
of what had been a captain's house. "Everybody was in
whaling," said his landlady, Mrs. Newcombe. "All the
men in Wellfleet." She meant, he learned later, in 1700.
Her house had a large widow's walk, and furniture and
ornaments from the China trade.

He was sleeping with the daughter of a real estate
agent in town. Bonnie returned from her sophomore
year at Simmons to find the local boys inadequate; they
whistled and hooted at tourists, and lounged on the
Town Office steps. They made peace signs and shouted
"Flower Power!" and wore ponytails. They went drag
racing on the sand and passed out drinking beer. She
was small and blonde and sweetly submissive and had
hazel eyes. Her father would kill her, she said.

Mark had read that writers lived along the ponds.
He saw them on Main Street, buying papers or fish,
wearing beards. He watched them strolling on the dock,
wearing caps at jaunty angles, smoking pipes. He heard
them at The Lighthouse, conversing over coffee, and
at the public library, where they donated books. He

told himself he too would be a man with a mission, aloof.

His room had a view of the dock. He had a double bed with a board beneath the mattress and brass bars painted white; he had a chest of drawers and a rolltop desk beneath the window. He organized the pigeon-holes, the stacks of twenty-weight paper, the marmalade jar full of pens. The paraphernalia of habit codified, that summer, into ritual observance. He made himself strong coffee on a hot plate; he bought a blue tin cup. He played solitaire. This permitted him, he felt, to stay at his desk without restlessness; it engaged his hands but not attention. He could sit for hours, dealing cards.

He wrote his pages rapidly, then rewrote at length. The little ecstasy of correction, the page reworked if a syllable seemed inexact, or missing, the change of a comma that felt consequential, the tinkering and achieved finality: all this was new to Mark. He recited paragraphs aloud. He read chapters to the mirror, conscious of inflection, rhythm, emphasis. He blackened the blank pages with a sense of discovered delight.

Mrs. Newcombe's parlor shelf had Roger Tory Peterson and *Songs the Whalemen Sang*. An ancestor had figured in Thoreau's *Cape Cod*. She owned *The House of the Seven Gables* in a leather-bound edition; she had instruction books on quilting and *Just So Stories for Little Children* and *The Fountainhead*. He loved the smell and heft of books, the look of endpapers, the crackle of pages and literal flavor of print. He loved the way words edged against each other, the clashing, jangling sounds they made, the bulk of paragraphs and linear austerity of speech. He recited lines while driving or at Fort Hill gathering mussels; they formed his shoreline certainties while he watched the tide. A phrase like "shoreline certainties," for instance, seemed luminous with meaning; it served as his companion while he shuffled cards.

At Columbia he argued philosophy and baseball with his suite mates; he ate spareribs at midnight and went to double features at the Thalia and New Yorker and took his laundry home. His thesis had been focused on Karenin and Casaubon—the stiff unyielding husbands in *Anna Karenina* and *Middlemarch*. There were parallels, also, between Vronsky and Ladislaw, those weak romancing men. The question most urgently posed, he wrote, is how to live a life alone when urged by a secular power to succeed, a secular temptation to accede—or, as Lewis Carroll put it, "Will you, won't you join the dance?"

We each have known conviction, the sudden flush of rightness; Mark came to feel it then. His book had a blue cover and its title was handsomely lettered. A bird ascended—framed by temple columns—from the sea. The stages of production grew familiar. But that his work would be transformed—that strangers in another town would take his words and reproduce them—this careful rendering in multiples provided his first sense of public presence, the work existing elsewhere also. We grow used to the private response. When someone speaks our name we assume we are nearby to hear. We answer questions asked; we find ourselves aroused by provocation, flattered by flattery, angered by insult—part of a nexus of action and talk. But his career, he understood, was in the hands of strangers—someone who might read the book to whom he had not handed it, someone who might help or hinder from an indifferent distance. The recognition startled Mark. He was

the master of his soul, perhaps, but not the captain of
his fate. He was reading Joseph Conrad and could re-
cite Henley's "Invictus"; such comparatives came read-
ily to mind.

"I don't know you," Bonnie said.

"Of course you do."

"No. Not any longer."

"I haven't changed," he said.

"You're changing. Yes, you are."

She turned her back to him. It was beautiful, un-
blemished; he traced the white ridge of her spine. She
shivered.

"I'll only be away three days."

"You won't come back."

"Of course I will."

"I mean you won't come back to me." She fingered the pillow.

"Make up something for your parents. That way
you could come along."

"No."

"We'll figure something out."

"I wanted to be at the party. I'm so proud of you.
A publication party. I did want to celebrate."

"You'll be there anyhow," he lied. "You go with
me where I go."

" 'Parting is sweet sorrow . . .' "

" 'Such sweet sorrow,' " he corrected her. Mark
flushed at his involuntary pedantry and—to counteract
the rightness of her accusation—pressed her back down
in the bed. She was all the more exciting when she
cried.

                    *   *   *

His parents had scheduled a party. They were proud of his achievement and would celebrate on publication day. They lived in Rye, New York. His father took the train to Manhattan, working for an import-export firm. He dealt in bristles, hides, and furs; he placed orders for Kolinski, Chunking 2¼, Arctic fox, and seal. They were moderately prosperous and happy, they told him, to help. His job at the bicycle shop was therefore part time, a gesture; he drove an MG. It was British Racing Green, a graduation gift. "From here on," he promised his mother, "I'm enrolled in the school of real life."

She thought this phrase enchanting. Much of what he said enchanted her—his pronouncements on fashion, for instance, his sense of the cartographer as artist, mapping the imagined world from its available features. She had two vodka martinis every afternoon at five; he joined her on the porch.

"My son the poet," she said.

"Except it's fiction, Mom."

"You'll always be a poet." She swallowed the olive intact.

His mother liked occasions. She was not sociable and did not attend parties herself. But she welcomed the caterers' bustle at home, the porch festooned with lanterns, the garden sprouting tables and white plastic chairs. She gave birthday and anniversary parties, graduation parties, wedding parties. The house was large. She felt less lonely entertaining, she explained; they should put the place to use. She asked him for a guest list six weeks in advance.

He listed friends from Columbia, his editor, the publicity woman, his cousin, a classmate from high school who was an all-night D.J. His father invited business associates; his mother included the children or parents of friends. She disliked a party at which everyone knew everyone; a party ought to take you by surprise.

She made a habit of pronouncements, and then repeated them. One such repeated assertion had to do with variety, the spice of life, the way ingredients invariably vary. He humored her. He had come to recognize his parents needed humoring; his father's politics, for instance, had to be avoided when they met. His father admired Judge Julius Hoffman. He wished the judge had thrown the book at those impertinent Chicago-based conspirators; he was afraid of Hoffman's leniency, he said. He trusted Mark. He knew his son refused to bite the feeding hand.

On the Sunday of the party, he drove from Wellfleet to Rye. Trucks rumbled past at speed. He reached the Sagamore Bridge in a sudden cloudburst and pulled off the road to raise the convertible top. Tugs whistled in the canal; Mark saw the line squall receding. His book was coming out that day; he would celebrate that night. He opened his shirt to the rain.

There was much weekend traffic; he made New London by ten. He wondered if the tollbooth tenders worked eight-hour shifts. They would take coffee breaks. They would bring a heater with them in winter, soft drinks in Styrofoam cups; they would have portable radios for music and the news. They would have a grandson in Spokane. This grandson played the drums. Mark was learning to provide corroborative detail for his characters: birthday parties, a distaste for lima beans, a preference in socks. "Make a catalogue," his writing teacher had advised. "Make it on three-by-five cards. Know everything you can. Tell yourself the person despises lima beans. Try to decide if she likes snow peas or string beans better, and if she wears a girdle, and if she sleeps soundly at night."

He took the turnoff after Playland and reached his house by two. It was a sprawling half-timbered slate-roofed structure; there was a three-car garage. His mother met him at the kitchen door. "Congratulations," she said.

"I made it," Mark said, stretching. "Six hours on the nose."

"It's a wonderful review."

"What is?"

"You didn't know?"

He shook his head.

"A beautiful review," she said. "In this morning's Sunday *Times.* I thought they would have told you."

"No."

"They must have planned to make it a surprise. It's wonderful. You'll see."

The pantry was filled with salads. There were trays of deviled eggs. The review was prominent, and generous; he had heard of the reviewer, and she made much of his book. "Classic and unmannered cadences," she wrote. "Fidelity of mind and spirit, a tale told with economy and grace." The novel avoided those pitfalls young writers so rarely avoid; she hailed "an auspicious debut." His mother clapped her hands. "They've been calling all day long," she said. "We tried you up in Wellfleet but you'd gone already. Everyone who's anyone reads the Sunday *Times.*"

We all have been assessed in public, whether by

report card, hiring, or review. Our system incorporates rank. We are used to reading how we've done, what we are doing, and in which percentile. But this was new and newly exciting—far more so than the notice in trade journals earlier. He had never heard of the *Library Journal* or *The Kirkus Reviews* prior to their praise. To read himself described as "brilliantly inventive," "persuasively original," was a "heady, yet heartfelt experience"; he took his duffel to his room, and then he showered and changed.

His parents knew an author who wrote children's books. Ernest the dog was anything but earnest—was, in fact, mischief itself. Ernest got into and barely escaped from trouble; he was a cross between a dachshund and Dalmatian—known as a dachmatian to his friends. Mark, nine, disliked the books. His parents thought them cute, however, and gave him *Ernest in the Monkeyhouse, Ernest Goes to Boarding School, Ernest and the Alligator Swamp.* There were elaborate inscriptions from the author for his birthday, for Christmas, or when he was sick. Ernest had a pal called Busy Bee. They helped each other out—when Ernest was being chased by the men from the dog pound, for instance, Busy Bee distracted them; when Busy Bee was slated for the honeymill, Ernest picked the lock.

One day the author came to lunch. His name was Harold Weber, and he had a big white beard and was completely bald. Like one of his own characters, he wore a blue velvet vest. His wife, who died three years before, had been Mark's mother's cousin; they kept distantly in touch. Harold Weber drove a Lancia; his father admired the car. "This is your biggest fan," he said, presenting Mark. "He knows *Ernest Goes to Boarding School* by heart. And *The Frying Pan and Fire*. It's his favorite."

That November had been blustery; the last dark leaves of the Japanese maple beat at the bay window. Branches blew past. His father said, "Let's have a fire," and a voice from the chimney said, "Wait!" "What's that?" his father asked. "Wait, won't you?" called the voice. "I have to get my family out first. We fell asleep."

Mark approached the fireplace and put his ear to the wall. "Hello, little boy; what's your name?" He turned to his parents, shocked. "I've got it—you must be Mark. Ernest told me all about you. You're his favorite person on all Echo Lane." Then the voice changed register, grew gruff. "Hello, Mark. How've you been? Tell them not to start that fire till I get Busy Bee out."

Harold Weber leaned against the mantelpiece. He was smiling; his mouth moved slightly, and his Adam's apple worked. Yet the voice came from the chimney, not where he stood beneath it. Mark said, "You're doing that," and Harold Weber bent, shaking his bald head, raking his beard with his fingers, looking up the fireplace and saying from what seemed like the window, "He's not."

Then there were drinks. There were cheese biscuits and shrimp with plastic toothpicks impaling them on a cabbage, so it looked as if the cabbage grew multicolored quills. "Don't poke me," said the cabbage. "I get ticklish if you poke." Then the cabbage giggled, and Harold Weber laughed. "I guess we'll have that fire," he said to Mark's father. "I guess Ernest helped old Busy Bee to get his family out." "I guess," agreed Mark's father, and they laughed and swallowed shrimp.

That day he knew he'd witnessed magic—not the poor ventriloquy but the invented voice. A creature from a page had spoken to him, Mark, from a familiar place. He adored Harold Weber through lunch.

The party started at six. His father's business partners, his uncle from Arezzo, his neighbors arrived. They congratulated him. They offered wine and a leatherbound notebook and a subscription to *The New York Review of Books* and champagne. His sister's plane was late. She took a taxi from La Guardia and clattered in, exuberant, embracing him. "I knew you could do it," she said. She told him that Johns Hopkins was a prison, and medical school like some sort of boot camp or jail; she hadn't slept in weeks, and then just for an hour with the surgeon on the cot. She laughed with the open-mouthed braying hilarity that meant she did not mean it. "I love the place," she said. "Seriously, kid."

The caterers served drinks. They set out food. There were several pâtés and salmon mousse and sliced roast beef and a whole ham and veal in aspic and caviar and water chestnuts and vegetable dip. Bill Winterton drove down from Rhinecliff. He accepted scotch. "It's quite a spread," he said. Mark was uncertain if he referred to the tables piled with food or to the house itself. "It's a question of proportion," Winterton observed. "Your folks are spending more for this than we paid for the book."

His friends appeared. They drove from Manhattan and Riverdale and Westport and Larchmont and Barnegat Light. They arrived in pairs or carloads and three of them came on the train. Betty Allentuck traveled alone. She had been living with Sam Harwood, his close

friend; she and Sam had broken up that spring. Sam
was on a Fulbright in Brazil.

Betty had thick chestnut hair, long legs and high
wide hips. Her breasts were full. She smoked and drank
and swore with what he thought of as erotic frankness;
he had envied Sam. They brushed against each other
in the foyer, and she kissed him happily. "Your big
night," she said.

"I'm glad you're here."

She kissed him again. "Later," she promised, and
they went out on the porch.

That promise hovered where she stood in the
gathering dark on the lawn. Spotlights in the oak trees
lit the far stone wall. There were lanterns and torches
as well. There were aromatic candles in glass jars. His
father moved among the guests, wearing a pinstriped
blazer, looking like a politician, pumping hands. The
punch was good.

His friends attended him. They asked about the
Cape, they praised his tan, they asked for free copies
or where they could buy one or if he would sign books
they brought. They talked about themselves. They were
in law school and business school and advertising agen-
cies; they were moving to Los Angeles and Spain. There
was a rope hammock, slung between two maples; Betty
lay inside it, swinging, sandals off. His father's accountant said, "Mazeltov," pointing in what seemed to be
her direction; his uncle asked about his plans, what he
was planning next. There were checkered tablecloths
and helium balloons in clusters anchored by his book.
The balloons were blue and white.

Then there were toasts. Bill Winterton said he was
pleased, and Mark should get to work. He hoped and

trusted this was the beginning of a long career. There was applause. Mark's sister said, I want to tell you, everyone, his handwriting is rotten. Scribble, scribble, scribble, Mr. Gibbon. People laughed. There was a toast to the reviewer for the *Times:* may her judgment be repeated. I'm proud of you, Mark's father said, I'm grateful you folks came. Imagine what this food will look like in the morning, said his mother; please everybody take seconds. Help yourselves.

By the time dessert arrived, he had grown impatient. A party in your honor is supposed to be more fun than this, he told Betty in the hammock; it was nine o'clock. Dessert was cake. His mother said, "You cut it, dear," and led him to the serving table. They made space. The cake was large, rectangular, its icing fashioned in a perfect likeness of the cover of his novel. The blue sky and the bird outstretched against it and the pillars with his name inscribed—all were reproduced. He was embarrassed. "Beautiful," they chorused. "It's magnificent." "The word made sugar," said Billy the D.J. "Take of my body. Eat, eat."

There were photographs. Flashbulbs popped repeatedly while he smiled and blinked. His mother provided a knife. "You cut the first slice, author."

"I can't."

"It's the book's birthday. We made it a cake."

"I don't want to."

"Please," she said.

He took the knife and flourished it, then stabbed the air. He wielded it as if it were a saber, impaling, conducting. In the angle of his vision he saw his mother's face, shocked. He advanced as might a fencer, left arm curled above the shoulder, wrist cocked, thrusting.

She would construct indulgence yet again. There were a hundred portions, and he hacked.

"You were wonderful," said Betty.

"When?"

"With the cake. I loved it."

"You're in the minority."

She put her hand on his arm. "When the party's over would you take me home?"

"Is that a proposition?"

"Yes."

The guests dispersed. They took their leave of him as if he were a host. There were pots of coffee for those who had to drive. The caterers cleaned up. His parents and his sister rocked companionably on the porch. "You'd never make a surgeon, Mark," she said. "Look what you did to that cake."

He told them he was taking Betty to New York. He claimed a bottle of champagne, said thank you to his parents, and promised to return by dawn. "Drive carefully," they said. "To the victor," said his sister, and they laughed.

The MG's top was down. The seats were wet. He dried them with his handkerchief, and Betty leaned against him, and they kissed. Headlights from a turning car illuminated their embrace; she did not turn away.

What followed was delight. They drove into Manhattan in their own created wind; she rested her hand on his thigh. The city spread beneath them like a neon maze through which he knew the track, a necklace suspended from the dark neck of the river. At the Triboro Bridge toll booth the attendant said, "Fine night." He found a parking space in front of her apartment, and they closed the car. "I've wanted this all year," she said. "Haven't we been virtuous? It seems like I've waited all spring."

The sex was a promise delivered. Betty took him into her with a high keening wail, a fierce enfolding heat; she flailed against him in the bed, repeating to his rhythm, "God, my God, my God." He was proving something, celebrating, displacing his friend in her flesh; he battered at her till she cried, "I love you, Mark." He wondered, was that true. They drank champagne. The ache in his knees, in his back, the plenitude of travel and arrival and release, the long day waning, the radio's jazz, the whites of her eyes rolling back—all this was bounty, a gift. Each time he entered her she begged him, "Stop. Don't stop."

On Tuesday he and Winterton met again for lunch. This time they ate at Lutece. "Word is the *Newsweek* is good. And *The Saturday Review*." He handed Mark *The Saturday Review*. There was his photograph, and a review entitled "Timeless Parable." Again he had heard of the critic; again the assessment was kind. "I wish I could have written a book this good at twenty-two. I could not, and very few do. There's a major talent here. Hats off."

"Publicity is ringing off the hook," said Winterton. "Don't let it go to your head."

The bumblebee, he said, is by all scientific measure too slow and fat to fly. Cheerfully ignorant of this, however, and to the dismay of scientists, the bumblebee just flies. Winterton flapped his arms. He drank. You've got to learn, he said, to be like that bumblebee flying: just go ahead and buzz.

"I'm working on a story," Mark announced.

"Good."

"It's about discovery. Self-discovery. A boy who sleeps with his best friend's girlfriend, then finds out she's the Muse."

"Don't spoil it by analysis."

"I'm not. I'm only telling you."

"Well, don't." He pressed his palms to his temples and then extracted glasses from his coat. He had not worn glasses before in Mark's presence; he studied the menu with care. "There's nothing that can happen now," he said, "that's anything but a distraction to your work. If the praise continues, if it dies down or changes or stops. All of this"—he waved his hand—"it's beside the point. The point is to keep working, to not stop."

He said this with bitterness, smiling. The first course arrived. Thereafter the mood lightened, and Winterton grew expansive. Ernest Hemingway drank rum, and Scott drank French 75's, and Bill Faulkner drank Jack Daniels; he emulated them all. You can tell a writer's models by which drink he orders, at which bar.

His tennis game was off. He had lost his backhand and his overhead. His marriage was a warring truce, his boy a diabetic, and his secretary couldn't tell the difference between Tolstoi and Mickey Spillane if her raise depended on it; his eyes hurt. No one read Galsworthy now. No book buyer in this room—he raised his arm, inclusive—could tell him, he was certain, where "The apple tree, the singing and the gold," came from, and what was its original.

Mark too recited a verse. "Samuel Smith he sells good beer / His company will please. / The way is lit and very near / It's just beyond the trees."

"What's that?" asked Winterton, incurious, and Mark said he read it in Wellfleet. It was a tavern motto from a tavern washed away. The whalers weighed anchor off Jeremy Point—but all they found was pewter now, a bowl or two, some spoons.

"Mine's Sophocles," said Winterton, "in the Gilbert Murray translation. 'Apples and singing and gold . . .' "

The garden room was full. Light slanted through the windows; women laughed. Mark had taken the train to Manhattan and would take it home again; his car was being serviced in the garage at Rye. They drank Italian wines, to honor what Bill Winterton described as his true provenance; it seemed important, somehow, to pretend they were in Italy. This went against the decor's grain; the waiters spoke in French. "You know where Napoleon comes from? It's a riddle." Winterton coughed. "The question is what nationality was Napoleon at birth? I ask you, 'Can you answer?,' and the answer's, 'Cors-I-can.' "

This seemed uproarious to Mark—witty, learned, apt. They celebrated lengthily, and there was nothing he could not attain, no prospect unattainable. Walking to Grand Central he breathed deeply, weaving. He made the 4:18.

Between self-pity and aggrandisement, there is little room to maneuver. His stomach churned; his shirt felt rank. The train was old. Mark wandered to the forward car; the conductor waved him in. The gray seats were unoccupied, the windows dark. He sat sprawling in the windowseat while the train filled up.

A woman with two shopping bags settled beside

him. She wore a pink knit suit and had a purple handbag and white hair. He made space. She produced *The
Saturday Review.* The train lurched and rumbled forward, and he told himself his father made this trip five
hundred times a year. They stopped at 125th Street,
and then they gathered speed.

He needed water. He wanted to sleep. His neighbor read the magazine with absorbed attention and came,
on page 23, to his photograph. He was sitting on a
rock in front of Long Island Sound. His tie had blown
over his shoulder, his hair was engagingly tousled by
the propitious breeze. He wanted to tell her, "That's
me." He wanted her to know that she was sitting next
to Mark Fusco, novelist, whose first book earned such
praise. He imagined her shocked disbelief, then recognition. She would tell her husband, when she got off
the train at Pelham or Greenwich or wherever she was
getting off, "Guess who I sat next to, guess who I met
on the train?"

Mark was on the verge of telling her, clearing his
throat to begin, when the train braked. Momentum
threw him forward; he jerked back. They had no
scheduled stop. His neighbor had her handbag open,
and its contents spilled. "What was that?" she asked.
The whistle shrieked. He bent to help her gather pens,
a tube of lipstick, Kleenex, keys. "What was that?" she
asked again, as if he might have known.

They remained there without explanation. The train
lights flickered, dimmed. He tried to open his window,
but it had been sealed shut. Brown grime adhered to
his hands. His head hurt. He excused himself to drink
from the water dispenser, but there were no paper cups.
He pressed the lever nonetheless, and water trickled

out. In the space between the cars conductors huddled, conferring. They looked at their logbooks, their watches. The next stop was Larchmont, he knew. He tried to see the Larchmont station down along the track; he saw the New England Thruway and apartment buildings and gas stations and what looked like a supermarket and a lumberyard. The train had been stopped in its tracks. He understood, of a sudden, the force of that expression; he returned to his seat and repeated it. "The train has been stopped in its tracks."

Then there were rumors. The train had hit a dog. It had hit a car. It had narrowly avoided a collision with a freight; the switching devices failed. The President was on his way to New Rochelle, and traffic had therefore been halted. There was trouble ahead with the switches, and they would wait it out here. There were work slowdowns, strikes. The woman to his right protested the delay. Her husband would be worried silly; he was a worrier. He liked to feed the cat and canary just so, in sequence, and if there was some change in the schedule, some reason to feed the canary first, he worried for the cat.

Her husband would be waiting at Mamaroneck. He would keep the motor running and fret about the wasted gas and fret about the timer oven since this was the maid's Tuesday off; since her husband had retired, she called him worrywart. She went to New York once a week. It wasn't for the shopping, really, it was to escape—a freedom spree, she called it, not a shopping spree.

Mark drifted, nodding, sweating. They would know him at Lutece. He would buy a pipe and captain's hat and lounge along the dock.

* * *

The grandmother from Agrigento buried donkey bones. She told her children there was treasure at the temple site, and they ought to dig. They were greedy; they vied for attention. She lay dying by the seawall, seeing her progeny fight, watching them swing shovels and threaten each other with picks.

Her favorite nephew watched too. He had flown to Sicily on a visit from the north; he was torn between two women—a big city sophisticate and the girl next door. The grandmother stretched out a finger like a claw. He mopped her brow with flannel soaked in lemon water; he ground rosemary and garlic and fed her moistened mouthfuls of bread and olive oil. Her house was bright with broken glass embedded in cement. Barbed wire clung to the doorframe like a climbing rose.

"Giovanni?" she said.

"Grandmother?"

Her voice was as the sea on gravel. "When there's treasure, *stupido,* you look for it here." She scratched at her ribcage, then nodded. "You understand, *caro,* the heart?"

He understood, he said. Dolphins played in the white surf. This teetered on the verge of sentiment, said Winterton, but it might be profound.

Then the conductor appeared. His hair was brown, and he wore a handlebar moustache. He stood at the front of the car, expectant, gathering an audience. They quieted. "We're sorry to inform you"—he cleared his throat, repeated it—"I'm sorry to inform you of the cause of our delay. There has been an accident. A person or persons unknown has been discovered on the track. That's all I can reliably report." His voice was high. He relished the attention, clearly, and refused to answer questions. "That's the statement, folks."

Police appeared beneath the window, with leashed dogs. There were stretcher-bearers and photographers; it was beginning to rain. He said to the woman beside him, "I need air." Then he followed the conductor to the space between the cars. "Can I get out and walk?" he asked. "I'm late. I know the way." They would not let him leave. "I might be sick," he said. They pointed to the bathroom door, unlocked.

The bathroom reeked of urine; the toilet would not flush. He held his nose and gagged. He braced himself upon the sink and stared at his reflection— hawking, blear-eyed, pinched. " 'The apple tree . . .' " he mouthed. What was out there on the track found him irrelevant; it proceeded at its chosen pace, and Mark was not a witness they would call.

In the next two hours, waiting, he learned what he could of the story. He heard it in bits and fragments, the narrative disjunct. A body was found on the tracks. It had been covered with branches and pine boughs and leaves. It had been a suicide, perhaps, or murder. It was female and, judging by hair color, young. The engineer had noticed the leaf pile ahead and slowed but failed to stop. By the time he identified clothing underneath the branches, and what looked like a reaching hand, he could not halt the train. No blame attached to his action. The body had been crushed. There were few identifying marks. Bone and flesh and clothing shreds were scattered on the engine, spattered on the crossties and beneath the first two cars. If the act were suicide imagine the anticipation, the self-control awaiting death; if murder, the disposal of the corpse. Forensic experts had arrived to gather evidence. Police were searching the approach roads to the overpass, and all nearby foliage. Traffic was delayed in both directions, therefore, while they combed the tracks.

"I'm leaving tomorrow," he said to his parents that night.

"For the Cape?" his father asked.

"So soon?" his mother asked.

"I need to get to work again."

"We wouldn't bother you," she said. "We'd leave a tray at the door."

"We'd screen your calls," his father said. "We'd say, 'No interviews.' "

"I didn't mean it that way. I left my work in Wellfleet."

"Coffee?"

"Please."

They settled in the living room. He tried to tell them, and could not, what had happened on the train— how his blithe assumption of the primacy of art was made to seem ridiculous by fact. It was flesh and not Karenina that spread across the track. It was rumor, not a cry for help, he heard. What impressed itself upon him was his picture in a magazine, and Betty's lush compliance in, enactment of his fantasy, was how much money they might spend for lunch. Mrs. Newcombe's ancestor spat in the coal grate. Bonnie will not take him back, will work in the Town Library; she runs off with the drummer from Spokane.

He would write it down, of course. Mark made

notes. It would become his subject; he would squeeze and absorb and digest it—as might have, once, the Barone P. P. He would throw his voice. It would take him time, of course, but if it took him twenty years he'd balance the account. He would feed the canary, then cat.

AND
WITH
ADVANTAGES

In the flush of his first manhood, he found himself courting old men. They wrote books. They looked less robust than in their photographs, but he had seen their photographs—less jowly, thicker-haired. They clapped him on the back. They inclined their heads toward him, shaking hands. They liked to see young people; it made them feel young, they declared. Old people need young people as the younger need the old.

This was not a proposition Ben believed in, though he seemed to—nodding, smiling, volunteering help with the woodpile or the canapes. He wanted their help, not advice. He flattered them by imitation, stroking his girlfriend's long thigh. He wanted them to know he would supplant them soon.

He was twenty-six years old. He had published his first book. It had been successful and, in some quarters, acclaimed. His present project, therefore, was the story of his life. It would be cast in fictive terms, but it was nonetheless and recognizably his own—the childhood in Alaska, the mother's early death, the series of surrogate mothers who either ignored or adored him, the loss of his virginity in Rome.

Ben admitted influence. Like Daedalus, he planned to forge the uncreated conscience of his race. Joyce mattered to him greatly, and he called the stockpot "Stately, plump Mulligan Stew." He liked to cook. Once a recipe for escargots worked on three successive nights with three successive partners; he made garlic butter in advance, and kept the white wine chilled. Women came to see him on the weekends, or while their husbands worked in town, or after a day's shopping spree. Often, making love, he considered the distinction between the colon, semicolon, and the serial comma; he had read that others, in order to postpone ejaculation, conjugated Latin verbs. *"Introit ad altare tei,"* he whispered in their ears. They called him elusive, allusive, charming; he did not disagree.

His father knew a lawyer with a client with a carriage house in Yorktown Heights. Ben settled there. He paid only for the telephone and heat—exchanging his weeklong presence and a kind of informal caretaking attention for rent. The manor house (it *was* one, really, in meticulous and detailed imitation of a Cotswold cottage) stood empty all week. On Friday night the bustle of arrival (heralded by headlights, the horn amicably blaring, the smell of woodsmoke on the wind, and, on mild evenings, the conversational clatter, laughter and music and ice) distracted him. On Sundays they would leave. Late afternoon departures (two or three cars often, in summer the convertibles, cars rented at the airport, a limousine with tinted windows) left him, inexplicably—half-glimpsing guests, half-hearing, waving—bereft. Of all the signs of speech, he wrote, the worst is the parenthesis; it heralded and then confirmed its own irrelevance.

The owner of the manor house was a writer too. He was seventy-seven years old. In his twenties he had known Kerensky, Trotsky, Lenin; he had consorted, briefly, with Eastman, Dell, and Reed. He had dabbled in the theater and in publishing; his most recent project was titled *Naming Names*. The first volume had to do with boyhood and young love, the second with his various adventures in the war. He was imposing, and knew it; his white mane of hair and thick-limbed bulk were leonine. This was a word he used. "Leonine" his belly laugh, his satisfied rumble at supper, his confident assumption that the guests about his table were enthralled. His habit of possession declared itself by pronouns. "My Chagall"—he pointed—"my memory of Einstein playing chess, my favorite spinach soufflé . . ."

Ben met him three weeks after having settled in. The afternoon was hot. He lay in the hammock, shirtless, reading Thomas Mann. The book was black-bound, heavy, and he had trouble focusing; *The Magic Mountain* seemed remote from all such buzzing plenitude, the summer's lazy passing. He heard dogs. He had heard them before and did not raise his head.

"Herr Settembrini, I presume."

Ben jerked awake.

"Herr Settembrini," said his landlord. "My name's Slote."

The trick of where he waited backlit him gaudily; sun enlarged him where he stood. "I've got some people up the hill. Why don't you join us for drinks?"

"Thank you very much."

"Six-thirty? See you then."

This conferral offered, he moved back through the trees. The golden retrievers rolled and tumbled noisily ahead. Slote wore a madras jacket and a shirt with pineapples and crimson slacks; the regalia did not seem absurd. It flattered, rather, the austerity of the white hair and head, the inward-facing melancholy of his face at rest. He walked with a slight, shoulder-rolling limp.

Ben showered, shaved, and dressed. He appeared at the agreed-on time; there were others on the porch. He knew the actress's name. He knew the television commentator in the rocking chair, the publisher with a cigar. He felt the dependent independence of a man who knows his worth but knows it not yet known. "Gin and tonic?" offered Slote. Ben set himself to politeness, a deferential attention. He had arrived where he wanted, and would stay.

"What will you do in September?" they asked.

"I'm hoping to be here."

"You've finished school?"

"I have."

"And what will you be doing in ten years?"

"I can't imagine. I know I'll be writing."

"You do?"

He nodded, solemn. "Yes. But where or how or

with what success I can't imagine, I just couldn't say."

He passed whatever test the invitation signified; he was charming, proclaimed Mrs. Slote. He must come and visit, he shouldn't feel confined to that sad cottage down the hill. "It's a beautiful place," he protested. "Isn't it," she said. He brought a presentation copy of his novel, *Widowswalk*. The inscription read "Please keep me on the shelf."

In the next weeks Ben came to grow familiar with the house. He offered to walk the retrievers; he collected groceries and mail. As summer waned he waited more and more for Friday night, its companionable summons from the hill. He wanted to be welcome where they reminisced, to sit in the firelit circle where they laughed and drank. He wanted to play Anagrams with members of the PEN Club and men who earned the Pulitzer and critics for the *Times*. It was not so much their prominence he courted as the sense of past attainment. He was sucking up to history, said his visitor that weekend, Jane; you shouldn't judge a life by liver spots.

"Why not?" he asked. "What better measure is there?"

"He's trying to screw me," she said.

"Who?"

"Slote."

"I don't believe it."

"Have it your own way." She shook her hair free.

The thought that the old man had propositioned her excited him; he took it as a compliment. "What did he do?"

"Licked his lips. Sent flowers. What do you want me to tell you?"

"Everything."

She watched him. "Jesus Christ."

"We're tenants in this house." Ben raised his arms, inclusive. "We can't insult the host."

"I thought it worked the other way. I thought the host gives up his chair. I thought he offers his wife."

"It's you I want," he said.

He bent above her then, and she received him greedily, lifting her knees to his neck.

Gretchen Slote was tall and spare and what Ben imagined as horsey; she would have been devoted to horses when young. Her hair was streaked with gray. She wore it to her shoulders—defiantly, he thought— and often she wore riding boots when tending to the garden. She told him, when he asked her, that no, she had never liked horses, it was the one obsession she had managed to avoid.

"How long have you been coming here? To York-town Heights," he asked.

"Oh, always. I was born here."

She gestured at the valley and the hospital, whose slate roof crested the opposing hill, whose chimneys matched her own. "You thought Slote bought it, didn't you?"

He watched her hands.

"They all think that. Slote wants them to. He married well," she said.

One night he stayed for dinner with three men. They were old and honored, longtime friends: a painter, a theatrical agent, and a judge. The painter kept an

unlit pipe clamped between his teeth; he had thick tufts
of hair in his ears. Hair sprouted from his nostrils also;
capillaries mapped the delta of his cheeks. The agent
wore a turtleneck and tweeds, the judge a leisure suit.
He stammered; the others seemed deaf. At ten Gretchen
excused herself and left them to their brandy. "It's been
a long day," she said.

They spat; they shook with glee. They shouted and
pounded the table and laughed great raucous laughs.
They told stories about women, other nights, themselves when young; they told the one about the chandelier, and poker with that blonde. "You filled the inside
straight, remember?" said the judge. The painter—
Quentin Wallace—took a red and black Pentel from
the marmalade jar by the phone. He took a piece of
paper also and sketched a naked woman with pendu-
lous breasts, long red hair. He did this rapidly, frown-
ing. Then he drew the four of them naked, on their
knees, their penises engorged and ruby-tipped. A deck
of cards emerged from her spread legs.

"Remember Sally?" asked the judge.

Slote laughed. "I carried her memory right to the
doctor."

"What a night," said Wallace. "What a night."

They talked in this manner at length. Ben waited
for the spark of wit, some proof of eminence earned.
They swallowed cashews and chocolate-covered al-
monds; they told elephant jokes. "How do you fit five
elephants in a Volkswagen?" asked the judge. "Two in
the front and three in the back," Slote answered. They
chortled and nodded and drank.

What of the larger life?—Ben asked himself, pouring—what of politics and art, the impersonal issues of

state? They spat into their handkerchiefs; they laughed
and shook and blew.

"You sonofabitch," said Alfred Wasserstrom. "You
cocksucking sonofabitch!"

"An inside straight!" said Slote.

"Come off it, Alfie," Wallace said. "You never took
her home."

This struck them as uproarious. "What happened
to her anyhow? She married, I remember that—some
lawyer from Atlanta."

"Coke, I think."

"He means Coca-Cola," Slote explained. "the Coca-
Cola fortune, am I right?"

They would tell him how careers are made, how
their own were fashioned; they could speak of the late
great. They might describe Manhattan when it was an
easy town, when Harlem was a friendly place to visit
after dark. They had known Theodore Dreiser, Babe
Ruth, Thomas Hart Benton, Josephine Baker, Chaplin,
Chaliapin, Pound. They could explain the usages of
smoke-filled rooms, the proper measure of ambition
with mete modesty, the secrets of longevity and growth.

"Can't drink like I used to," Slote said.

"No."

"You never could," said Wallace, and they laughed.

They had watched the rise and fall of fortunes,
tidelines, hula hoops, and wigs. The spinning wheel,
they might confide, was Sally's little counterweight, and
when she rolled her hips the fix was in. They would
define the wheel of fortune in the age of the com-
uter, missiles, and the laser beam; they could show him
how Arabia—its boundaries, the price of oil—was
rigged.

* * *

One Friday Gretchen came to him. "I have a favor to ask."

He stood.

"I've got to be away." She handed him tomatoes. "It would make me happy—make us all more comfortable, really—if you'd stay up at the house. Slote's been having trouble, and I hate to leave him alone."

"Of course. What kind of trouble?"

"Nothing serious. What they used to call the vapors." Gretchen smiled. "Only that was way back when, and woman's sickness, wasn't it? Now it's *petit mal*. He gets a little dizzy, and I don't like leaving . . ."

"Has he seen a doctor?"

"Yes." she spread her hands. "They've got him on so many drugs it's hard to remember how much to take. And what's for what, and which counteracts which, and what are only side effects. Don't ever grow old," Gretchen said.

"When are you going?"

"Tomorrow. Normally he'd stay in town, but this is the season he loves it out here—and if you wouldn't mind?"

She was wearing mascara, he noticed, and had not before. Her eyes were green. He could not tell if she were flirting with, flattering or condescending to him; these were the relations his experience encompassed. She pivoted on her boot's heel and, looking back over her shoulder, said, "Come for drinks. We'll talk about the details then," and left.

That afternoon he read no more. He balanced his checkbook instead.

* * *

She was going to Virginia, she told him over cocktails; her sister needed help. She would be gone for
four days. Her kid sister had married a golf pro, and
he was off on tour. Juliet had a hysterectomy scheduled for Tuesday, but the son of a bitch was in Hawaii
and not coming back; this was his first season with the
big boys, and he'd ironed out his swing. Gretchen had
offered to pay for the flight, but he'd said, no thank
you, not a chance.

They were drinking gin and tonics on the porch.
Slote had his feet up—thick woolen socks and sandals—and his glasses off. He rested in the chaise longue, half-attentive, drifting. The sun set. Gretchen said
her sister loved athletes and was a glutton for punish-
ment; she never learned, not Juliet. She was the cheer-
leader who believes the quarterback is wonderful, the
girl outside the locker room who could never get over
being cute. So now they'd scrape it out of her, and her
golfer husband was chasing the caddy through sand traps,
underneath the palms.

She apologized. She offered cheese. She didn't
mean to bore him with her troubles or her sister's
troubles. But Ben should know where she was going
and where she could be reached. Fleetingly he wondered if she spoke to him in code; she stared at him
unreadably while her husband slept.

When Gretchen left that Saturday (taking the
Mercedes, leaving him the Wagoneer, clattering down
the driveway as if she might be late, promising to call
from Kennedy and then again from Richmond, kissing
her husband, then him on the cheek), he felt his own
incompetence, the size of the space she filled. "Well,"
said Slote. "What's on TV?"

"It's newstime, isn't it?"

"Yes. Cronkite. The sickness. Do you know what *Krankheit* means?"

"Sickness in German?"

Slote cackled. "He knows." The laugh he gave was high-pitched, false, theatrical—as if there were an audience and the scene were written in advance.

"Can I make you a drink?"

"A fire. Make my fire first."

There was kindling by the hearth; he crisscrossed it in the ash. He crumpled newspaper also and went for logs; a wind arose. The first stars had appeared. A dog barked in the valley, accentuating silence. When he came back in with wood, Slote was in the wing chair, facing not the television but the wall. He had turned off the light. His hair above the headrest seemed dissevered somehow, a white aureole. He snored. Ben knelt to place wood in the grate, and the paper rustled and Slote woke.

"About time-lapse photography. That's what I've been dreaming . . ."

Ben checked the flue. He lit the ash, then paper.

"You know the way they show a crocus pushing up through frozen ground." Slote's speech was thick, laborious. "Then opening, then dying, all in the space of ten seconds. Or what we looked like when young."

The fire took. His face grew ruddy, watching it. "The sphincter valve, for instance. What a triumph of control." His mouth went slack; he slept. Ben poured himself a bourbon, neat, and wondered what he had agreed to. Slote's proprietary power had vanished with his wife. When he jerked awake at nine o'clock, he wanted frozen pizza. They boiled soup.

* * *

As the days wore on, however, he improved. Slote seemed alert at breakfast, high-spirited when working. He sat at his desk in the morning, rummaging through files and reading his old journals, making notes. The retrievers hovered, tails thumping, at his feet. He was compiling memories for Volume Three of *Naming Names*. Ben came down from where he woke to find Slote dressed, the coffee cold, the tabletop covered with sheets and the wastepaper basket full. He had assembled his notebooks, articles, and albums; he had photographs of friends. There were photographs of previous houses also, and naked women on the beach. He slid them across the green baize desk top as if for approval, their breasts emerging from the waves, their laughter-loving mouths displaying teeth. Or they wore jewelry. Or they stood with him, smoking, on dance floors, or waved from the railings of ships. On the back of every photograph, in pencil, he had written their names and the date.

"Gretchen doesn't like it," Slote confided. "Not that I blame her, of course. I used to have this photograph"—he pointed to a blonde in lederhosen, with a German shepherd puppy nipping at her heels—"there on the bulletin board. Christina, my first wife."

"She was German, was she?"

"Yes."

"She's beautiful."

" '*Das Ewig-Weibliche*,' yes. I've been writing how we met and how we married—in Karlsruhe. Long before Hitler, of course. *Habe nun, ach! Philosophie*—you understand German?"

"Not really."

"I'm making a bad joke by Faust. We were very young, we fell in love, we moved to this country, and then she went home." He stepped to the window and stood looking out. "It's the oldest story of them all."

He did not elaborate. He placed the picture carefully back in the file marked "C." "My recollections will be shocking only in their innocence, their pitiable fervor. You're older already, your whole generation is old."

"We were born after Hitler."

"Of course. That has something to do with it also. But during the Weimar Republic there was no such thing as hopelessness. We affected it, naturally. We smoked cigars and drank schnapps and stayed in bed till noon. But everything seemed hopeful, everything was grounds for hope." He laughed. "It's easier to be romantic when you don't know the language. The accent of untruth . . ."

They moved outside. "How's Gretchen?"

"Fine. She's fine. She sends her best."

"And how's her sister doing?"

"We recuperate so quickly when we're young. They're talking of a trip. Gretchen always wants to see Uxmal; I tell her it's too hot for me, and so she takes her sister."

This was at odds with the story she had offered Ben. The tamaracks were yellowing, the Japanese maple crimson, and the wind was high. Slote walked with a black burnished cane, its handle shiny from use. He decapitated goldenrod and slashed Indian paintbrush and grass.

"When do you expect her back?"

"Who? Gretchen? I don't really know. I should
have gone with her, of course."

"She's going to the Yucatán?"

"She might."

Consciously, Ben changed the subject. He was
planning dinner and wanted to know what to cook. He
wanted to show Slote his work. The dogs chased squirrels fruitlessly. He needed an imprimatur, a proof of
merited attention. He hoped for what he thought of as
a laying-on of hands. When he thought of those hands,
however, they were Gretchen's, and smoothing his shirt.

Then Gretchen did return. She was back the next
Wednesday, grateful, full of information about hospi-
tals in Richmond. "They're so *polite*," she said. "The
doctors there. Unless you're Edgar Poe."

In the kitchen, privately, she asked him how Slote
seemed.

"Well. A little tired, maybe."

"Did he show you all his pictures?"

"Some."

"We never had children, you see. I wanted to. He
didn't."

"We've been working hard," Ben said.

He was going to discuss the problem with the fictive life, the difficulty of completion when you know
where you are coming from but not where you will go.
His imagination faltered at the prospect of finality;
Widowswalk had ended with its closure incomplete. He
was planning a scene with a skater, an ice-clogged es-
tuary and the seals in bellowing alarm.

Gretchen said, "It's lonely here. He needs the city's
stimulus. It's time to shut up shop."

The woman skating backward on the ice was wearing gray. He could see it, was trying to write it. Snow would be falling; she let the flakes melt in her hair.

"What about the photographs?" Ben asked.

"When he starts speaking German, it's time to go back to New York."

"Will you come weekends?"

"Yes."

"*Frisch weht der Wind*," sang Slote in the dining room. "*Der Heimat zu . . .*"

"You see what I'm saying," said Gretchen, and rested her hand on Ben's cheek.

That winter they flew to Bermuda. There were available doctors, but not excessive heat. The Slotes rented a house in Tucker's Town—and there was room, Gretchen said. They would welcome Ben's visit and help. They had established a beachhead on the beach; he should join them for a week.

He had a cold; his throat hurt. On the flight south from Kennedy he tried to read, to sleep; his imaginings were fretful. He saw himself behind Slote's wheelchair, with the old man naked and the wheels locked irretrievably; when he bent to free them, Gretchen laughed. She who did not smoke was wielding a cigarette holder; ash glowed and fluttered at the tip. He took a taxi at the airport; it was a dark, brief ride. The smell of salt assaulted him, and sweet fermenting rot on the night breeze.

"We're glad you're here," said Slote.

"Welcome," Gretchen said.

They stood in the doorway together.

"How was your trip?"

"You've eaten?"

He nodded. "Airplane food."

"Your room is back behind the kitchen," Gretchen said. "It's closest to the water and the bar."

"But we've had such terrible weather. Monsoon season." Slote coughed. "Maybe you'll change our luck."

"He beats me every night. At Anagrams, I mean."

"This house looks huge," said Ben.

"It is. It was built for a Grace liner Grace."

The walls were pink. There were candles in hurricane lamps. The floor was terracotta tile, and it extended to a patio with palms. In the dark beyond the railing, he could see the sea.

"How's your sister?"

"Better. She was here last week." Gretchen took a lemon and sliced it in quarters, then eighths. "Someday you should meet her. But she left."

"She's recovering," said Slote. "You should see her in that pink bikini. A delightful sight."

"He's recovered too," said Gretchen. "Can't you tell?"

She offered him a rum called Gosling's—local, dark. He excused himself to change and did so, swiftly, emptying his single suitcase into the bureau by the bed, setting up his typewriter on the desk provided. He was grateful for their welcome and glad to be a part of even this declining. His ears cleared. *Widowswalk* was on the coffee table. "I've been reading it," said Gretchen. "I haven't finished yet."

It rained. There was a fire in the study fireplace. They sat and talked and he would not later remember—though he tried to, though it would matter—what it was they spoke about and how Slote had behaved.

There had been nothing remarkable; he shifted in his seat. They played a game of Anagrams, and Gretchen lost. He and Slote seemed equal till Slote formed "cubeb" with his final letters; a cubeb, he explained, was what you smoked behind the barn in the days when cigarettes were scarce.

This archaism pleased him. He told Ben the language was conservative; it kept old words around in order to remind itself of youth. It did not so much relinquish as accrete. The phrase "relinquish as accrete," for instance, would signify, for Ben, a stuccoed room with cedar paneling, a gaunt woman crossing her ankles and scratching where she said she had a spider bite, the taste of rum and lemon and that inward drifting of the traveler at rest. It was the last phrase he remembered—and the white head wagging, the cuticle he bit that bled, the blur of his tilt toward sleep.

He woke to find Gretchen beside him. She was shaking his shoulder, not gently. "Wake up," she said. "He's dead." He knew he was dreaming; he rose to her breast. "He's dead," she said again. "He isn't breathing, Ben. You have to help him. Help."

Then he was wide awake but panicky; she handed him his clothes. "Dead," she said. "There's no pulse, nothing. I know he's dead."

And it was true, was manifest as soon as he saw Slote, though Ben had seen no corpse before—the eyes rolled back, tongue disengaged, pulse unrecoverable in

the stiff chill wrist. He tried to take it anyhow; he kept
his fingers there. "Forget it," Gretchen said. Her voice
was shrill. "Get a blanket. Cover him."

He did. The body bulked beneath the pink twill
clumsily. He opened the window. Outside, it was dark.
"Are you all right?" he asked.

"Yes."

"What happened?"

"I woke up. I heard, it was almost like, gargling.
Like clearing his throat." She made a vague, dismissive
gesture. "Then he tried to stand, I think, tried to get
out of the bed. And then he just fell back. Like
this. . . ."

She wilted; he held out his arms.

So it became a matter of arrangements, of calling
the police, the doctor, the funeral home. They were
efficient; they offered their condolences and their expertise. Through the long day that followed he felt
himself an actor, acting, emulating attitude—the play
of grief and shock. But in truth he felt embarrassed,
cheated of the sun outside, the intimacy he had anticipated, flying south—embarrassed by his ignorance
of what she felt, or how to offer comfort beyond
the managerial: attentiveness to doctors, certificates,
the albino travel agent who would help ready the
corpse.

He signed and countersigned and called and reserved and confirmed. The officials were polite. They
commiserated with him, nicely allocating sympathy—in
part for his unfortunate loss, in part for his bad luck.
They spoke about the methodology of death in Tucker's Town, and how much Slote had meant to him; they
asked if he had known the history of heart disease and

if the deceased were regular with pills.

"He had a long, full life," said Ben. "He lived each day with the conviction it could be his last." This phrase appeared, with attribution, in the morning paper; Ben was described as a "close family friend."

Gretchen sat dry-eyed throughout the procedures, drinking quantities of tea. She regarded him, he thought, as though he had been summoned for just such an occasion. She had made him welcome for her husband's sake, but he would be dismissed. He had failed her, he was certain, but he was uncertain how. When the body was released and the authorities withdrew, Ben asked her if she wanted dinner, and she told him no. He asked if she were tired, and she said, not really, no; he asked her what she wanted and she said to be alone.

Aggrieved, he sought his room. There, in the increasing silence (a map of Bermuda on the wall, a photograph of a koala bear in eucalyptus leaves, his bed unmade, the closet full of scuba gear—a wetsuit, flippers, oxygen, a mask) he knew he would fly north. " 'Who once flew north . . .' " he said aloud, and misted the mirror, saying it. Sea wrack festooned the rock beyond the window, and a stunted palm. It rained.

The memorial service was scheduled for Frank J. Campbell's. Ben arrived at two. By two-thirty a crowd had assembled, and there were no seats; he relinquished his to a white-haired lady who smiled at him, bobbing. "You're very kind," she said.

Gretchen wore dark glasses and a hat. She listened to the music, marking time.

"My name is Sally Donat. Thank you very much, young man."

He recognized faces: Belinda and Frank Simmons, Bobby Morris, Etta Sloane. Alfred Wasserstrom was there, sporting a velvet bow tie, and Quentin Wallace with an eye patch and a cane. There were faces out of magazines and television news.

The program was succinct. There was music, there were speeches, there were readings from Slote's work. He saw Jane enter, draped in black. She stared at him, or seemed to, and half-raised her hand. He thought of her bruised acquiescence in his earlier withdrawal; he had not seen her in weeks.

They spoke of Slote's embrace of life, the pleasures of his conversation. "There's no point," said Wallace, "no point pretending he's a plaster saint. We should honor what he was. A man with clay feet to his eyebrows, and all the more noble for that." He coughed. "A glutton for life's what Slote was. And a voracious eater at the feast."

"How are you?" he asked Jane.

"I thought you might be here."

"I was with them in Bermuda. When he died."

They stood in the foyer. She wore a black skirt and black boots. "It must have been sudden."

"I don't really know."

"How's Gretchen? How's she taking it?"

He raised his hands, uncertain. "You look well."

"Was it sunny in Bermuda? You didn't get much sun."

"We turned around. I went for a walk once. That's all."

"Are you working?"

"No."

"It's good to see you too," she said.

Alfred Wasserstrom kissed Sally Donat on the cheek. There were limousines waiting outside.

"Are you busy? Later?"

"Tonight I might be." Then she smiled. "But not this afternoon."

She took him back to her apartment, and they opened wine. The rooms were familiar, not strange. The bear rug by the bricked-in fireplace, the Indian clubs and basket of dried flowers, the Miró prints and picture of the swimming team at Smith, the Marimekko bedspread and the rubber tree, the Exercycle by the dressing room and mirror on the mantel—all these remained in place. She said that she would quit the advertising business, it wasn't going anywhere, *she* wasn't going anywhere, she was thinking of production work instead. She was going on location to Nepal. All those sexy little Sherpas, all those Lhasa apsos; wasn't it just typical? Jane asked; I tell them that I'm quitting and they send me to Nepal. Kathmandu or bust, that's me, I wonder if Slote would approve.

"He approved of you," Ben said.

"He was a randy old bastard."

"Yes."

"He loved to celebrate. The idea of celebration, anyhow."

"Let's celebrate," he said.

She moved toward him teasingly. "You want to come to Kathmandu?"

"I've missed you."

"Don't say that."

"It's true."

"You're a randy young bastard."

He bowed. "At your service, ma'am."

"Well, aren't you?"

He placed his hand on her neck.

"Well, aren't you?" she repeated.

"From time to time," he said.

In the country of the blind the one-eyed man is king. He can follow trails that would be trackless to the populace; he may scale a battlement by watching where to climb. He need not be fine-fingered or sure-footed to succeed; he need only keep the claw at a safe distance, and avoid conjunctivitis and the fistful of flung lye. Jane lay with her eyes shut. Without her clothes on, beneath him, she seemed nonetheless aloof.

It is, he wanted to tell her, not always or predictably the fittest who survive. They had made love often, months before; she said, "I'd know you anywhere," and he said the same. They knew each other's rhythm, and kept pace. On the cosmetics shelf behind the bed he saw Slote's photograph—at fifty, windswept, cuddling a goat—inscribed "To Darling Jane." There were violets there also, and a jar of facial cream.

In the morning he drove north. There was ice by the side of the highway, and brown snow heaped at the crossings; the air was thick and gray. His heater was fitful. He would organize the files. He would learn what could be made of *Naming Names*. "How often did you see each other?" he had asked her, leaving.

She drew her bathrobe tight. "Not often."

" 'The randy old bastard.' Is that what you called him?"

"Correct."

He studied her. "Do you want to come with me?"

"To Yorktown Heights?"

"Are you all right?"

She shook her head. The glare of the overhead fixture was ungenerous. He kissed her cheek. She shrank from him. He left.

There was sleet when he arrived. It coagulated on his windshield thickly; the wipers grew ice-lined. His cottage was cold, unlit. The lights did not respond. He stood in the dark foyer, and sleet rattled at the window like a drum. He called the power company and was told that lines were down, were being fixed; the problem had been located, and he should just hold tight. "Hold tight?" he asked, and the woman at the switchboard said, "That's what we're saying. What we're telling everyone. It'll all be over soon."

Ben walked up the hill to the house. He wore a yellow slicker and a pair of stiff gardener's gloves. Where first he had seen Slote in full possession, glorying, where women lay in bathing suits and men of consequence, attended by retainers, laughed, and the lawns were carefully attended to, and the swimming pool, and ivy trained to trellises—where all had been immaculate was wreckage now, hail-pocked. A Coleman lantern hung hissing at the entryway, its light intense. He knocked. The lion on the door, he noticed now, was snoutless.

"It's open," Gretchen said.

"Hello."

"You're back."

"I came to see if I could help. If there's anything or any . . ."

"There isn't. But how kind."

She was sitting in the dark, in what had been Slote's chair. She made no move to greet him, and it took time before his eyes adjusted. The lantern seemed to dance suspended in the air. She was alone. She wore sweatpants and an overcoat and thick ski socks and had a bowl of popcorn at her side.

"I got so used to taking care of him," said Gretchen. "And now there's nothing to do."

"You did so much."

"That's what they mean by comfort. Those are words of comfort, am I right? That's what you say when there's someone in mourning. That's what they mean by condolence."

"I'm sorry."

"Yes."

"You shouldn't be alone," he said.

"I shouldn't? I'll get used to it."

"I wanted to tell you I'm sorry."

"Yes. You offered me words of condolence."

"I'll be leaving."

"Yes, you will."

He rose and said, "The power's out. In my house also, I mean. I didn't mean to bother you . . ."

But she was lost to him, oblivious, her left hand in the popcorn bowl, her right across her mouth.

The path was dark. He descended cautiously; the rutted clay grew slick. He understood nothing, he knew. He had not understood the usage Slote had made of him, the service he performed or what Gretchen knew of Jane. He did not know, for instance, if he should remain. Why should he feel so canceled, derided by vanity; how share in the general loss?

The lights of his cottage switched on as if tripped by a wire; the furnace clicked in. Behind him, on the pond, Ben heard the susurrus of skates. He stretched his hands in front of him as if to break a fall. He could hear the chimney hum. He could see it, thickening, cylindrical, a vertical column of air. What deeds he did that day.

You
Can Use
My Name

"I'll call you tomorrow, OK?"

"OK."

"I'll be in touch, I promise."

"Fine."

"Wait just a minute, will you? Let me get rid of that call. The other goddam line."

"All right."

"I'll be right back, OK?"

"I'll wait."

"Terrific. Great."

So Adam Friedberg waited until the phone went dead. He had expected it; he expected nothing now except such interruption. He had known Richard since

Iowa, and they kept in touch. It was important, they said; it mattered to them both.

Yet Richard seemed to thrive on discontinuity; there were other calls to take. There was always someone waiting, something urgent from the coast. There were always conflicting engagements, a party later on. He called at midnight, two o'clock; he seemed to need no sleep. Since Richard had grown famous, his ability to pay attention—provisional, erratic—had wholly disappeared.

That was what his old friends said; that was how they dealt with it when he drifted off. "He's changed," they said. "He's not himself."

Adam disagreed. To prepare for disappointment is to lessen its effect. "Oh yes he is. Completely himself."

"It's cocaine," they argued. "It's because he's hooked on drugs."

"No," Adam said. "It isn't. He just tries them on for size."

"He's too rich," they said. "Too famous. It's too much too soon. The only calls he answers are from gossip columnists."

"How different would you be?" he asked. "How else would we behave?"

In Iowa City, in 1979, Adam and Richard shared a house: a dilapidated clapboard structure with a wraparound screen porch. They were first-year students in the writers' program—a two-year course of study for the M.F.A. The rental notice had been posted on the Department Office bulletin board. "Writers Preferred," it said. "John Irving lived next door!"

The house was small, steep-roofed, with eyebrow windows on the second floor; the trim had been painted pale blue. The owner was Rutherford Greene. He sold insurance for a living but liked graduate student writers; he understood, he said, what they were going through. He supervised the furnace installation when the furnace broke and had to be replaced. He dropped by to check on things and brought along a six-pack and told long, disjointed anecdotes about his clientele.

Adam and Richard grew close. It was a two-minute drive or six-minute bike ride to campus; on clear days, they walked. They took the same fiction workshop and admired the same books. All that fall they argued principles of narrative, dialogue, anachrony, synesthesia, parataxis, the fallacy of imitative form. "The eighth type of ambiguity," Richard would declare. "That's what we're after, isn't it? The one Empson never dreamed of is the one we're living out. Enacting."

"Which one's that?"

Richard dropped his head and lowered his glasses and assumed his mock-professorial accent. "The eighth variety of ambiguity. Dot's simple, *boychik,* don't you know nuzzink? It's when the writer doesn't know what in hell he's up to. Why he's writing, or who for."

"For *whom.*"

Richard had an ear for accent and Adam an eye for grammar; between the two of them they licked the platter clean. Syntax is the art of subjugation, they agreed; it's knowing what depends on, is subordinate to what.

That first winter they spent time, together, with a girl called Marian. She was a second-year student and had been published already and was an optimist. "If you're good enough," she said, "they'll notice you. They will."

"What they notice her for, *boychik,*" Richard said,

"ain't going to help the two of us. No way."

They discussed their prospects. "With this information explosion," Marian maintained, "there's much less chance that great work goes unpublished."

"How can you tell?" asked Adam.

"We can't. Except all editors depend on making discoveries. And there's so much talent out there now, and so much competition. They've got to find new blood."

" 'Son of The Scarlet Letter.' " Adam laughed. "I've got this book I'm writing."

Richard leered and pulled imaginary postcards from his raincoat pocket. "*Feelthy* pictures stressing togetherness. You like, Miss Miss? You buy?"

She had freckles and thick, springy hair and a swimmer's body; she came from California and wrote poetry. She was twenty-three. She had the kind of exuberance Adam at first believed feigned. He had noticed her that fall, at the "Welcome to the Workshop, Don't be Bashful Bash." She wore a Cedar Rapids Miss Wet T-Shirt Contest First Prize T-shirt; the fabric appeared to be wet. The shirt was pink and red.

Marian was having an affair with a member of the wrestling team; only when it ended did she make herself available. She would sit drinking coffee at The Mocha Cow or wine at The Brown Jug, and call him over and produce the current issue of *Lachesis* or *The Running Dog* and say, "Can you believe this?"— jabbing her finger at the page. There she would be listed as a contributor, and sometimes her photo was also included—wide-eyed, large-mouthed, smiling at the camera and sun.

One of the professors gave a party at his farm. He lived five miles outside of town, and owned thirty acres.

The idea of the party was that poetry and prose should mix; the second-year students played host. "Welcome to Iowa," said Marian. "We're number one in corn."

She was wearing a yellow parka and tight Gore-Tex pants. The sun was bright and cold. It had snowed the night before, and the driveway to the farm was being used as a toboggan run. There were two-person toboggans, and cross-country skis. "Want to try it?" Marian inquired. She smiled at Richard and Adam, proprietary. "Both of you. One at a time."

Adam joined her, lying down, and they pushed off together and she squealed and clung to him, shouting, as they gathered speed. At the bottom of the hill they lay an instant, tangled, panting. Then they climbed the driveway and she lay down again and Richard lay beside her and they did the same.

There were kegs of beer and lamb chops on a grill that the professor supervised, and baked potatoes and cider and bourbon and an open fire, later, under the full moon. "It always makes me crazy," she confessed to Adam.

"What does?"

"That ol' devil moon. When it's full."

"What are you doing, later?"

"Going home with you," said Marian. "They say that story you workshopped last week was really something."

"Oh?"

"The one about the circus barker and the dancing pony. You'll show it to me, right?"

She never slept with poets, she told Adam the next day. It would be too confusing. She loved his prose and his cute little ass and his use of dialogue and that scene on the trapeze.

Marian drew the line at poets, but Richard wrote prose, and the three of them spent happy times together, reading work-in-progress and discussing their shared present and their separate futures. They took a trip to Cozumel, leaving Cedar Rapids in the dank, chill morning and flying through Chicago to Cancún. In Cozumel, however, Adam got food poisoning, and he stayed in the hotel while his companions went to the beach, telling him to rest up, not to worry. They returned that evening, laughing, sunburned, regaling each other with stories of turtles and the astonishing fish. Adam understood that they had slept together and asked—with the lucid, self-pitying clarity of fever—if Marian's choice of Richard meant things were over between them, or if they would continue, and she said of course not and of course.

Later he would wonder if this was a form of betrayal. But at the time it seemed an extension of friendship, an enlargement even. They had shared their work, its pain, and now they added pleasure; this was an additional experience to share.

They spent five days in Cozumel. Adam recovered quickly and ate turtle steak on their last night with no trace of revulsion. Richard's story, "Coral Reef"—in which he wrote about the double-dealing pilot of a glass-bottom boat, and his twin brother the client—was taken six weeks later by *The Iowa Review*.

"I brought him luck," said Marian. "I brought you luck, now didn't I?"

"My muse," declared Richard. "My inspiration."

"Our mistress of fine arts," said Adam.

"*Nous nous amusons*," she said.

*   *   *

When they separated late next spring, it was without regret. Adam went to Kennebunkport, where he found a job with the local newspaper; he wrote obituary notices and covered the courthouse and tried to write feature stories about tourism in Maine and fishing and unemployment and management procedures at L. L. Bean. Marian drove to Arizona and wrote long, romantic letters about the integrity of landscape and a group of potters who were living off the land. Her poetry became a ritual observance; she composed it, naked, after meditation and a pot of tea at sunset; she missed the taste of Adam, the feel of him, and urged him to come visiting and write her every week. He did write her, often, and said he missed her very much and was finding it hard to make friends. Richard had moved to New York.

"How goes it?" he would call to ask.

"It's raining," Adam said.

"And the inner weather?"

"Wet. What's up with you?"

"I'm working," Richard told him. "I'm getting down to it."

"The novel?"

"Yeah. 'Move over, Moby Dick.' How's 'Son of Scarlet Letter'?"

"Slow. I can't seem to get to B. The letter B, I mean."

"This connection's terrible. Is it ship-to-shore, or what? Don't they have telephones up there?"

"SOS," said Adam. "Buddy, I wish you were here."

The professor with the farm had introduced them to his editor. "This guy can help," he said. The editor had curly hair and wore leather clothes and smoked

cigarillos. He and the professor talked about duck
hunting and a buck they'd stalked with bow and arrow
and how the steelhead ran that season up in Michigan.
The editor had offered, "When you have a manuscript,
when you're pleased with something, show me. Really
pleased, I mean."

Adam had no manuscript, but Richard completed
a draft of *Isle of Women* and did send it on and, miracle
of miracles, he called to say, wonder of wonders, the
book had been bought. It was accepted, no ifs ands or
buts. They were bringing it out in the fall. The scene
with the shark and the glass-bottom boat was on the
cover mock-up; he wanted Adam to see.

"What shark and boat?"

"The one where she gets off on the air hose, remember?"

"Air hose?"

"Well, anyway, I want you here. I want you to come
to the party."

"When?"

"Next Thursday. Don't be late."

"That's New Year's Eve!"

"You got it. The start of a new era, *boychik*. Ours."

"Congratulations," Adam said.

"There's movie-talk already. Ryan O'Neal. Mi-
chael Caine."

"That's wonderful," he said.

"So get your act together, baby. Get yourself in
gear."

Of the graduating M.F.A.s, Richard was the first
to sell a book. He would not, however, be the only.
Billy Benton wrote a novel about baseball, and Karen

Adelman published a collection of short stories about life in Hudson Bay. Eric Thurlow won the George Schmidt Poetry Award, and Gillian McDermott produced an account of growing up her father's daughter, hooked on heroin in the fashionable suburb where he ran a clinic for substance abusers. In the two years after Iowa, a dozen of the students made their debut—modestly, in magazines—in print.

Richard proved the success. His book became a movie, and he commuted from New York to Hollywood. He made the best-seller list in Italy. His second novel went up for auction with "a high six-figure floor." The critics despised him; their insults sold books. He displayed a kind of genius for publicity; his new friends all were famous, and he was mentioned at the parties where rock stars and politicians and movie stars would congregate. He modeled clothes for *Esquire* and *G.Q.* Armani sent him suits. Photographs of blondes in strapless dresses, passionate and thin-armed, festooned his bulletin board. Their cheekbones were pronounced.

Adam watched. With decreasing irony, he described himself as one of the "crowd." What he came to understand was that Richard flourished in a ruckus of attention; his subject, he claimed, was "the scene." He planned to chronicle the eighties as Fitzgerald had the Jazz Age and Salinger the fifties. He became a corporation; he appeared on David Letterman and *Good Morning America* and MTV and *Donahue*. He was gathering material for a comedy of manners, a modern-day *Satyricon*. The artist ought to party until the party's over, he told Adam on the phone, since everything's grist to the mill. The pressure of celebrity is a topic too. Burn the candle at both ends; there's double the wax and flame.

"I worry for you."

"Don't."

"I mean, about your health," said Adam.

"No."

"I mean, that stuff they say you take."

"It's good for the digestion, *boychik*. It's called a reality pill."

Adam married Carol in 1982. They had met in Boston, in a Chinese restaurant, when the man that she was sitting with passed out from eating fish. "That's what he calls it," she said. "Really, it's bourbon." Adam assisted them with coats. "I wonder, are you busy?" Carol asked.

He had not been busy, had been nursing his spareribs and soup through the hour till the movie—a romantic triangle, French—began. He told her this. "I've just provided you with plans," she said. "It's lucky, isn't it?" Her escort slumped against the doorjamb, a purple silk scarf wound around his mouth. She wondered if Adam very much minded seeing the two of them home. She looked at him without embarrassment, with what even then he recognized as impersonal desire. It had been compounded by disdain. He did not mind, he told her, although he should have minded, although in time to come he minded very much.

They put Alexander to bed. She was visiting, she said, and had only just arrived. Alexander was her cousin and a problem drinker and a bore. He lived on the outskirts of Concord, in a white frame house too large for him alone. So he had invited Carol to visit, to help with the shopping and furnishing and redecorating and such. "Brandy," she asked, not making it a question. Then she produced snifters and poured. "What else do you help with?" Adam asked. She laughed. "That's for me to know"—she spread her arms—"and you to find out, cousin."

Those were the years when he pretended kinship with the rich, when he "dabbled in the market" or was "involved in real estate." So the names she dropped were names he knew, and her need to confer lineage on any man she slept with was one he understood. Her anti-Semitism, for instance, did not emerge until Antigua and their honeymoon. He had taken as self-evident her distrust of blacks. Her mother tended graveyards where they buried members of the D.A.R.; her father was a barber in Dubuque. She said he had abused her until she was fifteen. "He used to shave me," Carol said. "He liked the lather hot."

At eighteen she set off alone. She became a model in Chicago, briefly, then a buyer for Hudsons, and then a designer for Field's. She lived with the floor manager, then left him for a lawyer she met in a delicatessen; they each reached for the same can of soup. It was Campbell's split pea and ham. Through this man she met other lawyers, commodity brokers, the upwardly mobile and the already entrenched. So she invented a history of boarding school, a childhood love of horses, a proficiency at tennis until her ankle shattered. And distant claim sufficed for Carol; "Blood's thicker than water," she said. She was the second cousin of Alexander's ex-wife. Cousin Beatrice had had the Mayflower people empty the whole house. They came to Concord one morning and packed up all the furniture—the carpets, plate, and pictures—and drove away that night.

Then Carol (with her expertise in furniture, her decorator's eye) moved in. Alexander had money; she, glinting allure. She was twenty-five years old, with a close-fitting cap of curls, high cheekbones, bright blue eyes. Alexander collected his gentleman callers from every streetcorner in town. And as diversion, some-times—although he called it "variety"—he wanted someone to bring in the boys. She complied. That had been why they accosted Adam, she told him, except Alexander was drunk. He had been on a weeklong bender, and the MSG and bourbon did not mix. She had thought maybe rice and fish would help, and all that lukewarm tasteless tea. She had been growing tired of her role as consort, her position as decoy and host-ess. And because she was tired of sleeping alone, while Alexander squealed in the adjacent bedroom, she in-vited Adam to drive them both back home.

Carol was expert in bed. He left her at three in the morning, and they promised to meet the next night. Three weeks later they were married; it seemed the thing to do. She said Sedgewicks and Channings and Bradfords would celebrate when they returned. He did not believe her, but it made no difference; he was trying out the random act, the unconsidered response.

His parents were in Europe. Her parents sent flowers to Concord and a telegram that offered "Many Happy Returns of the Day." "It's the wrong holiday," said Adam, and she said, "That's my family. There you have them. Clowns." Alexander owned a summer place in Truro, and he offered them a long-term lease on condition that they winterize, with a purchase option

in two years. This seemed as good a way as any to settle into marriage and what Carol persisted in calling
connubial bliss.

That had been seven years ago; they did not last
the year. What it took him time to see was that all of
this was fleeting, fraud—an impersonation like others
she would have tried before. Carol's passion for pedi-
greed status, when he confronted it, ebbed. "This too
will pass," she said. Connubial bliss is a lie, she maintained, it's only playacting, it's just playing house.

His wife changed characters, it seemed to him,
constructing a new history. She decked herself in thrift-
shop shawls and gypsy skirts; she wore a barber's razor
on a chain around her neck. She called him Daddy Adam
and started smoking pipes. She stared into the fire
nightly, rapt, arms around her knees. Her women's
support group in Provincetown turned out to be a ma-
crobiotic coven with connections to Tibet.

Their leader, Sara Wigglesworth, had not in fact
been to Tibet. She had been turned back at the border,
but had received there, Carol said, an illumination—an
experience of light. The mountain passes of Nepal were
not unlike the hills of Wales or, come to that, Big Sur.
Kashmir was ineluctably related to Plymouth, and
Bradford's plantation could still be accomplished; Sri-
nagar and Eastham were as one. The point was, Carol
said, to recognize the similarities in seeming opposition, the constant contrariety, the body's single map
and country of the mind. Her sisters, Swami Sara taught,
were the permeable membrane through which life-liquid
poured.

"You don't mean that."

"We do."

"Osmosis?" Adam asked. "That's what you've been studying?"

"Plasmolysis," said Carol. "You've got it turned around. Swami Sara knows much more about molecular transference than you do. She studied it in flounder, for your information, she worked three whole years in Woods Hole. The point is not to take in liquid but to yield it up."

"To whom?"

"To the receptacle," she said. "To the deserving sisterhood."

"That's snobbery again."

She presented her white back to him, the perfect shoulder blades. "You wouldn't understand," she said. "You've never understood. Go back where you came from. Get out."

Where he went was to Manhattan and Richard's apartment on West Eleventh Street. Richard made him welcome. Their reunion was enthusiastic; they had not seen each other in a year. They would have a chance to talk. "A port in a storm," Adam said. "It's exactly what I need."

The apartment had eight rooms. The ceilings had been decorated with plaster pineapples from which were suspended Tiffany lamps; the drapes were in the pattern of the Bayeux tapestry. Framed copies of advertisements for Richard's books (in French, Italian, German, Japanese) filled the entrance hall.

It was elk season, however. Richard apologized; he had forgotten all about a promise to go hunting, a trip he was committed—contracted, really—to make. A magazine was sending him; he hoped Adam understood. He knew Adam wouldn't mind. He repeated his welcome and left for Montana next morning, leaving the key. He would return in two weeks.

There was a study facing south, and Adam sat for hours in the bay window, looking down, watching the pattern of traffic and the sideways scuttling motion of the heads beneath his feet. He was writing stories in the manner of Chekhov and John Cheever; he was influenced, too, by Paul Bowles. So he made Greenwich Village into a kind of marketplace, and what they sold there were the wares of fleshly commerce: influence, survival, a body for the night.

The stories did not work. While Richard moved seemingly-effortlessly from *dojo* to disco to pup tent to castle (his English editor had a "country place" in Scotland, and now the refrigerator was covered with photos of the writer and his editor and wolfhounds and long, pale girls with riding boots, staring; "Have you noticed" Richard asked, "how amateur photography shows everybody smiling? The family album's all smiles. But professionals just glare at you, nobody grins at the camera—right?"), Adam felt adrift. His writing was unearned. The clothes in the cedar-lined closets fit another man. The phone rang frequently but did not ring for him. When he finished the Beefeater and Remy Martin and Laphroaig, he used Richard's charge account to stock the shelves again. "Success, like water," Adam wrote, "seeks its own level. Except it runs uphill."

This was the single sentence he retained; he threw the rest away. He took baths. He thought of Marian often, and attempted to locate her. She had moved from Arizona and left no forwarding address with the Iowa Writers' Workshop and there were forty-seven entries with her parents' last name in the L.A. telephone directory and in any case, he told himself, he would not have known what to say. Then Richard called to announce he would be home tomorrow. He was bringing company, a lady he'd met in Missoula, and they really needed to be alone together and hoped Adam wouldn't mind; he hoped New York had worked for him and how was the weather and how goes the work? "It was splendid," Adam said. "Terrific. You've been the perfect host."

In 1986 he married Esther Mermelstein. She was small and dark and earnest, a potter. She worked at The Left Bank, a gallery in Chatham, and tried to sell to Cape Cod tourists what she produced off-season. She had been born in Riverdale and spent her junior year in Paris and then dropped out of Smith. Esther wanted to travel before settling down; the two sets of parents agreed. She said, whither thou goest I'll follow, I've been in the boonies too long.

The wedding reception took place at Tavern-on-the-Green. She danced the hora with him, and at some point in the evening he pulled out his handkerchief and danced a Greek handkerchief dance. Richard arrived at the party late, wearing dark glasses and a double-breasted white silk suit. He sat at a table, smiling, signing autographs, doing a star turn for strangers, and so entirely vacant Adam feared he might pass out. "Are you all right?"

"I'm fine. Just fine." His speech was thick. "Introduce me to the bride."

"We're glad you came."

"Wouldn't miss it"—Richard pronounced each syllable. "Wouldn't miss this party. Not for the world."

The bride and bridegroom flew to Istanbul, then Sicily, and then the south of France. They rented a house in the Lubéron range; there Esther studied Vasarely and Brancusi and Cézanne. He drank. She had her third miscarriage in Pertuis and came back from the clinic whey-faced, inconsolable. "This isn't working," she said. "It wasn't meant to work."

The Café Ollier was where he drank—its bright beaded curtains clicking in the constant wind. Men in blue coveralls played cards and read the papers carefully; cats foraged by the bar. Sitting in his corner on the day that Esther told him, insisting she had to go back to America and would do so by herself if he preferred to remain (the pastis suspended in water, the hard-boiled egg and bread a stay against confusion, the Cavaillon melons in crates at the door, the flyers for the dog show coming to Cadenet on Tuesday, the mechanic next to him explaining what he could not translate, why their secondhand Renault needed a valve job, was losing its oil), Adam saw—so clearly the vision was tactile; he could close his eyes and taste it—that he had to get to work and that he worked better alone.

They flew to Boston from Paris. The flight was difficult; she cried soundlessly for hours. He drank her splits of wine and every cocktail he could get the stewardess to serve. "I'm empty," Esther said. "I'm drained. I'm all used up."

"It wasn't so awful," said Adam.

"Pertuis." She spat out the word.

"Our marriage, I mean."

"Not for you."

"You said you wanted to travel."

"That's true," she conceded. "But not to Pertuis."
"I liked it there," he said.

It might have been like this, he felt—the random
act, the gratuitous choice—when Noah picked out animals to double in his ark. They barely knew each other
and would have to learn to share. You two will do, the
captain says, you can use the stateroom for your pleasure; you two we'll save from the flood. This is natural
selection, folks; this is the pairing I want. But it did
not mean the gates must close or gangway draw up on
the deck; it need not mean that others are excluded
from the ark. You could not close it off. You could
not draw the bridge.

And there *had* been pleasure in the coupling, he
tried to tell her at Logan; the two years of their journey had brought him much delight. He had made
brothers whose names he forgot and fashioned a goat's
likeness out of *chèvre* from their landlord's farm. He
learned the names of the thirty-two winds of Provence.
He had named them from the parapet of the Pont du
Gard, and in Ialova Spa watched a brother called Ufuk
swallow raki upside down. In Palermo he had seen three
men machine-gunned in the street, and in Catania
watched a car blow up. He had admired Cézanne.
He was glad she went along with him and glad to say
good-bye.

Esther shook his hand at Customs and walked,
formally, quickly, away. His own bags—the steamer
trunk tied shut with rope, the leather pack, the duffel—were searched with meticulous care. He needed
to go to the bathroom, and an agent accompanied him,
saying, "Don't mind me. I'll wait." They made him empty
his pockets; they studied his notebook and emptied his

bottles of aspirin, making certain of the brand.

But there was nothing to discover, nothing he wanted to hide. He had been well past thirty then, with a list of professions too long for the passport—and none of them serious, none of them what he would claim. As a pilgrim he had failed to find salvation, and the very word *sannyasin* seemed disjunct from *moksha*. He did not find instruction in the thirty-two winds of Provence. He would embrace sobriety, drinking only beer. He grew a beard, then shaved it, then shaved his head completely, then grew a beard again.

Richard was in trouble, he told Adam when he called. He'd lost it, whatever it was. "You remember how we used to argue over Empson?"

"Yes."

"What the hell did we argue about?"

"Ambiguity," said Adam. "Its various guises, remember?"

"No."

"Anachrony and parataxis. Stuff like that."

"There's another call," said Richard. "Hold on. Just stay there."

"Fine."

"I'll be right back, OK?"

"OK."

"Parataxis. Christ."

This time he came back on the line and said he needed company. They met in his apartment; it was eleven o'clock. The lights were dim. The air smelled rank, and Adam—who did not shock easily—was shocked. Richard's grip felt slack; he had lost weight. His breath was acetone. You name it, he'd had it, he said; it had been a bitch of a year. He'd lost his confidence. He'd lost the moves. You know how when you start to walk you think about it, practicing, and then you know how to do it—like riding a bicycle, swimming—and don't think about it and get good. But maybe something happens like you break a leg or wreck your inner ear and lose your equilibrium and therefore have to start again and suddenly it's hard, hell, it's impossible, a miracle of balance just to stand. It used to be so simple, it used to be—remember Iowa? Maid Marian?—that all you had to do was ask and the answer would be yes.

"What happened to her?" Adam asked.

"Who?"

"Marian. Any idea?"

"She's in town, she left a message. The world comes to Manhattan."

"I'd like to see her."

"Right. It's class reunion time."

Richard subsided. He sat. Then it was Adam's turn. The sound of sirens in the street, the radiator clanking, the fitful music from next door—all these made him expansive. He spoke about the novelist as nomad—a rootlessness, a restlessness—and how it became second nature. He loved, he said, the traveler's oblivion: the sense that no one knows your name and nobody who knows it knows where to locate you. There are ways to wander that do not entail first class; he had gone unrecognized for years.

"You can use mine," Richard said. "My name, I mean. For all the good it does you. Or did me."

Then he grew animated. He asked Adam how he planned to earn a living, where, and what he had been up to after all. What if he and Adam traded lives, replaced each other for a day, a week, a month—Richard was pacing, gesticulating—hell, a year! They knew enough about each other's pasts to pull it off. He thought it might just work. He'd made so much money he ought to be rich, but somehow—here his voice went shrill—he was spending more than that cocksucking accountant of his allowed. He, Richard, would go underground and Adam could go to the parties. They could trade their clothes and habits and bank accounts and bills. They could do a book together, in alternating chapters, about the way it felt to be an alter ego, to eat each other's breakfasts and write each other's books. He was sweating, urgent, laughing, giddy at the prospect of escape.

They met at *The Right Stuff*. Marian gave him her hand: an elegant, tall woman, with close-cropped curly hair. She carried a red leather briefcase and was wearing heels. "At last," she said. "At last."

"It's been too long," said Adam.

"Hasn't it?"

She took his arm. "I'm so glad I reached you," Adam said. She ordered cappuccino and strawberries; she was in town for a week. She was using the apartment of her in-laws—ex. The only good thing about Harry—that son of a bitch in Chicago—was his parents, Roz and Irv. She loved them like her own actual parents, and better than their son. Harry had his virtues, but all of them were obvious and none of them lasted the month.

Marian was talkative; she ordered a glass of red wine. She complained to Adam about the terms of her separation agreement; she was thirty-three years old and part of the workforce at last. This was a business trip. She had given up on poetry and given up on pottery and her experiment in holy matrimony was a holy mess. Except she wanted children. She wanted them a lot. They'd lost track of each other, hadn't they, after Arizona; was he married now? Did he worry about Richard and didn't it make sense for him to enter a de-tox clinic and did Adam remember Cozumel, that enormous anaconda outside their hotel? She had given up toboggans and sonnets and suchlike; she smiled at him indulgently. Did he remember that Wet T-Shirt Contest and his attitude of perfect outrage even though she won? With her napkin, she patted her lips. Their old professor was dead. Adam was looking wonderful; was he writing and what was he writing and where did he live now?

"No place special. I'm not sure. I'm trying to decide."

"Decide?"

"Richard wants me to move in."

"You're not serious."

"*À la recherche,* or something. I think he thinks I'll keep the creditors away."

"Those demented children."

"Who?"

"The clones, the look-alikes. The ones who want to *be* him."

"So you've discussed it with Richard?"

"He's using you," she said. "He's got this, this *pathological* need to be admired. Don't you see?"

He had traveled here to find—what?—a body touched as his had been by the quickening bloodbeat of grief. He shook his head to clear it; consciously, he blinked. It was not so much her presence that disturbed him—one chatty woman, spooning fruit—as the vivid tactile certainty that they had been intimate once. He saw as if already enacted the way he would approach her, the processional to her borrowed apartment, the keys, the doublelock. He imagined as if actual the way she would receive him, the comfort in mourning, the candlelit dark. Marian would hunt in him as he in her the trace of their shared passion, how they were abandoned together. "Excuse me," he said, leaving. "I've got to make a call."

HIS
MASQUERADE

This happened at Clint's farm. You know the place. Cossayuna is a village twenty miles from Saratoga Springs; it waited, with a kind of grim gentility, for the prediction of real estate agents ("Can't miss," the agents promised—"Just look at this beaming, this vista, do the demographics . . .") to come true. Clint bought the farm before he married Kathryn, in 1978. He would sell it four years later, at a loss. He had a small inheritance and large ambitions then—and the place approximated a gentleman's retreat. He called it "Farm and Content," and, sometimes, "Symbolic Farm."

He was hoping for tenure at Skidmore, and working on a book. He wanted to combine the poem and

the essay; they married in the spring. The house was
brick, with a central chimney and slate roof. There were
three outbuildings: one used as a garage and two for
storing hay. There were sixty acres, "more or less," according to the deed; the land had been measured in
chains.

His wife came from Chicago. She had been raised
with horses in the summer, and she wanted to fix the
small barn. They intended to add a corral. That winter
the pipes froze, and the barn's east-facing roof buckled
under ice. He and Kathryn sat huddled in the kitchen;
he was certain the windows would crack. How can glass
be so warm on the inside, he asked her, and be so
bitter out? This house has stood two hundred years,
she told him; it will last one more.

He doubted it. His work was going poorly. He
had been teaching Melville, and the power of darkness
compelled him. He said, "November in my soul" at
intervals, aloud. Between Bartleby and Billy Budd
there's not much margin for hope; between the tongue-
tied and the resolutely silent, how to stake out speech?

"You've got what they call writer's block," said
Kathryn. "That's the trouble, isn't it?"

"No."

"So what's the trouble? What do you need?"

"Something to write for. About."

"The world is full of instances." She was admoni-
tory this way often, possessed of a kind of conviction
he both envied and disliked. She could dismiss in a
minute what it took him months to accept.

He added wood to the Resolute. "I'm trying to
find one. One instance, I mean."

Kathryn had been baking bread. She cleaned the
marble slab.

"Like what happens to this window when it's twenty below and eighty degrees by the stove. Why it freezes, why it melts."

"It's time to order seeds."

"I love you very much," said Clint. "Except I wonder why we're here."

"The spring list came from Burpee's." She pointed to the catalogue. "That's one good reason, isn't it?"

"Is this the asparagus year?"

"It's a commitment," she said.

Asparagus beds take three years to establish, and he doubted if they would be there to eat the first result. It was an act of faith in continuity that rendered him uncertain. Belgian endive is a two-year proposition; he proposed endive instead. Their own third anniversary would come on April 10.

"Let's have some music," she said.

The dark outside was palpable. He saw ripples in the window glass. No matter how he misted it, the asparagus fern turned brown. He played Fats Waller and then the Mendelssohn octet and added wood at intervals to the hissing stove. He would speak next afternoon on the undercutting irony of Melville's title *The Confidence Man*. All confidence had fled. There were raisins and walnuts and honey in Kathryn's rising loaf; he did not know how to proceed.

That Wednesday night they gave a party for the poet passing through. He was coming to Skidmore to read. His name was Samuel Tench Hazeltine—and, as they would come to learn, he called himself by all three names at whim. He came to dinner with Clint's chairman, and their wives. It snowed.

Kathryn prepared boeuf en daube. She used the

recipe from *To the Lighthouse,* and looked—distracted,
fine-boned, inward—just like Virginia Woolf. Clint told
her this while they were setting the table. She smiled.
"Have you made salad dressing?"

"No. I will."

"Eloise Macallister's a bore." She produced the
garlic and the garlic press. "I feel as if she's judging us.
As if she thinks *she's* chairman, and the question of your
tenure rides on the dessert . . ."

"What's for dessert?" he asked.

"I'm serious. She's so *judgmental.* Coeur à la crème.
Mousse torte."

He smacked his lips. "My favorite."

"Who is this poet anyhow?"

"Hazeltine. He's good, I think. He comes from
upper Michigan and writes complicated rhyming things
about bears and sleeping with his leman in the
snow."

"Leman?"

"Darling. It's an early word for darling."

"Christ," she said. "I bet Eloise just loves him."

"No," said Clint. "I mean it. He is good."

They worked, then, in companionable silence—
setting out the candles, her family's silver, letting the
wine breathe. Outside, the snow had slackened; a plow
passed. The moon appeared. He was responsible for
college functions of this sort—the reader's series, the
symposium on Caribbean literature, the memorial lec-
ture endowed by the widow of the previous department chairman, having to do with myth.

Hazeltine, however, had not been Clint's idea. He
had been sponsored the previous year by the senior
poet at Skidmore. Then the poet—intensely anxious,

ferrety, with a red wisp of beard—took a leave of absence. He claimed he needed drying out, but Clint
maintained the preposition was wrong; he needed drying
up. He was not missed. His skin had flaked in patches.
He went to Florence with his lover, the quattrocento
art historian "big in Botticelli"; they adored Italian
cooking and called each other *caro* in the halls.

Hazeltine's *Selected Poems* had recently appeared.
Clint stocked six at the college bookstore, and bought
one. He read "Caribou and Booster Chair," "Both
Beautiful, One a Gazebo," and "Pica's Pique" with irritation; they were too clever by half. They preened.
Yet something contrary struck him in the formulaic
punning, the wordplay and formal invention—some
undercurrent to the verse he wanted to call bardic: a
dark demented chanting held in check by wit. It was as
if the poet, knowing his own power, declined or was
fearful to use it—"growing grim about the mouth."

"What about his wife?" she asked. "Do I take her
shopping? Or is that part up to Eloise?"

"Don't be angry. I'm grateful. You know that."

"Of course." She went into the downstairs bathroom to apply her face.

They arrived two hours late. Frank Macallister, the
chairman, came in first. "Whooeee!" He clapped his
hands. "Not fit outside for man nor beast." He did his
imitation of W. C. Fields. "We've got to be crazy," he
said.

Dark shapes surged behind him, slapping at the
air. Kim Hazeltine was blond. She was, he knew from
jacket copy, born on the same day as Samuel; they were
forty-six. There was much bustling apology—the plane

was late at Albany, the roads bad, the luggage lost—
not lost exactly but delayed, the change in Pittsburgh,
the weather advisory, and having made the wrong turn
at that intersection three miles back; how did you ever
find this place? how about a little privacy? are all those
cows your neighbors? I could use a drink. . . . It took
him some time, therefore, to disentangle his guests from
each other, their coats. The mudroom was cold. He
closed his eyes an instant, tilting up against his own
blue parka ("The Down Syndrome," Kathryn called it),
making space.

"I'm glad you're here," he said. "We're very glad
you made it. Welcome, all."

"I know your work," said Hazeltine.

His hand was limp. He was taller than Clint, pot-
bellied, oddly awry—as if he had gained weight or lost
it recently. His cheek twitched. He produced a pipe.
"What can I get you to drink?" Clint asked. Macallister
was pouring.

"You're good," said Hazeltine. "That's the reason
I came. I'm here to teach you everything you don't
already know."

"He means it," said his wife. "He wants to save
you. Scotch."

She had a wide engaging smile that he thought in-
sincere. He found the J & B. "They're real," she said.
"These emeralds." She lifted her chin at him, arching
her neck. "I know you're asking, are they real? They
are."

Kathryn offered cheese.

"What are you working on?" the poet asked. "What
have you been up to, lately?" He filled and lit his
pipe.

Eloise Macallister had substituted heels for boots. "These winters. I don't understand how we manage. Every year I tell myself it's positively final, it can't go on like this . . ."

"Are you hungry?" Kathryn asked.

Macallister gazed at her greedily. "I am, my dear. I am."

They moved toward the Resolute, its spreading warmth. "We never see you anymore," Eloise complained. "Hiding out here, just you two. Rusticating."

"Is that what they call it?" asked Kim.

Hazeltine held out his glass. "What are you working on?" he asked again.

Then Kim was at his side. "Poor darling. No convert in *weeks*."

"Her husband's keeper. Call me Sam." He jangled ice. "It's scotch."

Clint poured. "Not much," he said. "Old Herman."

"Your poem on 'His Masquerade.'" They drank. "It's good, you know. You're good."

"This food won't wait," said Kathryn. "I *am* sorry."

"It's our fault," pronounced Macallister. "We're starved."

"The trouble with poems," said Eloise, "is nobody remembers them. It's impossible these days to remember poetry. Because it doesn't rhyme. The poems, I mean."

"His do." Clint raised his glass to their guest. There was salmon soufflé, and dill sauce. There were Kathryn's own baguettes.

" 'In Flanders Fields,' " Eloise persisted. "I was

forced to learn that one. I forget who wrote it, even, but I learned it all in second grade. I stood up in front of the class. 'In Flanders fields the poppies blow . . .' "

" 'Between the crosses, row on row,' her husband joined in, and they both recited. " 'If ye break faith with us that die, we shall not sleep, though poppies lie . . .' "

"It's 'us that go,' " said Kim. "And then 'the poppies blow.' "

"Well anyway," said Eloise. "You get what I'm trying to say."

"This soufflé is terrific," said Clint. He made a point of praising Kathryn's cooking, and it did deserve the praise. "Anyone ready for seconds?" Hazeltine held out his glass.

In this fashion the evening proceeded. The poet drank great quantities of scotch. He spoke in high, staccato bursts about the town of Charlevoix, the Indians, the French, the lilac bushes that the voyagers there planted, and the indiscriminate screwing—Excuse me, he turned to Eloise, but there's nothing else to say—they're not like the English, not fastidious or racist, they left lilacs and babies all over northern Michigan, but they weren't what you'd have to call settlers, not the Jesuits, not Père Marquette. The inward exploration, westward ho!, synecdoche, the part representing the whole . . . Synecdoche, said Kim, isn't that a town near this one, the one catercorner to Troy? They laughed. They spoke rapidly, shrilly, of life on the road, the woodpecker nattering jargon of praise, the strangers with their hands held out—not you, of course, he turned to Clint: you're exempted, brother, *ego te absolvo*—for

healing and reference letters and book jacket blurbs
and advice.

The boeuf en daube was a success. Macallister said
"Encantado" to Kathryn, and he kissed the fork. Clint
wondered what she thought. Her composure was gla-
cial and subject to cracks. He asked her, "Can I help?"

"What you don't understand," Hazeltine continued, "is coming up short at the fence. Is just simply
losing your nerve. Is figuring that all the games aren't
worth the candle. Help?"

"He means with the dishes," said Kim. "I'm sure
that's what he means."

"Our Clint is always helpful," said Macallister. "He's
always there in the department pinch." Then he leaned
across the table and pinched Kathryn's cheek. She drew
back.

"Like when the Dean was cutting your budget, remember?" Eloise appeared not to notice; she turned to
Clint, benign. "When he took a head count at that
reading last November, and came to the conclusion
poetry's not popular."

"Cost-efficient, was how he put it. It was the yard-
stick he used."

"We'll pack 'em in tomorrow."

Clint went to the kitchen for salad.

"Of course. Now Tench is back in town." Kim said
this with a high, bright laugh.

"Scotch," the poet said.

There were reserves in their abandon, assessments
of inconsequence Clint shared. He was gratified to think
they were in league. They drank their way through salad
and dessert. "If someone asked me," Eloise declared,
"what tree I'd be—we play that game—I'd answer the

Dutch elm. There are so few examples of them left."

"What *twee* are you?" asked Hazeltine, making his voice shrill. "What twee are you, fwiend Clinton?"

"Elm," asked Kathryn. "Why elm? They're blighted mostly, aren't they?"

"Maybe that explains it," said Macallister, sentenious. "The noble elm at risk."

And suddenly the six of them were busily assessing trees—the kinds of tree or bush they'd be, the varieties of weather, scent, time, taste. He himself was willow, Hazeltine proclaimed. Large and spreading and yellow in springtime and sucking up liquid and sentimental and trash: a trash tree, willow is . . .

"What's all this got to do with poetry readings?" asked Eloise. There was strawberry sauce on her cheek. " 'In Flanders Fields,' remember? That's what we were discussing."

"You were, darling," said her husband. "Only you discussed it."

"I prefer not to," said Clint.

They left at two. He and Kathryn carried in the dishes; there was much stumbling about in the snow. The car lights flickered, blazed. He watched them through the pantry window, wreathed in the white smoke of the exhaust. They seemed ceremonial, wiping windshields with attention, meticulous about the doors. Snow was falling lightly, noiselessly; he watched the car drift down the hill. "What did you think of them?" he asked.

She scraped plates. "We don't need to do this. We can leave it for the morning."

"Just the food." Clint produced Saran Wrap, flourished and tore it. "I'll put the cheese away."

"He seemed desperate."

"Hazeltine?"

"Yes. He was talking to himself. He was making connections like crazy, but they made no sense."

"I'm not sure I agree with that."

"You heard him better, maybe. I was in the kitchen, being pawed at by Macallister." Kathryn shook her head. "What sort of sense did he make?"

"Huck Finn and Mickey Mouse. Don't laugh: there's the problem of how to approach them. Do we read them the same way? Arguably they're masterworks, creatures of inspired inventiveness, right?"

"Right."

"And they both give pleasure, both engage our interest and make us laugh or cry." He stretched. "So what's the difference, really; why should we as readers think the one must be taught and the other ignored?"

"He can take care of himself." She pondered this. "He doesn't need the sponsoring. Mickey Mouse, I mean."

Clint wrapped the mousse torte carefully. "Why is *Moby Dick* a better book than *Jaws*?"

"Did you notice?" Kathryn asked, "how Eloise pricked up her ears? When he was praising you."

"The argument from weakness. My enemy's enemy can't be all bad—so too with my friend's friend."

"If that's what happens to success, I'd rather be a . . ."

"Failure?"

"Let's get some sleep," she said.

*   *   *

Next morning he drove to the school. He followed a snow plow on Route 29, and trucks spewing
sand. Hazeltine was in his office, holding forth. There
were students at his feet: Betsy with the long black
hair, Jill the tennis player, the twins from New Orleans. They wore sweaters and high leather boots. They
had their notebooks open and were taking notes. "Hey,
buddy," said the poet. "We're using your office, OK?"

They were asking Hazeltine whom they should
read; they asked him how he wrote—if he used a typewriter or pen. They asked him what hours he worked,
and how he first got published, and when he discovered he wanted to write, and what he was working
on now.

Hazeltine wore the same clothes as on the night
before; he had not shaved. He chewed his pipe; his
eyes were red. "Bright kids here," he wagged his head.
"Except they don't know shit from Shinola. What have
you been teaching them?"

"The usual."

"Apollonius of Rhodes," he said. "That's who they
ought to be reading." He swept his hand dismissively
across the shelf. "Not this anthology shit."

Outside, the wind was high. The pines by Pala-
mountain Hall were snapping, shaking, sprung. Snow
cascaded whitely. " 'Pied beauty,' " Clint announced.
"Until I knew you'd come to class, we had Hopkins
scheduled. He's up for discussion today."

"Let's talk about *your* book."

Betsy with the long black hair leaned forward,
showing cleavage.

"Let's find out why you're writing it," said Hazeltine. "Or not."

The twins from New Orleans—Kiki and Kay Kay, though he never could be certain which was which—turned to him, expectant. "Oh please," they urged him. "*Do.*"

"Let's talk about your work instead," Clint said. "We've been reading 'Quahaug Chowdown.' 'The Sunrise Downer.' " He smiled. "The ones in the anthology."

"I asked first," said Hazeltine.

"You *never* tell us what you're writing," said the tennis player. "*Please.*"

Trapped by all their emphases, cornered in his office, Clint began. He wanted to write the chapter on whaling from the whale's point of view. He knew that sounded hopeless. He knew it smacked of good intentions, bumper-sticker pap like "Save the Whales." Remember, he asked them, that great blue plastic whale in the Museum of Natural History—its enormous hanging shell? Well, imagine what it feels like to be polishing the eye, suspended with a feather duster and a mop, snouting up through impossible watery bone-crushing weight after air, then diving again, blowhole full. Imagine the bottoms of boats. That was what—he warmed to this—a whale would see, or sense, inconsequential timber preparing to be jetsam where it yawed. There would be wood. The chapter would splinter to stanzas. There would be metal, no more than a pinprick but lasting. There would be rope, the pilot fish, the plankton; the school in its tail's wake would scatter. Down, down, down it sounded: blubber, blood, and hemp.

He stopped, surprised. He did not usually permit himself such language, the intricate echo of lies. Hazeltine was grinning, lighting up his pipe. "It's fine insofar as it goes."

"But?"

"But it goes insufficiently far."

They looked at each other in pure opposition. "Professor talk," said Clint.

His students closed their notebooks. It was time for class. They apologized. They stood.

Confidence, Clint told them, is the mutuality of trust. That is its root meaning, the force of the term; we confide in each other, we grow confidential. A man who trusts himself is confident, as if the body knows the mind, the mind the spirit, the right hand the left. Yet a "confidence man" is not to be trusted, though he engender confidence—being of respectable appearance and address.

We have all had the experience of dislocation, a sudden ringing in our ears or floaters in our sight. Vertigo and masquerade and the question of identity are commonplace in film and fact; what do we know and how do we know it and when do we make up our minds? Imagine for a moment that a stranger comes toward you, smiling, affable, rolling up his sleeves as if to demonstrate that there is nothing hidden there. He praises you; he if full of high-flown flattery because you volunteer. His hat has a rabbit, however, and his handkerchiefs are knotted and his rings ring hollow; he says he can cause you to levitate, to rise in the air on a chair.

There is something pleasing about his assurance, his smug conviction he can manage because he has managed before. He takes your weight into account.

He places your hands on your knees; he tells you to relax. He waves his hand near the slats of the chair in order to prove there are no wires; he avoids the filaments attached to the headrest and legs. Throughout his patter and performance, he glances into the wings.

Why confide in strangers when we keep silent with friends? Why give ourselves to lovers when their files are confidential, their health histories unknown? Melville's book is "Dedicated to Victims of Auto Da Fe." Are we not all such victims; do we not walk through doors routinely, or drive into enclosing darkness, or dive into clear water of uncertain depth? We speak of chance encounters or an accident narrowly missed. What we mean is we are confident of gravity: the chair will not rise up unaided. Confidence is not the spurious confession, the revelation opaque in its false clarity, the card up the dealer's rolled sleeve. It is knowing what you will accomplish, what you won't; it is knowing what you know and what you don't.

Kim and Eloise and Kathryn had been shopping. They met at Mrs. London's Restaurant and displayed to the men what they had bought. The table seemed too small. There were angora sweaters and a photograph of Saratoga Water being sold from a horse-drawn wagon. Kim loved to shop, she said. She confessed she was compulsive but could always give it back. Or to the Salvation Army, or we can have a tag sale; I've spent your check already, dear, she said. Whenever we're too crowded we just buy a bigger house . . .

There were garnet cuff links; there was a box of chocolates; there were coral beads, a pair of gloves, black ankle boots, a hat. Eloise, too, was talkative. She had bought an espresso machine. "After last night's feast," she said, "we decided we just had to have one. We need it, don't we; it's a business expense. You can go a lifetime not knowing what you need." She put her hand on Kathryn's wrist. "You'll show me how to use it, won't you, the proportion of coffee exactly?"

Kathryn promised. Samuel—he was referring to himself in the third person now—said they must come to Michigan and visit Tench and Kim. The dogs, the horses, whitefish, the dunes, the anapestic trimeter of town names, their involuntary wisdom: Betty Groeze. It means *Bête Grise,* he said, a place where bear roamed freely once, or something tameable only by pronunciation, ignorance, and guns. He studied Clint. "But you're suspicious, aren't you? You wonder what Samuel's after."

"Yes."

"Greatness."

"He's joking," Kim said. "Pay no attention."

"He has never been more serious," said Hazeltine. "Not ever in his life."

"He means it," Kim told the others. "He does."

"Either you come back with us or Sam's staying here."

In the motel, after lunch, he expatiated on art. It was not a luxury but a necessity, not only light but air. When they made shelter in the caves they started painting walls. In the long winter nights we whittle shape. We whistle when alone. Why then should this be just a pastime or sport, a casual encounter for the weekend or on Wednesday night; why should we let jealousy distract us, or petty envy, ambition's shrunk shank? "Don't piss away your life." He rubbed his low belly; he yawned. "Don't get suckered in by this, by what you think you're working for." He waved at the boxes in front of the closet, piled about the bureau: Kim's booty for the day. "A nice place you got here. A nice place to visit." He sat on the complaining bed, then threw himself backward and slept.

Clint and Kathryn, the previous summer, had gone to Nova Scotia; they talked about it as a way to live. It was cheap and manageable, protected by the Cabot Trail and beyond the reach of academe; if they had to leave Cossayuna, this could be a refuge and escape. The sea was cold. The lobsters, however, were plentiful; on Cape Breton they made camp. They joked about life lived among subarctic flora, the edible tundra for lunch. "Let's have some edible tundra," Clint would say, and make camp coffee and Spam. They spent ten days on the Cabot Trail, clambering on rock.

In Dingwall, near Meat Cove, they found a house for sale. The schoolteacher, Mrs. Helen Borden, was planning to retire. Her husband had recently died. She showed them through the rooms and pointed to the bay, a neck of rocks where the property line ended, a garden, a toolshed glazed with rain.

The price was low. "There's a carpenter," she said. "His name is Alec Moore. He'd like to have a go at it. He'd live here when you don't." She regaled him with the virtues of the neighborhood, the value of the property, the pleasurable prospect of a future in the Maritimes; there would be positions in the school system for literate persons; Clint could have her job. The post office, too, needed help. "Alec lost an arm," she said, "when he was a fisherman. But you should see the things he manages with just the one he's got."

The afternoon wore on. Her enthusiasm wearied them. The more she praised the place, the more they grew suspicious of her decision to sell. "Real oak," she said, "this flooring. And we've never had a leak. Not since he patched the roofing in, let's see now, '64."

They met Moore in the driveway, his sleeve pinned to his shirt. He had close-cropped hair, a sailor's lurch, advancing. He reeked. "This is Alec Moore," she said. "How nice he happened by." Alec proferred his good right hand. His nose was bulbous, red. He said they'd find it dull in winter unless they had a hobby; he had a hobby, himself. He was interested in model planes and fashioned them from balsa wood; there's nothing like a helicopter made of balsa wood to help you pass the time. He lifted his sleeve at Kathryn, smiling. He'd gotten used to making do, to doing without, he wasn't complaining, but eighteen foot of snow could make a person impatient, he hoped they had hobbies to help pass the winter, young marrieds like you are, you two.

Mrs. Borden said, "Come out of the rain, would you kindly?"

Beer bottles littered the shingle. Gulls preened. "Excuse me," Alec said. "I need to get on with it, Helen." He bowed. "Good afternoon to you both." His courtesy was drunken, his deference excessive. The thin band of light on the western horizon shut off as if with a switch.

Later, at the lodge, they talked about a winter with eighteen feet of snow. "No wonder they drink," Clint said. "No wonder it's so cheap."

"This too will pass," Kathryn said.

They both used that expression. It gave a kind of certainty to progress, the promise of endurance before anything endured.

* * *

The hall was full. Clint thanked the audience for coming, the department for its sponsorship, the memory of that deceased chairman who made this evening possible. He tried to be yet parody the smiling public man. He shifted tone, however, when introducing Hazeltine; he borrowed phraseology from our guest tonight. The arc of the intelligence, the vector of the metric drive, the circumference of reference, the radical radius squared—all these figure in what I would like to call the geometry of love. Whatever we might mean by this has something to do with poetry also, the feel of the moss underfoot while you wait, the way the black bear and steelhead conspire, or, in that memorable stanza, copulate in foam that is not sea spume but sludge, the industrial park of the soul. He ended with a flourish, to applause.

What followed was astonishing. Hazeltine wore black. He had brought a mandolin and flute. He strummed and blew and spoke with a high, keening wail; he stamped his foot for emphasis and overstated rhyme. "Howl," and "Who'll," for instance, and "gravid" and "beloved" were matched pairs. His voice was thin, his music mediocre, his attitude both self-effacing and pretentious; he kept his eyes closed. Clint laughed, or wanted to; he did not look at Kathryn, for fear she would laugh too. Macallister coughed, shifting in his seat. "Whatever you were ever," chanted Hazeltine, "come over here, come near; whatever you wear never, don; come on." This rhythmic burble soothed him, seemingly; he swayed and rocked and sang.

His body *was* the language, his thick throat the flute. "Bear, bear, bear," he chanted, cuffing the microphone as if it were salmon, pawing the stage like a rock.

"The showman, the shaman." He danced. His face went slick with sweat. He had the long poems by heart. He looked at the twins, reciting, as if it were to them he spoke, for them he wrote; he worked his way—in the second stanza of "Victus"—up to fever pitch. "In the transept of the birch cathedral / they rise above us, tetrahedral / reeking where / there once was bear / the spoor / of you, locked leman, poor / bloody remnant"—here he flourished the mandolin—"of the scrotal, fetal sack / come back!"

Clint, listening, dreamed Arrowhead, that dark expanse of wood, the meadow behind him, the sun on the poplars, the tree pollen drifting, Melville with a waistcoat and gray beard and tankard and great anxious intelligence declining—saw further how the whole of what he had been working for was represented as burlesque by the man above him strutting, his wife in the audience twisting her rings, the flower child gone weedy, the bard with nothing consequent to sing, codified in self-indulgence by the indulgence of just such admiring acolytes as he, Clint, had become (and what of his colleague in Italy now, the fifty-five-year-old with black shoes and dungarees and a leather vest and boy that he brought to the Piazza della Signoria, hoping to impress on him the marmoreal grace of David, the dispassionate homage a witness must pay to that most potent curving thigh, the way that the boy, if sufficiently urged, might return with the poet to their pensione, hear how he was misunderstood in Saratoga Springs by Philistines, how his companion, the Botticelli expert, had decamped for Siena with Angelo, and therefore they might share a grappa, an evening, a bed—this too in the service of art, the crease of the bedsheet, the pillow, the cry, the curvature of clothesline at the window, *et in Arcadia ego, ego, ego*), the dream of the hunter, the long line baited, the perception fading, fading Clint's sense of resolve, of the thick-bearded failure in Pittsfield—and as the reading tilted to completion, as Hazeltine wound down, hoarse now, wrung by effort, the associate professor of European history asleep, the composition teacher correcting texts, dealing with serial commas, and Betsy with her skirt hiked up, a scar on her knee he had not noticed, and all of this predictable—applause, the books to sign, his self-revulsion at the prospect of security, small daring, and large scorn—this was the candle, not game; the process, not result—saw the reception afterward, with cheese and apple slices and white wine and cider and doughnuts and beer, and then they would repair to someone's house for drinks, the die-hard remnant and the recently divorced—where Hazeltine was holding forth, backed against the counter, saying "In my opinion," often, discoursing on renegade verse, the notion of the "sacred fire," the *vates,* the poet possessed, talking rapidly, coherently, his eyes blear, blank ("I'm tired," he would say to Clint, "whipped." "It takes it out of you, right?" "It does. I need a drink." "Scotch?" He nodded.)—Kathryn in the corner, inattentive, patient, discussing asparagus still in the kitchen until they might withdraw, offering apologies, their explanations and farewells and the promise, absolutely, to remain in touch, to get to work, the long cold drive to Cossayuna, the chance still of snow, their escape.

In bed that night he turned to her. "We can't stay here."

Kathryn feigned sleep, or was sleeping.

"We've got to go."

"To Michigan?"

"No. And not to Dingwall either."

"It's one o'clock," she said. "Let's sleep on it, darling."

"I can't."

She gathered herself in the pillows, then heaved upright. He watched her breasts.

"This sucking up to college students. Jockeying for tenure. Wondering if Melville merits the attention. Christ," he said. "I quit."

"It will come your way."

"I doubt it."

"Those are actual emeralds," said Kathryn. She was reaching for a cigarette. She liked to smoke in bed.

"Whose? Kim's?"

She nodded and inhaled. "That's why he can rail at the academy. That's how they afford such scorn."

"You wanted a horse barn," he said.

"I want a child." She knocked out ash. She had not said this before.

"What changed your mind?"

She dropped the sheet and would not say. He bent above her, rapt.

The night was clear and cold. A crescent moon hung framed by the top left-hand pane, its edges iced. Tomorrow it might snow again; the moon seemed sheathed in light. " 'In Flanders Fields,' " he found himself repeating, as silent inward litany, " 'In Flanders Fields.' " The Morgan in his neighbor's stall stirred in its sleep. He had been moved by Hazeltine, impelled by the great thrashing malice of the invocation, invitation to the dance: here's a doubloon for him who finds the fish. Everywhere about him they were singing whaling songs, they were doling out a tot of rum and doffing their caps to the breeze. The wind stood fair. While Kathryn moved beneath him, her white breasts roiling, spume at her neck, he studied The Book of the Quick.

THE
DAY'S
CATCH

THE
DAYS
CATCH

I

Everywhere they told him stories; all of them wanted to talk. Everyone confided in him elaborately. It was not so much his reaction they wanted as his respectful attention; let me tell you, they would say, the story of my life.

David listened. He told himself this was useful, a lesson, the way a writer works. The difference, for example, between someone who would get the car and someone who would fetch it was a difference to record. It was not so obvious as "trunk" and "boot," or "let" and "rent"—but it did signify; someone who would "fetch" the car had spent his childhood in England, or New England, or tried to make it seem so. Appearances deceived. The glitter of surface, the glimmering sheen of the harbor at night, the focused diffusion of light—these were their subjects, therefore his. He made notes.

Why do we distrust those men who will not talk to others, those women who talk to themselves? Some poke their way through garbage continually muttering; others keep mute. If eyes be called the window of the soul, then surely the mouth is the hallway, the ear the door. What he heard was confident or confidential, full of mock or true humility; he heard it in diners and restaurants and cabs.

Voice, he came to understand, is the play of utterance—its registered timbre and range. It may confound or confirm expectation: so deep a sound from so small a throat, so nasal a twang from such elegant lips. Who has not been astonished by the barrel-chested athlete in the tenor section, the sultry alto burble from a child next door? Voice amplifies the eye; it travels as slowly as sound.

At any rate he listened. He watched the smile belying anger, the gesture of evasion, the passionate avowal or pretense of indifference, the sharp rushing intake of breath. The way it all happened, they said, the way it used to be, you'll never believe this, you'll never, the story of my life. He wrote it down every day.

In 1968 David Lewin moved to Martha's Vineyard. His parents approved. He was twenty-two years old, a Harvard graduate, and classified 4-F; he arrived

in May. He rented a shack at the edge of Quitsa Pond—
a shack that would be sold, ten years later, for four
hundred thousand dollars. It sat on two acres of land
and had been the schoolhouse privy. A black kerosene
stove offered heat. The plumbing was erratic; the roof
leaked in a northeast rain. He knew the leaks' locations
and could gather the water in pails; he rigged himself a
shower stall outside. He had been trying to write.

He believed, that season, in a return to ancient
techniques. He wrote fables, parables. He had completed three. He felt invaded by the beauty of the
scene—the heather and spear grass at his doorstep,
the soft slope to the pond and glimpse of dunes and the
south shore beyond, the ocean a distant, deep blur. Gulls
wheeled above him, then dove. A great blue heron
nested nearby; often, in the mornings, he would watch
it preen. He had no lock on his door. The shack was
one large room, with partitions for the kitchen and the
toilet and the bed.

He had many visitors. He was young and single
and heterosexual, and there weren't enough of those,
they told him, to go around. Their fathers or their boy-
friends or their husbands wouldn't mind; they were di-
vorcing anyhow, or separated, or on vacation. He was
in demand. They liked his car or hair or laughter or
paragraphs or hut. He had no telephone, and therefore
they dropped by. They came to take him sailing or to
dinner; they brought him wine and peyotl, and one
woman brought her own sheets. His bed was double,
with tarnished brass bars. Its mattress was thin, its frame
sagged. He had nailed a reading light to the beam above.
Once he returned to find a garter snake coiled to the
lamp, hunting heat; he did not recognize the snake as

harmless and, panicky, cut off its head.

David held two part-time jobs. He drove a delivery truck for the Menemsha fish market seven mornings a week. He rose at dawn and dressed in rubber boots and army surplus khakis; he arrived at six. The owner was there before him, an unlit pipe clamped in his teeth; he had been bringing in the boats and buying fish and putting up orders since four. On slow mornings they had coffee; then the fish cutters arrived. The market had holding tanks for lobster and an ice room for the larger fish; it opened on a retail basis at nine-thirty every day. By then he had loaded the truck. He delivered swordfish and lobster and bushels of quahaugs to the island restaurants and to the Vineyard Haven ferry slip.

David liked the work. Thick slabs of swordfish bulked gleaming in the truck bed, and he would carry two or three whole fish. The wooden lobster crates leaked. Their weight when loaded was greater than their delivered weight; the lobsters were packed in seaweed, and they yielded water. He needed help unloading; there was camaraderie in the delivery bays. He learned the island gossip, learned the backroads and shortcuts between the towns and, on his return trip, if he ran ahead of schedule, could stop for a swim or cigar.

Part of David's salary was fish. He collected fish scraps from the cutting table, or a ragged fillet, or lobsters with no claws. He learned to shuck shellfish expertly, and at cocktail parties he was called upon to open oysters and clams. He was back at his shack before noon, and he had the afternoon to write. On clear days he took his typewriter outside. He set up a table beneath the shingled overhang and kept his carbon copies in a doorless Kelvinator by the western wall.

He also worked twice weekly as the paid companion to a twelve-year-old blind boy. Anton Longley Mackin, Jr., was fatherless. His cousin had gone to college with David and asked him as a favor if he'd be a friend to Tony, a pair of male eyes. It would be worth his while. The kid was surrounded by women, he said; he needed to go bowling or talk about baseball instead.

"Where would we go bowling?"

"He should get out of the house. Mom-mom wants to meet you. It's arranged."

So David drove to a great gabled home beside the bay and was ushered in while Tony waited, docile, in the hall. The boy loved jazz. He had been blind from birth, and his aural memory was extensive and exact. They played a game called "Blind Man's Bluff"; Tony proposed the name. David selected a record, selected a side and a cut. If Tony failed to identify the song and the performance within five seconds, he lost. He rarely lost. Once he confused a Jelly Roll Morton solo in terms of the date of the recording; once he could not place a Muggsy Spanier performance until twelve seconds had passed.

"Mom-mom" was rich. She wore flowing caftans and used a cigarette holder and said "*Dah*ling" as if she'd studied for the part. This turned out to be the case. She had been an actress, David learned, acquired in Cleveland by Mr. Mackin when Mr. Mackin was drunk. He had been drunk for years. He had wanted, she told David, to be the youngest of his set to succumb to cirrhosis; he thought cirrhosis of the liver had cachet. There was no distinction to a heart attack, or

cancer; it took a special kind of perseverance to die of
alcohol. That was a distinction, she said, conferred upon
the very poor and rich; that was the reason opposites
attract.

She had been sufficiently his opposite, she said,
and attractive. There was a prosy, truth-telling side of
her that David came to trust. Anton Mackin had spirited her from backstage at the Cleveland Playhouse like
the seducer of showgirls in some melodrama or farce.
He plied her with champagne and telegrams and roses;
his great black car purred in the alley. Only there was
such studied nonchalance in the gestures he made that
she spotted them as studied; she learned to see the
parody behind the high romance. There had been more
self-mockery than mockery about him; there had been
a cold-eyed calculation in the operatic ardor and the
fistful of rings that he asked her to wear once engaged.
She did want David to understand—as her husband had
once wanted her to understand—that money was a
means, not end; it was a shared illusion, a conventional
acceptance of what was merely scrip. Why should a
check mean money? Why should a broker call one day
to say we've made a thousand dollars or a hundred
thousand dollars or five hundred thousand dollars, since
the takeover bid? It was a dream people dreamed. It
was a God more persuasive than God; whole societies
were organized by the convention of wealth.

For those with wealth, however, and no capacity
for dreaming, it also was a joke. It divided and multi-
plied and reproduced itself like cells. There were men
in Wall Street and Chicago and Cleveland who were
working overtime so Anton need not work. Slowly she
too came to see the comedy in things; there was noth-

ing they could buy that would not increase their pur-
chasing power, no expenditure so great it would not be
recouped. Did David know the Billie Holiday re-
frain—" 'Them that's got shall get, them that's not shall
lose. So the Bible says, and it still is news . . .' "

Therefore he made random gestures, and one of
those gestures was marriage when he knew he was going
to die. He told her this, in San Francisco, almost as an
afterthought. "By the way," he said, "I ought to tell
you. I've got six months to live." She had not believed
him, of course. They were staying at the Fairmont,
dressing for dinner; he was tying his tie at the window,
looking out. His back was to her, and she asked him
to repeat it, and he said he had cirrhosis and did not
choose to die a bachelor; he hoped she understood.
She would remember forever the way he tied his tie.
His fingers seemed translucent and the brown stains at
his fingertips looked suddenly like blood. The tie was
a bow tie, dark blue. She came and stood beside him,
and he put his hand on her shoulder and said, "I want
a child."

Anton Jr. had been born with his father still alive.
But they had been on different floors of the same hospital, and when she brought the mewling blinded pre-
mature bundle down for inspection, her husband had
not known his son; he kept his eyes closed also, and
failed to acknowledge their presence. He died when
Tony was seven weeks old; she had been bereaved. That
was the word, said Mom-mom, even if *bereaved* was
foolish, the kind of word you read in newspapers or
flower shops. Yet it was how she felt. She told her
story to David in twenty-minute segments, drinking tea.
It all happened years ago, but years ago was yesterday,

since every day she lived with the abiding presence of
the past. She could not help it; she minded; she had
been bereft.

One month she had been living in a third-floor
walk-up in Cleveland, hoping to play Ado Annie in the
Oklahoma revival. She had been offered the Janis Paige
part in a bus-and-truck company version of *The Pajama
Game*. Next month she was in Venice, at the Gritti
Palace, with a man she barely knew whose last name
had become her own legal name, whose fingers were
translucent and who bought her whatever she paused
to admire. She fell in love with him then. She had not
married for love. She had not married for money, precisely, although the money helped. There was no point
pretending it did not help. It was the collective dream;
it made her own dreams come true.

Yet what she elected to marry was the clear-eyed
chilly assessment in Anton, his gambler's sense of risk.
She would have liked to know him better; he had surprised her, as she surprised him. She had surprised him,
for instance, with her knowledge of the Tiepolo ceilings and how they used perspective. She had had what
Anton called more than a pretty face. Mom-mom
laughed. He, David, mustn't pay attention; she had been
fishing for praise. It was a bad habit. No man could
walk into her home without arousing in her what she
recognized as sorrow, a passionate nostalgia for her own
lithe youth. They had had a gondolier to escort them
everywhere. Her memory of Venice was a wash of
marble and green water, the wine Anton ordered for
lunch, the lanterns, Torcello, the pastry, the light. In
Venice her true love was born, and what is born
must die.

So when he told her, some weeks later in their
suite at the Fairmont, that the doctors could not save
him, that it was irreversible—when he said he was dying
and wanted a child she took that as a general truth: we
all die, we desire children to strew flowers on our grave.
And it had not seemed specific, had not meant his liver
would quit. Cirrhosis meant nothing particular; it did
not mean him lying sweating, shaking, unable to swallow; it had not meant she'd continue with a child born
blind.

Mom-mom was thirty-eight now and not recon-
ciled. She had had too little of her husband; it was a
brief, waking dream. She had married a stranger dead
twelve years ago, and now she was nearly his age. He
had been thirty-nine, so possibly he had not been the
youngest of his circle to die of cirrhosis—but from her
newfound vantage he had been young enough. She and
Tony summered on the Vineyard and wintered in
Manhattan and Londonderry; they traveled to Barbados every March. She was not complaining. She had
little to complain of; she could have a private performance of *Oklahoma* if she chose. She could give so large
a sum in memory of her husband that the Cleveland
Playhouse would build a Mackin Wing; she was consid-
ering that. And Tony did not seem unhappy—he too
was content with his lot. He had a shy sweetness like
his father's, Mom-mom thought—only it had not yet
hardened into nonchalance.

"You'll like him," she finished.

"I do already."

She smiled. "He's sensitive to strangers. He notices more than you think."

David stood.

"It's like a dog," she said. "I don't mean to compare him to a dog, of course. But he can sense immediately if you're frightened of him, or pretending interest. He knows by someone's footsteps if that someone is a friend."

As if on cue, Tony entered. They walked together to the beach. "You didn't take a shower," Tony said. "What's that I smell on you—swordfish?"

"Three of them this morning," David said. "I brought you a present."

"What?"

"This." He handed Tony a dried swordfish sword. Nearly three feet long, and grainy, it seemed capable of skewering a rowboat. The boy was grateful. He veered between civility and childishness; he kicked off his shoes and waved the sword. They charged the surf. Tony galloped, whooping, and was both horse and rider. "Cavalree!"

They had many such routines. On clear days they would walk the shore or go horseback riding on the bridle trail behind the golf course. Tony owned a bicycle built for two, and he enjoyed tandem bicycle trips. "Two eyes and four feet and two seats," he would say. "What kind of animal do you suppose we make?"

He joked about his blindness. It was a running patter, a continual allusion. "You should have seen Mom-mom last night," he said. "I swear she was blind drunk. And that old bag across the street, Mrs. Tillotson. She came over with Jenny, you know? They couldn't walk a straight line. They all needed blinders last night."

On rainy days they listened to music, or David read

The Last of the Mohicans, Kim, or *Oliver Twist.* Once
he collected Tony and took him on the fish run. Tony
enjoyed it, he said. But the way he traced the dash-
board with his fingertips seemed fretful; he scratched
at the blue vinyl seat. He positioned the radio buttons
and the treble knob. He inclined his head, absorbed,
and his attention to the banter of the men at the ferry
loading slip felt excessive. "What's a portagee?" he asked.

"Portagee?" David reversed the truck.

"They were mentioning a portagee. They said it
couldn't add."

He swung into traffic. "Portuguese. They were
joking about Johnny over in Woods Hole. His daughter kept the books. And apparently she's pregnant now
so Johnny's going broke."

Tony laughed. He slapped at his knee. Yet the
laughter had been dutiful; they both knew the joke was
not funny. He did not ask to join in the fish run again,
but he always inquired after the men in the market or
at the restaurants or dock. "How's Ted?" he'd ask.
"How's Bill? How's Johnny Portagee?"

One Thursday it rained and they followed Mom-
mom to Vineyard Haven. She had some errands, she
said, and they might as well have a soda or something;
they could poke around the Goodwill store while she
assessed the breakfront Harrison had found. You
couldn't trust him, naturally; he'd claim a piece was
Chippendale before the varnish dried. But Harrison did
have an eye and know what she wanted and claim to
have found it, and therefore it was worth a look since
tennis was out of the question.

The rain was warm. David lingered for an instant

at the Goodwill door. He held it open. Later he would ask himself, if it had not been raining, if Mom-mom had not dropped them there, if Tony were not blind—if any single one of all the things that *were* the case was *not* the case, would he and Alice have met?

She had been looking at clothes. She stood in the rear of the long, littered room. There was a rack of children's clothes, a rack of women's dresses, an aisle of men's trousers and coats. She emerged from this last. Hooked rugs showed deer on the wall. The shoes were dingy, the appliances secondhand; there were glass plates and used blenders and a chess game with one knight missing. Tony hunted records beneath the paperbacks. He would insist on extracting the disks—running his fine fingers along the countertops, rummaging in cartons. Then David read out the titles and Tony said, "There, that one. Yes," or shook his head.

Alice approached. She was looking for a mirror; she held a man's hunting jacket with red and black woolen checks. There was no mirror. She worked herself into the coat, then belted the belt. "It looks terrific," he said.

"What does?" Tony asked. He held a selection of Fred Waring 78's.

"The jacket. Tell her that you think so too."

"Which one is this?" David read the titles and the girl moved away, comprehending that Tony was blind.

They met again at the register. "Did you decide?" he asked.

She nodded.

"My name is David. Lewin."

"Alice." She held out her hand.

"And this is Mr. Jazz," he said. "Tony. We come here for records."

"I see that." Alice colored. Tony touched his arm.

"You should have bought a raincoat," David said. Mom-mom would reimburse him for the records. The lady at the register cracked open a brown paper bag.

"We could give you a ride?" Tony asked.

She refused him, gravely. "I work across the street. I work at the jewelry shop. It's the end of my lunch break, you see."

Later he would tell her that she'd told him to return. She said, "Don't flatter yourself." Later still, in his arms, she whispered she was glad he listened, glad she told him where she worked. "Imagine," Alice said, "how close I came to missing you. Imagine how that would have been."

He could not imagine it. He tried to, in the years to come, but failed. Her hair was thick and blond; it fell to the small of her back. Her nose was acquiline. She smiled at him at six o'clock, when he entered the jewelry shop, saying without surprise, "It's you." He said, "It isn't raining. Would you like to take a walk?" She switched off the light at her work desk. She made a pile of shavings, arranged the necklaces—turquoise and coral, on thin silver strands—and asked him, "Where's your brother?" The display case had a scallop-shell motif. He told her that he had no brother, Tony Mackin was a friend. "I have a car," he said. "We could go up-island, if you'd like."

They drove to Indian Hill. He followed the road through the woods, then parked where the path ended at the forest ranger station; there were tracks in the sand. There was no one in the fire tower, however, and they climbed in silence. An Indian burial ground and a replica of Reverend Thomas Mayhew's chapel lay to the west; they climbed above the trees. The stair slats were wet. At every landing stage they paused; the farms assumed dimension, and the shore appeared. He pointed out the visible landmarks; he knew the island well. She wore the hunting jacket he had seen her buy that afternoon. Wind took her hair. "I'm glad you're showing me this," Alice said. "I get so sick of beaches. Everybody and his brother has a favorite beach."

They reached the ranger's cabin, but the trapdoor at the entrance had been padlocked shut. The sun was roseate. It was August 14, 1968. Later he and Alice would disagree over the date; she thought it had been August 12. He remembered standing with her on the topmost platform, the sun descending, sea birds beneath, and telling her this whole display was for her benefit.

"You've been to Versailles?" Alice asked. He said, yes, he had been to Versailles. Somehow their shared knowledge of that royal pleasure-perch, how queens and princes could survey from balcony or window what those watching from ground level had to gape to see— the possibility that they had been together at Versailles, had glimpsed each other in the halls or down a green allée, had stood in the same ticket line or heard the same interpreter or admired identical portraits— that shared invented meeting made this seem a second chance. "A third," said David, "if you count this morning."

They remained on the tower, not touching. A ferry made for Cuttyhunk, and day sailors beat before the

wind to Lambert's Cove. A chimney on the mainland
gave out smoke like a white fan. "I have to go now,"
Alice said. "I do want to see you again."

They saw each other daily, and on Labor Day she
moved into his shack. Things changed for David, were
transfigured; the jeweler closed down for the season.
The days grew briefer, the light more clear. He whistled love songs while he worked and relinquished his
cigars. He started a novella about life at the fish market, the tall tales he heard. Her skin was fair, her body
lean; she was not adept at sex. The first time he entered her she seemed to be in pain. She lay beneath
him, eyes wide, resistant, staring at the ceiling. He asked
her, was he hurting her, and she shook her head. He
asked, did she want him to stop, and again she shook
her head.

Alice came from Chapel Hill. Her father was a
lawyer, and her parents had divorced. She had two sisters—one still at home. Her mother had once trained
to be a pianist; she married on a whim. Then the whim
became a household full of squalling argumentative
children, and she couldn't concentrate or go to audi-
tions or, when the opportunity came to perform, remember the music. She always used to remember
instead—so she told her daughter—that she'd left the
right rear burner on or maybe the porch door unlocked; she'd failed to feed the dogs or get the guest-
room ready. She drank. She grew partial to pink gin.
A pink-gin fizz at lunch helped make the world accept-
able; without pink gin at hand, Estelle found it unac-
ceptable—the way we maim and slaughter animals, for
instance, the inequity of wealth.

Her father had been in the air force during the Korean War. His family was army, and his decision to join the air force had been greeted not so much with disapproval as shock: why trust yourself, they asked him, to all that untested machinery? His answer had been speed. A pilot got involved in combat more quickly than did combat troops; he had a stronger, swifter sense of purpose in the air. He was sent to the Pacific, and he came back changed. Alice could not remember him before he left; she had been a baby, and her mother was pregnant with Beth. But she did remember how he came back pole-thin, bald, impassive, not smiling at their mother or his children or their "Welcome Home Daddy Hero" sign, not wanting to be touched. He allowed himself to be handled, but there was no answering pressure, no sense of quickening warmth. If he mentioned aircraft carriers or landing or the enemy, that was all he ever said, not answering her questions about the bamboo cage. She had heard he spent a year in China in a bamboo cage. "I can't talk about it," her father said. "Not yet."

He dreamed about it, however, and Alice could remember waking in the dark because she heard him shouting, screaming, "No!" He would launch into unintelligible speeches in what she guessed was Chinese; he would jump out of bed or cover his eyes while they tried fruitlessly to wake him; he had been engaged, for years, in a tortured private wrangling they were powerless to halt. Her mother helped, at first. At first she sat by his side for as long as it took, holding his hand, stroking his forehead, speaking with that soothing croon she used when the children were sick. She had been the picture of compassionate patience for years.

Then imperceptibly—or by so slow a gradation and shift that Alice barely noticed—her father improved. He composed himself at mealtimes; he took an interest in the paper and the television news. He tended their garden with skill. He pruned the shrubbery around the walk. Alice returned from school one morning to find her father at the hedge, a neat, boxed section behind him and an overgrown straggle to tend to ahead. He was trimming things, setting things straight.

Then as if all Chapel Hill waited on his recovery, his neighbors and associates welcomed him back to the fold. They made as much of his return as if he had been Lazarus. He could have gotten the keys to the city, if Chapel Hill had a key. He resumed law practice, and cases came his way. He sported a moustache. He still had a reserve about him, but it seemed appropriate; it was civil, *civilian,* and often someone in the streets would remark to Alice how lucky and proud she must be.

That was when her mother started in to drink. Alice had it all muddled; her childhood was a muddle just like everybody else's, and she couldn't say this happened and then that happened and then that. You don't get over shellshock overnight. Neither do you go from sober to sodden, from painstaking nurse to failed musician in a nightgown, drinking gin at noon, sweeping the coffee cups into the sink, showing more leg to the gardener than the gardener thought proper—neither did her mother go from support to burden overnight.

So there might have been a moment when the prisoner of war believed his wife angelic and thought himself beloved. Florence Nightingale had syphilis; she wondered if David knew that? She died in the Crimea, having ministered to soldiers there a little too particularly; that's what her mother said. Her father took business trips. He acquired from his wife what she was visibly losing, and there might have been a month or year when they met as equals in the house and bed.

But Alice could remember no such time. She remembered only imbalance, the way the walls would seem to tilt, the argument between them that was spoken or unspoken, and the way the doors would slam or be closed so gently, precisely, as to constitute reproach. She and her sisters would huddle in the playroom, playing Monopoly or Crazy Eights or with their grandmother's dollhouse, the one that had real marble pillars on the porch. It was a white plantation house, with antebellum furnishings and pickaninnies in the kitchen and a stately entrance hall. The whole stood four feet high. She remembered playing with the fervor of belief: everything could be adjusted, perfect; all the cups and saucers would be put back on the shelf.

In springtime they would flee outside, and there too the world was in order. They had a pony and chickens and, when their father returned to his guns, bluetick hounds. He refurbished the cinderblock privy by the chicken run. It became her playhouse, with curtains on the windows, whitewash, and a screen door. She and Beth—Mary Kate had grown too old for this— would sit for hours on the windowseat that had been the three-holer and play "Who Do You Like Better?" or "Sleeping Beauty" or, later, with the portable radio, sing along with that week's hit parade. She knew the hit parade from 1958 through 1963 by heart. She could remember the first time she heard Elvis Presley, for instance. She had been taking a bath. He sang "Heart-

break Hotel," and his voice warbled as though there
were water in her ear; she wasn't certain, till she heard
it several times, that she was hearing right.

Later she headed for Memphis just to see his house.
Bobby McKelroy from U.N.C. said he knew Colonel
Parker, and all they'd have to do was go to the front
door and knock. He came for her one Saturday morning on his Harley; he called it a hog. They had pretended they were going swimming, and she packed a
picnic and bikini and, for when she would be introduced to Elvis, a makeup kit and her see-through cro-
cheted top. They rode for hours on the Interstate, and
it was hot and boring and he had a blowout at eighty
miles an hour on a curve. She would never forget the
way it sounded, the tearing roar beneath her and the
jolting skid and rubber screaming on concrete. She knew
she was going to die. She closed her eyes and held to
Bobby like salvation, like her father's dream of Chapel
Hill when he was nose down, diving, metal shearing
everywhere; they bounced and teetered and bucked.
Impossibly they stayed upright; impossibly the cycle
slowed; he shouted "Jump!" and they landed in the grass.

Bobby was sick. He stayed on all fours, retching,
while she felt for broken bones. Her wrists were
skinned, her hair a mess, but she was otherwise unhurt.
Alice tried to pray. All she seemed able to remember
was the grace beginning, "Give us this day our daily
bread," and the Twenty-third Psalm. She began to re-
cite these and stopped. Her father too had faced a green
oblivion when landing on the terrace by the riverbed
that, from his plummeting distance, might well have
looked like grass. He too refused to pray. Bobby came
to her, wan-faced, stinking, and said, "I ain't never met

no Colonel Parker. I just wanted to get you to Memphis. Just you and me in Memphis, off alone."

He looked so hangdog, standing there, she hadn't the heart to be angry. Mostly she had felt embarrassed for him, and ashamed. She collected his toolkit and wiped his bloody nose with her bikini top. He blew his nose in it, crying, "I'm no good. I'm shit." She did not contradict him, but she did not tell the trooper, either, that he had spirited this minor, her, across state lines. They were in Tennessee, and he could have been arrested, but instead they fixed the tire and made their way back home. She could never hear Elvis again without that rush inside that meant they were exploding and would crash; she watched him gyrate on TV and saw the state troopers above her, Bobby on his knees.

David lay beside her in the dark. Her breathy voice, her series of secrets, made him hold his breath. "You don't want to know this," she said, and he told her yes he did. "You don't have to listen," she said, and he rubbed her back and shoulders while she talked. Her elder sister married when Alice was fifteen. They had had the most beautiful wedding, all silk and lilies and champagne, and when the bridal couple left her father called his three remaining women to the den. "Take off your shoes," he said to Beth and Alice. "Make yourselves comfortable."

Their mother had done so, ostentatiously, kicking off her heels and stretching and sitting with her legs splayed on the ottoman. The girls sat in the black leather chairs in a room that, without being precisely off limits, was so clearly his haven that they seldom entered. It reeked of pipe tobacco, leather-bound law texts, and oil. Alice faced his gun rack, she remembered. He poured them flat champagne. "Your mother and I have something to tell you," he said. "Something you should know."

The scene that followed was banal. She had guessed it in advance, had understood recrimination and control and tears not quite spilled and shock not quite genuine would be the order of the day. "Your father is leaving," their mother announced. "Mary Kate has gone her way and he'll be going his."

"I've taken a house at the Kerr's. It's not as if I'm leaving. Think of it," their father said, "as if we bought an extra home."

She had had too much to drink. She had french-kissed Geoffrey Williams in the TV room; he said her tongue was like solid champagne. She wasn't sure she heard him right, like the time she wasn't sure she heard Elvis sing "Heartbreak Hotel" on purpose as if he were gargling—but by the time she had had an answer Geoffrey was gone. That Saturday she stopped him, saying, "What a peculiar thing to say," and it was clear from his open-faced puzzlement he hadn't known what she meant. "Solid champagne," she reminded him, and still his expression stayed blank. Yet in her father's den, respectful, trying not to hiccough, all she could think of was "solid champagne" and the feel of his tongue on her tongue and if she would be sick; she could not listen to the hackneyed consolation they offered her and Beth.

It wasn't, she wanted to say, as if they were in need of consoling; it was water spilled so long ago you couldn't find the bridge. Alice laughed: there were proverbs somewhere struggling to be free. You cried

over spilled milk but shouldn't, while water spilled under the bridge. You took a stitch in time, and birds in
hand were worth two in the bush. She was his bird
in the hand. You made your bed to lie in, but stitches
in time would save nine; she muddled the proverbs and
hiccoughed and, sitting in her father's chair, curled and
uncurled her toes.

David too wiggled his toes. Had he noticed how
his toes curled back when he came? Each time he had
an orgasm his toes turned in and pressed. She knew his
breath would quicken and his pulse increase and muscles tense; she watched him carefully. She loved to watch
him come. He coiled in the bed like a spring. She came
to take such pleasure in sex that she felt like a kid with
a first set of skates or some long-desired doll; she ex-
amined him minutely, asking, "How does this feel? How
does *this* make you feel, how does this?" Alice shifted
in his arms. "If everybody stayed in bed, the world would
have no problems."

"Population," David said.

"OK. If everybody stayed in bed and used birth
control."

"And lived on an island like this one," he said.

"You're making fun of me."

"Yes."

In retrospect it all seemed fun, loud childish fits
of laughter in the middle of the night. They wrestled;
they had pillow fights; they tickled each other exuber-
antly. "Let's go to bed," she said, and he said, "No, I'm
tired. Let's play three sets of tennis instead." She left
him notes beneath the pillow, or in the sugar bowl or
above the soda shelf in the refrigerator; they read,

"Darling, I adore you." Or, "You have such a great big
juicy beautiful"—and then, beneath the fold— "ear."
"Don't ever leave me," she lettered, and pinned to his
fish clothes where they flapped drying on the line. Once,
after an argument, Alice wrote, "I love you very much.
And that makes me very happy." He could not remember what they argued over, what lilt of voice or lift of
chin or topic had occasioned disagreement—but he remembered with no trouble the trouble she took with
that note: the pen she used, the open blue print, the
lined yellow paper, and the curling initial in the lower
right-hand corner with which she signed off: A.

He was her first love, she said. He was her first
and only love and would remain that way. She had had
other lovers, of course. She ran through men about as
frequently as he did women, though what it meant in
her case had been something very different: a baseball
saved, or dance card, or ticket to the double feature
where she had had her first kiss. She had, she said, a
promiscuous imagination: she watched each man who
passed her by—or those who watched her passing—as
if he could be stripped. Did David find that shocking?
Did he behave the same way? Only he could act on it,
had acted in the Goodwill store and later at her jewelry
desk and later in his hut.

She could think and feel the same, of course, but
couldn't let him know. She'd have to smile and bat her
eyes and cross her legs and look away. It was amazing,
really, it came from the Pleistocene epoch. It was—
what was the word? she ran her hand around his knee—
antediluvian. Her first boyfriend, Henry, had spouted
a jingle. He was very proud of it, it expressed his whole
theory of life. "Higamus, hogamus, woman's monoga-

mous. Hogamus, higamus, man is polygamous." He had
flexed his muscles, smiled, and posed in front of what
he thought to be the admiring mirror of her eyes. "That's
the difference," he proclaimed. "We men just can't be
tied down."

Alice had not needed him. She was learning about
freedom, and one of the principal freedoms was to learn
to say no thanks. She had said no thanks to Henry, as
she said no to most of those who gave her baseballs or
orchids or wolf whistles at the swimming pool or from
the front seats of cars. And if she said yes instead, yes
why not, that too was freedom; she would not be cajoled. She refused the second baseman. He was all
puffed up with his picture in the papers and his charley
horse from headfirst sliding and the rumor that the Cubs
had sent a scout. She told him she would rather take
the bat boy home, or that gangly left fielder with acne.
So she dispensed her favors—Alice giggled at the phrase:
"These are my favors," she said, "what a way to describe them," placing his hands on her breasts—with
the mindlessness of fate. That was how she liked to
think of it and what she liked to say. When Henry announced, "Higamus, hogamus, woman's monogamous,"
she quoted Augustine to him instead. " 'Do not de-
spair,' " she said, " 'one of the thieves was saved. Do
not presume; one of the thieves was damned.' "

He stared at her, wide-eyed, and she said, "Don't
worry, Henry, it's the doctrine of election. There's
nothing you can do about it. The answer is no." The
way he had looked at her was indescribable, as if a cautious swimmer had discovered the sandbar drops off.
There are fish and coral and riptides in the water;
everything's precarious, at risk. And what you took for

granted you cannot take for granted; your beauty, youth, and prowess each will go. If there's anything to take for granted, Alice said, take that. She didn't want to worry him; it wasn't something, really, there was any point in worrying about, but what Henry took for granted—her—was not his to take. The gift had been bestowed and now would be withdrawn. It had meant nothing, would mean nothing: one of them was saved and one was damned.

She laughed. There's nothing like Saint Augustine to take the wind out of a man. He can strut past, full of beer and pumped-up-cock-of-the-roost boastfulness, and all you have to do is turn away. All you have to point to is the dunghill where he struts. She had been prepared to do so in the Goodwill store. She had seen David coming, had gauged him from across the room behind the coats. Then he took that blind boy by the hand. They were reading record labels, and he read them carefully aloud. She watched him for some time.

"You sleeping enough?" Mathew asked. Mathew ran the grocery store. He worked twenty-hour days in summer and drank all winter long.

"Mm-mn. Why?"

"Just asking," Mathew said.

"I sleep."

"A beauty sleep," said Mathew. "Right?" He opened a carton of Nestle's Crunch and stacked them on the shelf.

David selected corn.

"That girl. That Alice who's moved in. You two on separate accounts?"

"No."

"Mostly she pays cash." He tore a Nestle's Crunch in two. "Just asking," Mathew said.

He paid. He was cultivating reticence. A customer entered and gathered tonic water bottles, two to each hand. "Might rain," said David.

"Not till tomorrow."

"Is that what they're predicting?"

"Well fedded and well bedded," Mathew said. "Don't take it personal."

She had dropped out of college that June. She spent two years at Hollins, playing tennis, riding her room-mate's Morgan, and wavering between majors in psychology or French. All the girls had crushes on the French professor, she told David; he managed to be both devilish and cuddly. He was better dressed than anyone and even when she sat at the foot of the French table and he sat at the head, she could inhale Old Spice. But her psychology professor played tennis; she liked the way he toyed with her at net.

He had a beard. He also had three daughters and a wife who brought iced tea and cookies to the courts. The students called her "How you doin', darling?" because that was what she asked. She always asked it, and he always answered, "Fine." He threw a pass at Alice one morning by the stables; he asked her if she knew what cathexis entailed. She said she thought so, yes, it was a series of emotions, a whole set of connections. He said, yes, there's emotional cathexis and sensory cathexis and he felt them both that morning and wondered if she felt the same.

His beard was sweat-soaked. He wiped his neck. She said maybe they should go off campus to discuss

it, because she couldn't handle a cathexis while her
roommate saddled up. He complied. He brought his
station wagon to the stable, and she knew without his
asking to meet him at the gate. She got in and pulled
her cap down over her eyes and turned toward him,
averting her face from the window. He seemed pleased.
He drove into the mountains, telling her that Roanoke
was not the town it used to be, that when he first arrived at Hollins College there were farms all around.
Now you have to drive for twenty miles to be alone—
that's progress, he supposed.

"Do you do this often?" Alice asked.

"Not often," he answered. "Do you?"

She had wanted to provoke him then; it all seemed
so routine to him, and foreordained. "Not since I
got VD."

He tightened his hands on the wheel. "You're
serious?"

"Yes."

He drove for some minutes in silence. "What did
you want to talk about?" she said. "About sensory
cathexis, I mean."

The joke had been on her, however, when she told
him it had only been a joke. He had been so sweaty,
panicky, so fearful of contamination that he couldn't
get aroused. She told him not to worry and he lay there
by the stream they'd found, being ravaged by mosquitoes while he said this never happened, not to him. She
said she was into Abraham Maslow and self-actualizing
personality; did he think a person could acquire the
power of self-actualization, or was it already too late?
He squeezed and poked her, kneading her nipples, and
she squeezed and prodded him. He pulled away. She

said, "This isn't working," and he slapped at a mosquito on his thigh so hard his fingers were imprinted there pinkly. She laughed; they looked like pricks. He asked her why she was laughing, and she couldn't tell him, wouldn't tell him when he urged her, and he put his pants back on and buckled his belt.

Then she knew she'd have to leave. Hollins College was not home to her and offered no cathexis; his lectures on Freud, Jung, and Erikson would be too hard to take. She had had to take them, of course. She sat in his class while he spoke about Jung, the collective unconscious, and the deep drive driving us all; she copied, with no conscious malice, what he said about the stages of men's growth. He called her to his office. He said she disconcerted him, he wished she'd stop giggling in class. She said she didn't giggle, and he said, well maybe not out loud. She said to give her love to "How you doin', darling?" and that she was going to leave.

Her suite mates were not shocked. Rather, they seemed envious; they asked her to describe how his penis hung limply, what color it was, how he explained himself to her while pulling off his pants. He had not been exploitative, she said. He knew what he was up to, psychologically, and how to go about it; he made it clear she could choose. Yet Alice felt exploited anyhow—exploited by his age and position and weight, the tennis courts, the black men mowing and raking and sweeping, the campus police, the circumstance of college while our air force strafed and burned. We were bombing villages while her teachers talked of foreign policy; we made craters out of mountain peaks, defoliating forests while she attended lectures on the Civil

War. She read "On Civil Disobedience," and then was told that protest permits had to be denied.

On the final day of spring semester she took Tracy—her roommate's Morgan—for a ride. The bridle path was overgrown in what seemed overnight. Everywhere things sprouted; every fruit tree was in flower; the sky was a blue canopy above a lush green bed. She couldn't help it, she told David, that was the way to describe it: everything at peace. Tracy trotted easily. She reined in, however. They stopped.

What happened to her next was hard to tell. She had an illumination, an experience of light. It was what she'd read of and they talked about in class. Had her psychology professor been along with her that morning, she'd have asked him for advice. But he was home washing the car; he was home taking out garbage, or dealing with his wife or scrubbing down the patio or helping his kids with New Math.

Tracy breathed in unison with every living thing; Alice saw the lung. The world was a lung, pumping, and she was a cell in the infinite cluster of cells. Leaves had no perimeter that marked them off from air. She felt the leaves, their veins and sides and indentations and microscopic particles, could see with perfect clarity how they were formed yet formless, how they inhabited air. Alice laughed. She knew it was hard to explain. She had not felt that way before and did not expect to again. The earth and sun and leaves were of a piece, she told him, and she too was of that wholeness, constituent, her body a membrane like his.

He touched her leg. "How long did this last?"

"I can't tell. It felt like—oh, I can't explain it—my

body was a membrane and everything inside of me and
everything outside was a balanced solution, perfect, so
it didn't make any difference if I was inside or outside,
or if the horse could talk. I know it sounds silly. You
have to accept that. I *saw* the bombing, *saw* the Me-
kong Delta in a branch of dogwood. Tracy was a plane.
We were intruders, we didn't belong. Not on this planet,
I mean."

"I understand."

"You don't. You can't."

It was in this fashion that he entered what he came
to think of as his outlaw state. Alice joined him. They
took mescaline and psilocybin and LSD and hashish and
cocaine together. She wanted to try heroin, but he said,
let's wait. They read the first page of *Finnegans Wake,*
convinced it held the key to everything that followed;
if they understood that page, he said, they wouldn't
have to read the rest. They pored over her catalogue
of "Treasures from the Louvre." The Louvre was the
place, she said, where wolves ran freely in the periods
of plague.

"Did they teach you that at Hollins?"

"No."

"Imagine," David said, "wolves on the rampage in
Paris."

"When are you leaving the island?"

"I haven't decided. You?"

So they stayed on for the fall. He had had enough
of schooling, he told his parents on the phone; he
needed a little more time. His work had begun to make
sense; he was listening to stories and filling the refrigerator with his second sheets. "Are you finding yourself?" asked his mother. "Is that what they call it these
days?"

* * *

It was a halcyon time for him; he woke up each morning replete. If he had to drive the fish truck, he crept out of bed without waking Alice and left. On those mornings when he did not need to work—and these increased as the autumn wore on; he met the noon ferry; the restaurants closed—David rose at dawn nevertheless. He stood on the front step a moment, letting the air wake him, watching the color soak into the sky. Then he brewed their coffee, poured himself a small black cup, and let the pot stand on the stove.

In November the days darkened early, and rain rinsed the pond. The wind was, continually, north northeast; the scrub oak trunks turned black. He and Alice took turns with the buckets, and if they went down-island for a movie or provisions they came back to water on the floor. They added their two sleeping bags to the nest of blankets. Squirrels scuttled in the eaves. He said, "Indian summer. It's got to come soon." But the tour buses ceased, and the Indian who sat at Gay Head in his headdress departed. The tennis court nets at the Community Center were removed; houses sprouted shutters and driveways were blocked off with chains. The parking lots were empty; there was no line for groceries or mail.

And something wintry entered also; Alice bought a radio and lay each evening listening to news. It was rarely good. She grew restless. She said she had no occupation, and fashioning trinkets for tourists was not work she wished to continue. Her peers were getting married or preparing for law school or graduate school; her friends were in the streets. This emerald glimmering place, this retreat for the famous and rich, this tourist brochure aimed at those who choose privacy—Alice laughed. The blacks in Oak Bluffs were all gingerbread blacks, cute enough to eat. They trimmed their houses neatly; they were glad to cut those lawns with power tools and keep on painting curlicues for the front porch. The Indians were getting drunk, they were lying in the cranberries and watching the celebrities and stars. Again she laughed. The sound was not mirthful; she sucked in her breath. It's one hell of a place, Alice said, it's good manners and ex-Cabinet members and the cunning little surf lapping at the cunning little beach. We're killing villagers in Vietnam so that you can write your fantasies at leisure.

"What do you want me to do?" David asked.

"I don't know."

"What do you want?"

"If you hadn't been 4-F," she asked, "would you have gone to Canada?"

"Irrelevant," he said. The army had rejected him, and it did not therefore matter if he would have rejected the army in turn. There had been no choice to make.

"Yes, but what *if* . . .?"

"The assumption is false." They were unpacking groceries. The paper bags had torn. "So the conclusion will be faulty."

"Every draftee in America didn't have rheumatic fever. Some of them are going. Some are getting killed."

"The categorical imperative," David countered, "fails to apply. If my behavior were the behavior of each potential inductee, there'd be no army. No war."

They argued this way often. They discoursed on civil disobedience, the effective forms of protest, and where to stake one's claim. Alice favored the Black

Panthers, a group on the West Coast. She said Huey
Newton, their jailed leader, had a real chance to be
free. The Alameda County Courthouse would prove a
testing ground. She said Bobby Seale and Eldridge
Cleaver and the rest were showing white men what
manhood could mean; if Angela Davis said "Shove it,"
she knew what she was saying and what her audience
wanted to hear. Men like H. Rap Brown and Stokely
Carmichael had this in common also: they knew which
way the wind blew, and which camera was working.
They were media creations who would bite the feeding
hand, but not so hard that toothmarks marred the palm.

Mom-mom sent a letter, saying, "You don't answer at the market now. We'll be there this weekend
and would love to have you visit. Just Tony and me
and some friends."

"And our little blind archer?" she asked. "Our
wealthy musical Cupid. Will he be there?"

"Others too."

"Just you and me and Mom-mom make thirty-
three," she said. "Will she mind if I come with you?
Tag along?"

That night he dreamed of banishment, the sense
that he would come to see as augury that something
evil entered, and their isolation could not be pre-
served. What walked abroad would stalk them too; it
could not be avoided, Alice said. He had no talent for
language; when he offered this opinion she did not disagree. "I'm leaving," Alice said. "I've got to get off this
island."

"When?"

"Not the next ferry. But soon."

Call it boredom, they agreed, belief or the convic-

tion of inequity that ought to be addressed—for where
Fred Hampton slept and woke to hear the Chicago police was by extension their bed also. A nation that permitted this would not permit them privacy. They were,
in the already hackneyed phrase, for the revolution or
against it, part of the solution or the problem—not
happily aloof no matter how protected by birth chance
or choice.

When the rain came south southeast it streamed
in through the window casings; shingling on the northern wall looked black. The nights were bleak. They
found a book on constellations and tried to identify
stars. He was proud of his ability to spot Orion's belt.
Some mornings she remained in bed; some afternoons
it seemed too much trouble to dress. She said he should
learn to relax. At times when he lay next to her, the
pattern on the wall—crosspieces of the rocking chair,
the paper sporting a motif of a captain with a beard
and pea jacket, smoking a pipe, holding a ship's wheel
in one hand, a threatless whale spouting to starboard—
appeared instructive. There was locution in the mist if
only he could follow it, a message in the wind, some
cipher cawed by starlings at the chimney. He felt on
the verge of clarity, the brink of change; she cupped
her hand to his neck.

In the morning, however, the weather cleared, and
they spent the day on the beach. They walked to where
the dunes began and took off their clothes. He spread
their towels on the slope of the first of Zack's Cliffs.
They faced Squibnocket Pond. Unbroken sand stretched
west and east; there was water before and behind them.
Geese rested there, and gulls. "I love you," Alice said.

"It makes a difference, doesn't it, this sun?"

She laughed. He said turn over, and she turned. There was no wind. He kissed her breasts, then stomach, then the slight rise of her abdomen. "I'm getting fat," she said. He shook his head. He worked his tongue along the inside of her legs the fluttering way that she liked it, lightly, from her ankle to her thigh to the lips of her cunt. She placed her hands on his hair. She burrowed a declivity by shifting weight in the sand. That scooping motion moved him—the sideways swing of her buttocks, weak sun on his back—and when he rose to enter her he felt completed, unafraid, the twinned half embracing, made whole.

II

Yet voice changes pitch over time. Strain and training alter it; so do cigarettes, whiskey, and age. Compare early Billie Holiday with late, the first recorded Armstrong vocals with the last. Mr. Jelly Roll gets hard to hear, the needle going blunt.

David wrote a story about a deaf boy who lip-read at speed. So rapid was "Allan," in fact, that he finished the phrase a stranger began, completing conversations by himself. In this way dialogue proved monologue, and the voices in his head were a chorale. Then he wrote a novella called *Wolf.* A philandering bass player discovers the "wolf" in his instrument, that dead space where vibrations cancel out. In the end he dies of lupus, dreaming himself back on stage.

Ventriloquy next engaged his attention. He wrote a piece about a Charlie McCarthy-like dummy who could throw his voice. The puppet imagined himself his own master, and that he went on TV. This happened. The puppet became, briefly, a celebrity—with T-shirts and beach towels and thermos bottles and lunch boxes emblazoned with his face. David, promoting his work, felt like just such a puppet on talk shows—given two minutes' air time only, and someone else's script. Through the years of his professional attainment (the job at Sarah Lawrence, the job with *The New Republic,* the television work, the time in Hollywood authoring the screenplay of *The Hut*) he felt himself a mouthpiece, not so much a writer as someone being written. His agent got pregnant and quit. His parents died. He edited anthologies. He met Mom-mom and Tony once, by accident, on location in Barbados; there was a strained silence between them. They were delighted, they said, they had so much in common and so much talking to do. It was terrible the way time flew, but aren't we looking well.

Voice is a function and aspect of speech. Yet it predates utterance; a child will voice complaint or pleasure with no language. Nor is language irreplaceable. The cries of love, of anger, the ululations of the hunter and the haunted—these too are voice. They resound. We are the sum of others' stories, and they the sum of others, and so on in a kind of chorus: a round, a catch, a half-heard snatch of song. Everywhere he went they told him, story of my life. . . .

The family flew to Tortola in 1983. It was their son Billy's school vacation. It would be, said Alice, a second honeymoon or—she raised her hands—that's that.

"That's what?" he asked.

"The end."

"Is this an ultimatum?"

"Yes." She had called the travel agent, made the reservations, and presented him with tickets. "Let's see if there's anything left."

"Why Tortola?" David asked.

She handed him a folder: British Virgin Islands, the *Welcome Tourist* guide. There was a cloudless sky, a seascape with islands, and a boat whose spinnaker looked like the Union Jack.

"A quiet place," said Alice. "Where there won't be many distractions. Just sun and sea, the two of us."

"And Billy. He can keep score."

"I can cancel," Alice said. "If you don't want to give it a try."

She was wearing her navy blue jumpsuit, and her hair in ringlets. "What the hell," he offered. "At least it isn't Virgin Gorda. All those Rockefeller intimates staying decent for each other's sake. Someone just came back from Little Dix."

"Who?"

"And they said it was so *comme il faut* you wanted to break plates."

"Who said that?"

"I can't remember." For the moment he honestly could not remember, and his irritation at forgetting flared. "It doesn't matter anyway. She wasn't pretty, if that's what you mean."

"I mean," said Alice, "everything we talk about turns into an argument. It did again, just now. I want to try to have a family vacation, to see if it can work again. That isn't too much to ask."

"No." He raised his hands, in conscious imitation of her previous gesture. "It isn't, is it? Let's see."

The flight was full. American Airlines had overbooked, and they offered cash to passengers who would be willing to wait. There were few of these, however, and the amount increased. Finally, prior to boarding, nine hundred dollars in travel vouchers were offered to three ticket holders, and seats on the next open flight. "What do you think?" David asked. "This flight's certain," Alice said. "The connecting flight's certain, the one from San Juan. I think we should do what we promised we'd do." Billy nodded, solemn, sleepy. She stubbed out her cigarette and stood.

It aggrieved him that she seemed so resolute—unwilling to take chances on a future trip. He compiled a list of grievances while they took their seats; he nursed them during takeoff and through dry martinis that seemed a single swallow in his clear plastic cup. Billy hated lunch. He said the chicken tasted yucky and he tore the salad dressing packet; it spilled across his cake. "Can I have yours?" Billy asked, and David told him no.

"You can have mine," Alice said. "But try to be more careful, darling." Billy spilled his Coke.

The air in San Juan was palpable; he felt as if he had walked into a steambath wearing clothes. Men in shorts brandished cigars; a woman in a sari tried to sell him pamphlets on the peace that comes from bliss. There was no one at the counter for Air British Virgin Islands; they proceeded to the gate. The woman in the

sari drifted through the terminal, soliciting. He thought
of her as someone's daughter, lost and far from home;
would her parents know her, passing through San Juan?
   The second flight, however, had about it something celebratory—a sense of actual distance traveled
and, therefore, impending release. The sun set as they
flew. They passed through Customs easily and walked
out under palm fronds in an evening breeze. Billy found
a shell. He held it up, delighted, and the taxi driver
was too.
   They rattled over a one-lane bridge. "The Queen
Elizabeth Bridge," their driver said. "This connects Beef
Island to Tortola. Queen Elizabeth herself arrived to
open it in 1966." He had been to England for three
months three years before; he said it was too cold. He
drove his aging Mercury on the left side of the road.
They passed goats and Land-Rovers and trucks alarm-
ingly. Every quarter mile or so, the driver slowed and
rocked across a ridge. "We call them sleeping policemen. It keep you from driving too quick."
   Their hotel fronted the water. Long-fluked fans beat
at the air above them, and a piano player adapted Bea-
tles songs. By the time they had unpacked, a saxo-
phonist arrived, and he played "Yesterday." Then they
played stately Calypso, stressing "Island in the Sun."
David had purchased rum at the airport. He poured
drinks. They had a double bed and rollaway bed in addition; there was a balcony. Sailboats clustered thickly
to the jetty at their left. "Your health," he said, and
Alice said, "To us."
   Billy fell asleep without his dinner. They sat on
the balcony, shoeless. "I'm glad we came," she offered.
"I'm glad we didn't trade our tickets for a later flight."

He sniffed the air for sugarcane and listened for the sound of a steel band. "What's that dance they do, the limbo?"

"You're thinking of Jamaica," Alice said.

What he was thinking of was youth—the glittering discovery of prowess, the future envisioned that now was their past. They used to dance. They used to make love on the floor; then they thought of middle age as their present age. He could remember couples on Squibnocket Beach, with picnic hampers and beach chairs and plastic inflatable boats and buckets and shovels and children on Donald Duck towels. He threaded his way past them once but would take his place there now. Billy muttered in his sleep. It was like those fairy tales in which the granted wish came all too literally true. When was the last time, he asked her, that they did the unexpected—took off all their clothes, for instance, and went for a midnight swim?

"Don't go getting maudlin," Alice said.

"See what I mean? I suggest we go for a swim, and you call it a midlife crisis."

"I didn't say that. Billy's sleeping."

"Wake him up. Or let him sleep."

"It's our first night here," she said. "He's seven years old. We can't just leave him sleeping in a strange hotel."

"Q.E.D." He finished his drink. "That which was about to be proven has been proved."

Next day they did go swimming; after breakfast they walked to the pool. There was an exercise class in the water, and a tape deck producing music; an instructor in a bathing cap smiled up at them expansively. David felt white and bloated and, even in dark glasses, forced to squint. Alice rubbed Billy with sunblock and made him wear a hat. He counted seven women in the pool. They wore water wings on their arms. "Why can't they swim?" asked Billy, and Alice said, "They can."

"Why are they wearing floaters, then?"

"It makes them move more slowly. It's like an added weight."

David lowered his chaise longue and lay in the sun. "One and two and three," the women chanted, bobbing. "Four and five and six." The song proclaimed the singer's intention to do it all night long. The women in the pool were plump and elderly; water lapped at their waists. It blurred their bending legs. "Ex*tend*," the teacher chanted. "Back and *two* and three."

"Can we go swimming, Daddy?"

"In a minute."

"Can we, Mommy?"

"Soon," she said.

"I'm hot. I'm boiling."

"You can go in by yourself."

"*Can* I, Mommy?"

"Daddy will take you," she said.

He let the sun invade him; he tried to hear nothing but music. "And *up* and down and *three* and four and up and *six* and hold!" There were palm trees by the guardrail, and an empty kiddy pool whose blue cement had cracked. In the fork of the palm trees fruit hung; he tried to distinguish if that which soared brightly above him was coconut or breadfruit. He tried to remember, also, the names of such tropical trees. There were trees called woman's tongue with long, rattling pods that clattered in the breeze; there were tulip and flamboyant trees, and many flowering bushes that he could not name. "I'm boiling," Billy said again, and David said, "Let's swim."

What he was hoping for, he wanted to tell them, was peace: no clamorous expectancy or bills. He wanted to sleep in the sun. He stood in the shallow end, helping his son do the dead man's float; he applauded the distance that Billy could swim. Alice read. The women in the exercise session smiled at him approvingly; a frigate bird flew past.

Alice praised his books. She did so, however, with a certain caution and what he thought was reserve. He resented this. He feared her pride in him masked disappointment, her flattery disdain. She said, "I'm sorry, he's working," when the phone rang in the morning and he was not yet at work. She said, "You *have* to read this. It's terrific," about the latest pan-flash, the coffee-table talent of the month. He thought this a betrayal. Her enthusiasm for the work of others should be tempered, he believed, by greater admiration of his own. That she never voiced a criticism—she who could be so severely critical of how he drank, or talked, or dressed—made him the more suspicious: she was holding back. Her silence had enlarged—the praise ringing hollow, the compliments false—to become an echo of David's own self-doubt.

"You're projecting," Alice said.

"No."

"What do you want me to tell you?"

"The truth."

"The whole truth." Alice raised her hand. "And nothing but the truth."

"So help you, God," he said.

"I mean it. I just love the story."

"Except?"

"Except I don't just love an inquisition. And you don't want my criticism, and it's simpler all around if we just leave it alone."

He pondered this. He had given her the galleys, not the typescript of *The Hut*. Some part of him had surely known she would not take it well. The story of their courtship had been tailored to his hero's past, then butchered for the benefit of plot. She said he was dishonest, and that art required honesty; he said the problem is that honesty needs art.

That afternoon they took a taxi on a tour. The roads were steep. A road called Joe's Hill led to the crest of the island; the switchbacks were continual and the climb abrupt. Billy had wanted to stay in the pool. "You don't want too much sun," said Alice. "Not our first day out . . ."

Their driver was thick-armed, affable. He wore a red cloth cap, an earring in his right ear, and a goatee. "Mac's my name," he said. "They call me Mac the Knife." He drove them to a restaurant at the island's highest point, from which they could survey Drake's Channel and the multicolored sea. "You got this only boy?" he asked. "You just beginning, Missus?"

"No. How many do you have?"

"The ones I know about?" Mac the Knife winked broadly. "Eight at the table and one in the oven."

He recited the names of his children, their ages, the name of his wife, the place they lived, how many brothers he himself was raised with—and this singsong

litany, half-comprehensible, became a kind of counterweight to David's own attempt at measure: what had
he accumulated and what was it worth? He was a member of the PEN Club, the Century Association, and the
Writers Guild; his third book was translated into seven
languages. Mac said, "I come back in an hour. Maybe
two."

A cement truck blew its horn. Mac turned on the
radio, made a U-turn, and rattled away. Clouds massed
above the bay, and the wind was easterly. At the restaurant entrance, Alice smiled. "It's beautiful here. That
island"—she pointed—"it's named for a pirate. Van
Dyke."

The sun was hot. They stood together at the
guardrail, watching the few whitecaps and the sailboats
and the ferryboats and what looked like a tanker in the
distance. "Jost Van Dyke," he said aloud. "What happened to us, do you think?"

Billy shouted from the observation deck above
them. "A *big* boat, Mommy."

"Happened to us?"

"Yes," he said. "The romance of the trade winds.
Galleons. All those one-eyed buccaneers, and maidens
walking the plank." He gestured at the horizon. "The
way it used to be."

A waiter said, "Your table, sir," and they ordered
rum. "The difference between us," said Alice, "is that
you refuse to grow up. You think the world owes you
attention, and I think we owe attention to the world."

This had the ring of rehearsal. "A fine phrase,"
he said.

"I mean it. You've got to grow up."

Billy clattered down the stairs. "Your mother thinks

I'm selfish," David said. "But she's wrong. Watch this. You can order ice cream—or a piece of that huge chocolate cake on the table there. And I won't take one bite."

Billy grinned, expectant. He went to examine the cake. "How could you call me selfish?" David asked.

Alice lit a cigarette. She did this in moments of anger, or concentration; she would not be deflected. "My hero." She stubbed out the match.

"Are you seeing someone else?" he asked.

"That's not the point."

"But are you?"

"Would it matter? No."

He studied her. In the bright light she looked pale. A sense of their shared history assaulted him, and its physical concomitant—Billy, the lines at her mouth, the weight of the flesh at her chin. "You're a beautiful woman," he said. His throat thickened at the waning of such beauty, and he took her hand. "I've been paying too little attention. I'm sorry."

Billy came back. "I want cake."

They ordered cake. He ate it, and David started whistling "Mac the Knife."

Alvin Prendergast had sparse white hair, a moustache stained by nicotine, and a stomach that seemed larger each time he and David met. They had known each other since Harvard, where Alvin studied architecture; by coincidence they moved into the same apartment building on West End Avenue and Ninety-seventh Street. Alvin loved David's novel, he said, and made him sign a dozen copies of *The Hut*; they would make Christmas gifts. He praised the second book lavishly also, and bought six copies of the collection *Reality Principle: Tales.* In 1976, however—and before the publication of David's most successful book, *Orison*—Alvin said he had had it with climate control, the rat race, and nuclear threat; he would rather build with cane and thatch than reinforced concrete.

He announced this, the writer remembered, at lunch. They ate together often, or the families had drinks. Alice and Carrie were friends. The women played tennis on Wednesdays and took the same aerobics class. Sometimes David thought of them, towel-swaddled, gleaming in the sauna, interchangeable. They would raise their legs from the hot cedar bench and open their four arms.

The Prendergasts' marriage went bad. Carrie said he was smothering her. He came back home and sprawled on the couch, she complained, and shed all over everything like a Great Pyrenees. If she wanted a lapdog, she said, it shouldn't have to be two hundred pounds and give her no personal space. "I'm an architect," he said to David, "right? The one thing I *know* is personal space. A room with a view, Christ, a room of her own . . ." Alvin twisted his napkin. He made distracted motions with his knife. "Does Alice give you that?"

He chewed carrots and celery sticks. He had been sailing that winter and come to a decision; he'd said to himself, Alvin, old boy, you're not getting any younger, there's nobody who needs you and precious little you need. Three of the things you need are right here: a steady breeze, manageable anchorage, and cheap abundant rum. He could live five times as well in Road Town for one fifth the price.

So he had moved to Tortola. He was one of the two licensed architects in town. Did David remember the Babar books; had he seen them lately? The town of Celesteville was Road Town; Alvin thought of it that way. The palm trees and the coconuts and pastel stucco houses and porches and light green shutters; that had been his first impression of the place. He expected to see elephants in costume on the dock. Your standards of beauty can change, he said, your expectations of what houses and women should look like. He, David, should come down. He could do a travel piece, or maybe one of those "far-flung correspondent" numbers for *The New Yorker,* or just let his typewriter rest. Alvin built a house from time to time, or helped with a government building, or provided a hotel with a patio and pool; it wasn't full-time work. He wanted it that way. He had "personal space" in the channel, and no disapproving first mate. He sent the Lewins postcards—of sunsets, beaches, girls in bikinis, and men wrestling game fish or standing proudly beside them. He always printed, in block letters, WISH YOU COULD BE HERE. When Alice came home with the tickets, and they looked at the hotel brochure, David said, "He's there."

"Who?"

"Alvin. You remember."

"That will be nice," Alice said.

When she was eleven, her family went to the Yukon. It was their first shared vacation, and it would be the last. Their father had wanted to camp past the tree line, where everything is visible. What comes at you comes from a distance, he said—you see elk miles away. Yet the ground got softer, springy, and she remem-

bered walking in a kind of marsh, sinking to her knees
each step and asking him if moss could freeze, if the
Arctic was just frozen mud.

Her sisters complained. Her mother refused to
complain, spreading out the picnic cloth and taking
sandwich meats from the hamper and pouring milk and
cold tea from the thermos with the kind of scrupulous
attention that meant she was furious, resigned, not about
to quarrel but past compromise already, totaling each
day's discomfort in the ledger labeled Grievance that
their marriage had become. Her mother had been a
good sport. She could go anywhere, uncomplaining; she
could rock-climb and fry ham with the best of them,
or serve tea in a marsh. But there was nothing yielding
in the gesture, no complicity; she sat apart.

Alice had a horror of sitting in that fashion; she
saw it these years in herself. Her father, for instance,
could never remember if she took milk in her tea. It
was silly to complain—but somehow his forgetfulness
had mattered a great deal to her. It stood for all his
years away, his conclaves with the Hunt Club or lawyers or district attorney while she waited in the hall.
She had thought that fathers were supposed to do the
waiting; they were proud to come and get you after
ballet school. They smoked a pipe outside the stable
while you worked the jumps. They waited, checking
the clock, for you to return from the prom. But it hadn't
seemed that way in Chapel Hill. She was the one who
waited. He would come out from the bowling league
twenty minutes late; he'd emerge from a meeting to
wink at her, saying, "Just a second, honey, I'll be right
along." He'd cover the telephone receiver while she sat
across the desk, and look up and whisper "Soon."

Once she asked him, "Daddy, why'd you keep me waiting?" It had not been easy, asking. Her manners rebelled, and her habit of obedience; she had smiled and asked offhandedly, as if the question just occurred to her and the answer didn't matter and was just a point of interest. He had ignored her, hands in his pockets, studying the floor. Bravely she repeated it; she knew he had some sense of time that was not hers, not theirs, not anyone's in Chapel Hill. " 'They also serve who only stand and wait,' " he said at last. "That's worth remembering."

Alice pondered this injunction—for it had been one, clearly, a way of checkreining her rush. He spoke of the virtues of patience. He was patient himself, explaining it, saying time that hurtles when you're young becomes all you ever have to deal with, dying of starvation in a prison camp. You die of boredom, really. It's no accident, he said, that another word for patience is the game of solitaire. It's what you learn when solitary, and it doesn't hurt in public either; patience is a game we all must learn to play.

She remembered her own childhood rhyme. "Patience is a virtue, virtue is a grace. Grace is a naughty girl who wouldn't wash her face." Patience wouldn't wash her face, she could remember cackling; patience was a naughty girl—and virtue didn't enter into it, or if it came it did so slantways, twenty yards from center stripe in the hockey field, whispered by Marsha Prentiss who had been french-kissed already and had seen Tommy Altschulter's thing.

Her father had no patience with anyone's imperatives but those he made his own. He preached silence and exile and cunning, chattily, from the screen porch.

He would freshen up her Shirley Temple with a sprig of mint. He had been born in their house; the house had belonged to his family since the first brick was fired: exile is easy to preach.

Two days after their arrival, Alvin came to the hotel. He drove an ancient Jaguar sedan with a bright blue right rear fender; he had acquired a limp. His white shirt sported pineapples and grapes, and the legend *Welcome to Daiquiri Country* on his chest. He had not shaved. "Davey boy," he said, and embraced Alice lingeringly. Then he held her at arm's length. "A sight for sore eyes, sweetie. You look terrific. Why don't you leave this bum and stay down here with me?"

She laughed. "You've got a lunch date, remember?"

"I'll leave the bum at lunch and we can sail away."

"Meet Billy," Alice said.

Billy presented himself. They shook hands.

"Well, all right then," said Alvin. "So what's-his-name and me will go to Rotary instead. Don't say I didn't ask you."

"When you're finished . . ." David said.

Alvin licked at a cigar. In the car he continued his banter. "Did you hear the one about the Irishman and Mexican? The Mexican asks the Irishman, 'In your language do you have a word for *mañana*?' 'Yes,' says Paddy. 'But it has less urgency.'" He repeated this, delighted. "*Mañana*'s too urgent, you see."

"How are you, really?"

"I'm good." He waved at a man in a doorway. "I like this way of living."

"You live alone?"

"With visitors." He pointed out the governor's house, and the hospital. A cruise ship had arrived and was disgorging passengers; taxis crowded to the pier. "I'm not in touch with Carrie, if that's what you mean. We parted, as the lawyers say, amicably. She sold the apartment, of course. She costs only half what I make."

"Is she still living in New York?"

"That's where the checks go," said Alvin. He made a left turn, and they started climbing. Schoolchildren idled past. He pulled into a hotel parking lot. "We meet here once a week. It's the one appointment I do try to keep."

The bar was full. A man sat at the door, with a checklist for members and guests. David gave his name, and the recording secretary—an Englishman in a beige linen suit—filled out a lapel card. "Alvin's guest," he said. "Well, we can't help that, can we?" The Englishman beamed, showing teeth. "You're welcome anyway. What brings you to us, Dave?"

"Pleasure," Alvin said. "This is an important man. This is the great writer. I'm buying. What's your drink?"

There was a swimming pool outside, and a view of the bay. Rotarians came up to Prendergast and clapped him on the back or took him by the elbow and then shook David's hand. Several were black. They spoke about the weather and the question of beach rights on Virgin Gorda and the proposed hospital addition. They discussed Prince Charles and whether he was as good as Prince Philip with horses.

"Philippos," someone said. "That means 'lover of horses' in Greek." This was the minister. He was being transferred to Nevis in a week. Alvin said to David that the minister was being censured; he had answered

the telephone, "Planned Parenthood; can we help you?" once too often. There was laughter at the bar. They asked him how long he would stay on the island, how long he had known Prendergast, and what kind of novels he wrote and if he liked to fish.

David tried to listen. He thought of Alice by the pool, and Billy with his flippers on. The recording secretary was assessing fines. One Rotarian had gotten in line before his guest; one brother had failed to maintain silence during grace; one had said there were an "awful lot" of visitors. This insult drew a fine of fifty cents. You should not call your visitors an "awful lot." There was laughter, then applause. There was a raffle. There was a speech about providing for the anticipated increase of tourism attendant on completion of Marina Cay. There was a round of applause for the minister, and best wishes from the membership of the Tortola chapter for his continued health, prosperity, and happiness.

The minister stood. He took small, cautious steps to the microphone; he wheezed at it, clearing his throat. He then made the sign of the cross. "You forget," he said, "my own immortal soul." He handed the microphone to the presiding officer, returned to his seat, and sat down. There was a moment's silence. Then the presiding officer—a black man with high sloping shoulders and white muttonchop whiskers—said, "That's your department, Father. We don't interfere."

Again there was laughter and prolonged applause. "Great bunch," said Alvin, "right? You always know just where you stand, this is a great bunch of guys." They left. The afternoon was bright; the leather seats of Alvin's car retained and gave off heat.

* * *

Orison is a novel, David explained, about voice.
He gave interviews. Remember how Claudius, kneel-
ing, says prayers rise to heaven while his thoughts remain below? Remember Hamlet saying, "Nymph, in
thy orisons, be all my sins remember'd"? It is not clear,
however—and staging must take this into account—if
the prince intends this as a question or imperative, if
he says so in her hearing or when she cannot hear.

Much of what we learn is voiceless—the body language of a friend or enemy, the caressing motions of
bereavement or maternity or sex. When we say we
"change our voice," we mean it changes pitch. But how
does this relate, the interviewer asked, to that scene
where Jack almost drowns in his kayak, off by Noman's
Land? If you have to ask, said David, the scene just
doesn't work; what I wrote is what I meant. Did you
always know, they asked him, that you would be a writer;
when did you first start writing, what are your favorite
books? Do you use a pen, they asked; what are your
work habits; what hours do you work?

We throw the reader "plot," he said, as the dog
trainer throws a bone: first to engage attention and second to reward it—but not because the bone as such
matters in the telling trick. If we are the sum of other
stories, others' stories, then the game is zero sum.
Thanks so much, they said, this has been very interest-
ing. We're not sure we can run it, we'll see how much
we can print.

That night Alvin joined the Lewins for dinner at
The Pub. It was, he said, the place for *tout* Tortola. His
exaggerated courtliness continued through the meal. He

referred to himself as Alice's ardent admirer; he said he hadn't been so happy since the last time they met. They should quit the rat race—all of them—and come to the island to stay. There were no tax problems; as a resident alien David could pay nickels on the dollar; that's what Alvin did. His whole tax bite—he clicked his tongue, demonstrating "bite" for Billy's sake—had been one hundred twenty-seven dollars this last year. You couldn't beat it, he said; he, Alvin, couldn't beat it and he doubted others could. They should try the tuna or the dolphin steak—he clicked his tongue again—grilled.

Men clustered to the bar. They played a game called "foosball"—with wooden soccer players on a rotating stick. They scored goals with golf balls when the goalie failed to block; there were seven balls. Billy went over to watch. Alice sat with her back to the water, the moonlight behind her, wearing a white shawl. "Two days of this," said David, "and I feel I've shed two weeks of winter." His skin felt pleasantly puckered by sun; he tasted the salt on his lips.

"You know why we came down here?" Alice asked.

"To see me," Alvin said.

"I'm being serious. Has David told you?"

"No."

He looked for his son at foosball.

"I want a divorce," Alice said.

Billy was standing, his head at table level, his back to them, absorbed.

"He's practicing avoidance," Alice said. "He could have mentioned it."

"I wanted to give you the pleasure. I knew you'd want the fun of making the announcement."

"I'm sorry," Alvin said.

"For what?"

He spread his hands. "Your trouble."

"It isn't your fault, Alvin. Don't apologize."

"It's nobody's fault," Alice said. "It's something that happens, that's all."

"I didn't know. I'm sorry."

The waitress appeared, checking drinks. "Another round?" she said.

"I've been through this, remember? I know what you kids feel."

"You don't know," Alice said. "You don't have any idea." She put her hand on David's forearm, not lightly. "I just thought I'd sound it out. I don't like the way it sounds."

Billy returned. "Can *I* play, Daddy? When they're finished." His hamburger arrived, and there were home fries and pickles.

Alvin leaned back on the bench. He locked his hands behind his head, stretching the pink shirt. "You two amaze me. You do. I'd forgotten how much fun it is to yank at the short hairs, correct?"

"Correct," said Alice. "As you so elegantly put it."

"Can I have another Shirley Temple?" Billy asked.

"Love," said David, in the intonation he knew his wife hated, "love is a spectator sport." Their waitress brought the dolphin, and he concentrated on that. By the cheesecake there was peace between them, camaraderie again, and they agreed to meet next morning to sail to Peter Island on Alvin's catamaran.

That night he dreamed of sailing, and the drone of the fan above him seemed like the sound of the surf. It was irregular, off-center, and the shift into rotation invaded his light sleep. They were on that blue-green water he could see beyond the bedroom, but it might equally have signified the Aegean or South China Sea. Natives pranced along the shore. He could not tell, however, if they welcomed or warned him away.

David woke. His wife was breathing heavily, her face slack. This made him tender toward her. He got out of bed and cracked open the balcony screen and sat on the balcony, smoking. In holding on, he asked himself, what was he holding on to, what attempting to retain that was not past retention, and would not memory go with him where he went? He was enacting, dutiful, his own imagined scene. He felt precisely centered, in an equilibrium not so much the consequence of balance as inertia self-opposed.

The last time Alice saw her father, he visited New York. He called to say he was in town and explained he was there on a case. He had depositions to take. Yet something in the timbre of his explanation—some pause to light a cigarette, the exhalation signaling not intimacy but pride, an after-dinner chattiness with brandy and unloosened tie—told her her father wasn't alone, was there on business not business as such. He asked her to meet him, by herself, at Jack's. The table was reserved for three—and she had been, if not prepared, unsurprised.

The maître d'hôtel bowed her in. Jack's was a good choice: the room well-lit but private, the decor unassuming to the point of ostentation. She ordered Dubonnet. She saw her father enter behind an Oriental woman—short and thick and gray, so absolutely not what she expected that Alice thought they were entering separately, strangers, and maybe she was wrong.

Then the pair approached. The woman smiled at her, showing gold teeth. Alice rose. "I'd like to introduce you," said her father. "Wa-Lee, this is Alice. Alice, Wa-Lee." Wa-Lee did not giggle but seemed to. They sat.

That night a tale unfolded—decorous, oblique, but unmistakably a tale of passion. Alice heard it out. Her father did most of the talking; Wa-Lee nodded for emphasis. When he came out of prison camp he had been sent, for the first stage of his debriefing and recovery, to Honolulu. There she attended him. Wa-Lee was a hospital orderly. "Not so much a nurse," she said, "as 'Assistant Nurse.' " At night she cleaned the ward. One night he beckoned her to talk, begging for companionship, unable to sleep in the bright dormitory light. In halting English she conveyed to him that blindness was best, that what you see is horror and better to keep your eyes closed. She massaged him skillfully. He shut his eyes and did not mind that he remained awake, that nothing induced him to dream.

She had seven sisters who worked in Maui, on a coffee plantation. One had married an overseer, and the other six were therefore also employed. The overseer, however, had made improper advances to her— Wa-Lee dimpled, giggling, as her father said "improper advances"—and she fled. Heaven only knew what the other six sisters were thinking, or what their response had been; heaven knew whether or not they responded to his provocation in the fields. Kau-ling had surely responded, for her twins had cauliflower ears and the same peculiar shade of red hair on their heads. She preferred the hospital; she did not think if you married one member of a family this entitled you to sleep with the sisters as well.

Wa-Lee had been nineteen and unused to the way

of the world. That was her expression, said Alice's father, "unused to the way of the world." When this tall, silent stranger—her father smiled, apologetic at this way of describing himself—asked her please to talk to him, to remain at night so he could sleep, she thought there need be neither gossip nor recrimination on the ward. She lost her job. The supervisor made rounds while she, Wa-Lee, was dozing, catnapping, her cheek on the pillow beside him and hand on his bare back. No matter how he explained, how she protested she was helping him to rest and must have fallen asleep, briefly, by his side, not intending to, not having any reason for exhaustion or having gotten underneath the covers as the supervisor could plainly observe—no matter how they argued, Wa-Lee was dismissed.

Jack greeted them. He hoped everything was to their satisfaction and they would try the soufflé. They ordered the crabmeat soufflé. They ordered a bottle of wine. It was only after the firing, her father confessed, that he awoke to responsibility; they released him for a weekend on the town. He walked out of the hospital whistling, a citizen on his own. He had never planned to talk about those months. He apologized to Alice. He had never felt the need or the ability before. But now she, Alice, was a wife and mother, and they were in this town together and this restaurant, and she should know that Wa-Lee was an angel, that her ministration brought this patient back to life. That night on the plantation (a driver had taken him there, had known the address and the place from the piece of paper she had scribbled, leaving, and wound out of town and into the hills and up beyond the smoke into the startling trees) was paradise on earth. He came for what he failed to claim while on the ward. For all those weeks of comfort there had been nothing sexual, nothing but her hand between his shoulder blades, her palm on his eyes till he slept.

And then the world's suspicion made it plausible to act. Then they might as well be damned for wolves as sheep. He took her for a walk. Then he took her, in the recommended fashion, to a hut overlooking the valley where the workers kept a Primus stove and mattress should they need to stay the night. She took off her clothes without shame. He would spare Alice the details but assured her it was paradise on earth.

Throughout this long recital Wa-Lee remained attentive. She too appeared to hear the story as if for the first time. She smiled at the end of it widely, showing her gold teeth. "Why are you telling me this?" Alice asked, and her father answered it was time she knew. For all those years in Chapel Hill he had been a man without allegiance, remembering the hut and sweet odors of the hillside and what sounded like a nightingale beyond the open window. It was time to make amends. It was long since overdue. He had lingered in Hawaii for two months. He had been no hero, had extended his sick leave and recuperation period, and returned only halfheartedly to his wife and family—you—still hearing the nightingale, hearing Wa-Lee.

He brought her to Chicago. She was a chiropodist; he saw her whenever he could. Did Alice remember *South Pacific;* did she remember their trip to the City Center to see the revival, how the whole family—her sisters complaining, playing "Booey" on the trip and singing "Three Little Maids from School Are We"— drove north and stayed at the Biltmore; did she recollect the original cast album, with Ezio Pinza and Mary Martin, the planter singing "This Nearly Was Mine"? That was their story too. She could have seen the stranger across a crowded room, but the stranger was Wa-Lee—so their story really was the story of the flier and Bloody Mary's daughter and prejudice. It was in *The King and I.* There they sang "We Kiss in a Shadow," and there too the tale was familiar: prejudice, unyieldingness, a cross burned on the lawn. Rodgers and Hammerstein knew all about it; it was everywhere you looked the second you went looking, and took no skill to find: intolerance, indifference, the leering supervisor on the plantation or ward.

He wanted to marry, of course. But Alice's mother had not offered a divorce. She knew this part of the story, the years in Chapel Hill while they snapped at each other or were polite, the warring neighborliness and his drinking problem, then hers. Then, when they were separated, when the divorce came through—the very same week—he had flown to Chicago and, as he had promised, proposed. They were no longer in the flush of youth, the blush of it—he smiled—but this was a promise delivered. Wa-Lee said no. She had made a life of her own in Chicago and she had relatives there. Chiropody was both an ancient and an honorable trade. They knew that in Illinois.

Wa-Lee had an acrid odor, a sharp perfume unfamiliar to Alice; her laugh was loud. Her father's tale wore on. Wa-Lee had been the moon and stars to him, the life raft for a drowning man. Alice could not remember ever having heard him talk so much, or with such sentiment. Each time he addressed a convention, or argued a case out of town, each chance he found they met and solaced each other like castaways. "Like castaways?" she asked, and he nodded solemnly. He was tired of legalistic distinctions, sicker than she'd ever guess of dotting the *i*'s crossing *t*'s. Life is a tempest-tossed ocean, he said, on which you are a shipwrecked sailor and you dream of shore. He proposed a toast. He hadn't had this much to drink or drunk it with two people he loved more since heaven knew when. He wanted them to understand how much this evening mattered. Wa-Lee's English is far better than you think, he said, she knows what I'm trying to say. She's been in Chicago since 1961 and has heard it all.

Wa-Lee ordered zabaglione for dessert. The waiter slipped, approaching them, and in a caricature-frantic attempt at a save, hurled the zabaglione into her lap. She shrieked. There were apologies. The maître d'hô-tel bestirred himself to wipe her, but she drew back from him, dripping. They stood. Alice thought about the songs from *South Pacific* and *The King and I,* her father in the prison camp, then hospital, and then re-ceiving comfort from a limber Wa-Lee in the hut.

He had lost, if not his birthright or familial pride in Chapel Hill, at least all sense of home there, home-coming, the center of things come unstuck. She thought about her father's baffled payment for the privilege of declaration, a confidence exchanged (though till that moment there had been no countervailing equivalent, no "Dad, I knew it all along, we all did, I'm so glad you're happy, I don't know what went wrong . . ."), showing his daughter a gap-toothed fat Hawaiian mas-seuse in this place aswarm now with waiters, an apron produced, Jack insisting that they send the bill to his personal attention, and if dry cleaning failed then buy

a dress on him—thought maybe it was true and Wa-
Lee had saved her father's life, saved anyhow his sense
of possibility, thought therefore her own childhood had
been shaped by something she herself had till then
known nothing about, no name to call it but absence,
no face to give it but blank.

Alvin came at nine. He had a picnic hamper on
the backseat of the Jaguar, and an extra life preserver.
He was apologetic. "I rode you pretty hard last night,"
he said. "This morning I'll behave myself, I promise.
Hey, Billy, you know why a lawyer can swim in this
water without fear of sharks?"

"No," said Billy. "Why?"

"Professional courtesy." Alvin guffawed. "He's got
professional courtesy, see?"

David explained to his son what professional courtesy meant; Billy laughed. There were whitecaps on the
water, and the wind was high. "We'll motor out," said
Alvin. "Then raise sail."

On water he seemed less of a buffoon. He positioned them expertly, readied the craft, and cast off.
There was no waste motion in him now; he worked
without talking. Ferry boats roared past. Tacking, he
told Billy to hold on. When the harbor receded, however, and they held a straight course in Drake's Channel and the jib was set to Alvin's satisfaction, he opened
a beer. He offered one to Alice, who declined. He told
them he had fishing gear, if anyone wanted to fish. "You
look like a pirate," she said.

"I don't feel well," said Billy.

"What's the matter, darling?"

He shrugged. "I just don't feel well, Mommy."

"Does your stomach hurt you?"

He nodded.

"Badly?"

"I need to upchuck," he said.

David laughed.

She turned on him. "I'm glad you find it funny."

"I don't," he said. "Just typical."

"Terrific." She bent over Billy.

"He'll get used to it," said Alvin. "Won't you, sport?"

Billy nodded, his face green.

"Take deep breaths," David advised. The catamaran pitched and rolled. "Lean over the side, if you have to. We're almost halfway there."

"Think of it like Popeye," Alvin said. "Like Popeye the Sailor Man." He grimaced, squinted, did a two-step. "I loves me spinach, yum-yum."

Billy did not love spinach. He buried his head in his hands. His mother rocked him cautiously, embracing the orange preserver, one hand on his neck. "Breathe deeply," David said again. Billy's shoulders shook. A pelican immelmanned past.

"Think of Columbus," Alvin said. "Discovering America. These are the waters he sailed."

Billy was sick. He gagged and retched. Alice held his waist. Alvin brought the boat into the wind, and they made their way in silence for what seemed like a long time. Then Billy collapsed back into place and David asked, "Feel better now?" and he nodded. "Seasickness," Alvin said. "It happens to everyone once."

Peter Island had a newly built resort. It was of brown wood, with roofs painted blindingly white, and a central structure with restaurants and gift shops and a swimming pool. The manager emerged. He knew Alvin from the Rotary Club, and David from the day before, and he made much of Billy and gave him a white golf cap with *Peter Island* on the bill. They had ice cream on the patio, and Billy said he felt much better. They boarded a golf cart and drove to the beach. These are vacation rituals, David said to Alice, this is what a family is supposed to do by way of enjoyment.

She lay in the shade of a palm tree, while the men lay in the sun. There was a raft in the water, and sunfish and paddle-wheelers for rent. There was an open-air bar, and David brought her rum and tonic in a plastic cup. The swizzle stick had a pink parasol on top. She smiled at him, accepting it. "It's beautiful here," Alice said.

"Yes."

"I've been imagining nuns. Dreaming of"—she smiled again—"the Holy Orders. Don't they renew their vows?"

"Something like that," David said.

"I don't know much about it. But I think that's what we're doing."

He put his hand on her knee. She did not move away. She was watching Billy as he shaped a sand castle with moats.

Alvin had a yellow pail. Big-bellied, absorbed, he was pouring water on the turrets of the structure. He was making stucco, he said, sand-driblets like Gaudi's best. "It's worth it?" David asked.

That night, however, it wasn't worth it; he knew this on the balcony and, later, in their bed. It hadn't been worth it for years. There was nothing between

them but Billy, and habit, and the self-affrighting solace of pressing on a bruise. She knew it too. She had
known it all along. He had been raised with the conviction that marriage lasts, and family, and that you
married once only till death did you part. Yet there
were little daily deaths, and the carapace of good behavior cracked to birth a corpse. He had fashioned a
career. He had written three books and was completing a fourth. He had used up their story. He was nothing on his own. He spent the next week swimming,
watching Billy learn to surface dive and stand on his
hands in the pool.

PANIC

It seemed to be the season for marriages again. Robert Potter was forty-three. In his twenties the weddings took place in September; this year, unaccountably, they filled every weekend in June. He was invited to six. Two of the couples were children of friends—romantic striplings fresh from college or completing business school. More of them were second marriages, or third—with complicated etiquette as to who invited whom. In one case the woman was pregnant and, in one case, blind. What interested Robert was the month: the late-spring sense of possibility and risk. He went to the weddings alone. Marriage represented—as someone said, making a toast—the triumph of hope over experience.

"I've heard that before," he told his partner at lunch. "Yes."

"Who said it?"

She was tall, black-haired. He tried to read her place card.

"Dr. Johnson." She had put on glasses to watch the round of toasts.

" 'The triumph of hope over experience,' " he repeated. "Lovely, isn't it?"

"It's lovely, yes," the woman said. She pursed her lips to drink.

The groom's name was Shem. His best man made a jingle: Shem would marry the *crème de la crème*. Robert barely knew the happy couple, but the bride's father was a college friend as well as neighbor, and he explained this to those who asked. The wedding luncheon was salmon and veal; the wines were good.

"What do you do?" the woman to his right inquired.

"I'm in real estate," he lied. "And you?"

"Photographer." She smiled at him. "And a philanthropist."

Shem and Katy make a team that will be the cream of the cream. A long and happy life was proposed, a marvelous honeymoon trip, and all the trips thereafter—this occasioned laughter from the ushers' table—a great day for the parents and grandmother of the bride. A bald man with a handlebar moustache toasted her dead grandfather. "He would have been so proud of you. He always called you his jewel. Ladies and gentlemen, friends, I speak for the elder generation when I call this girl a jewel."

The reception took place at the Explorers Club.

There were plaques and photographs and maps and
books about travel downstairs. Upstairs, on the landing, a polar bear loomed placidly above the receiving
line; someone draped a scarf across his paw. "He should
be holding the bridal bouquet," Robert said. The day
was hot. A group that called themselves The Separate
but Equal Circuit came to play. The girl who sang wore
an electric green Oriental-style sheath with side slits
high up her legs. He was offered, and accepted, a cigar.
He could not understand the lyrics, and the band was
loud. At three o'clock he excused himself, saying
"Congratulations" several times. The groom, gyrating,
bumped Robert as he left. "Sorry, old man," the groom
said.

He had been staying, since April, on the Connect-
icut coast. This weekend was the weekend he could
not have Jimmy; Jimmy and his mother were going to
Nahant. They were opening the house, she said, and
Jimmy at eleven was old enough to help. She and Robert had been divorced for two years. She could use a
man around the place—all that opening and closing,
with no one to carry the shutters or take down the
storms. Robert had offered to help. Janet hesitated
briefly before she refused. He could picture her, speculative, tapping a pencil, at the other end of the line.
"You can have him next weekend instead," she said.
"I'm sorry if it complicates your plans."
So he had gone to the wedding, arriving in time.
The minister intoned the service lengthily; the pews
were full. That Wednesday, in Old Lyme, he had attended The Burial of the Dead; the son of his first agent
had come home after school and gone to the attic and

taken his father's service revolver and shot himself in the mouth. The memorial service was brief.

"I'll miss you, Dad," said Jimmy.

"I'll miss you."

"I want a wet suit."

"Now?"

"For my birthday, OK?"

"We'll see."

"We'll see," in their negotiations, meant "yes."

"If I had it now," said Jimmy, "I could go swimming this weekend."

"No."

"Why not?"

"You're helping your mother, remember?"

"Not *all* the time."

"All the time she needs you."

"OK."

Robert smiled. He coiled the cord; he would give his son the wet suit when they met. "I want to be there when you put it on," he said. "To show you how to move in it."

"OK."

"What color do you want?"

"What colors are there?"

"Yellow," he said. "Red, I think. Mostly black."

"Black like frogmen wear?"

"That's right."

"It's what I want," Jimmy said.

The wedding one week earlier had taken place in Water Mill. Robert used the ferry from Bridgeport to Port Jefferson, then crossed Long Island in the late morning. He drove against the flow of traffic, unimpeded. The justice of the peace was garrulous; he had lost more weight sweating, he said, than he'd gained all winter. He and Robert waited for the happy couple on the porch. The bride and bridegroom gave themselves a party. The bridegroom was a novelist; he had just sold movie rights to *The Bronx Book of the Dead.* Their families were warring—the father and mother of the bride had not spoken for years, and it proved difficult to locate a city that would not be "taking sides." They had dismissed Winnetka, Asheville, and Grosse Point. So they rented a house in Water Mill and invited friends. There was a tent with a yellow and white striped awning, in case of rain. It rained. There would be a juggler and magician and steel band from Jamaica. There would be a clambake on the beach.

This wedding, said the J.P., put him fourteen short of six hundred; he'd seen all kinds. Last week, for example, at the Yacht Club there were two hours of cocktails and they had to prop up the groom. His talk, he said, would last four minutes exactly. "The first part's mine. And then I'll ask the groom a question, and his answer is 'I will.' Then the bride answers, 'I will,' then you as witness"—he nodded—"give him the ring and he gives it to her and then the last part's mine again, the legal bit."

He was planning to retire after one more term. He and the wife had a piece of land in Florida, and they figured six months here and six months there was one whole year of paradise; between you and I and the lamppost, he said, this burg gets dull in winter. What with the parking tickets, the felony charges, and the D.W.I., it's hopping all July.

"Ceremony," the groom told Robert. "I hate it. I

hate it for *me,* understand." They stood alone in the hall. "I feel like a trained seal. I really should get back to work."

"You're working?"

"No. Are you?"

The house had been recently shingled; the wedding took place on the porch. Behind the swimming pool three horses grazed, switching their tails. There were cherrystones and littlenecks waiting in abundance, and champagne. "Ceremony," the groom repeated. "Not my cup of tea."

There had also been a christening that week. At ten-thirty Robert drove to St. Peter's—a white stone pile near the center of Mystic—but the doors were locked. A man with a flower bouquet met him at the steps. "It says ten-thirty," he said. "I'm to deliver this— Pratt? You're with the Pratt party, correct? I hate to leave them sitting here," and he handed Robert the vase.

So he waited in front of St. Peter's, holding a stranger's bouquet. During the service his attention wandered, and he scanned the walls and pews. Then he joined in the responses and complimented the mother of the child. They said how brave a boy he'd be, how strong a swimmer, happy in water, how much like his mother he looked. The child was wearing, they said, his grandfather's chemise. He thought of how that other boy, eighteen years old, came home from school and looked in the kitchen, looked in the living room maybe, found nobody home and went up to the attic—the walls lined with photographs of his own father holding up bear, up antlers, up fish, with hunting knives and rod and tackle and Spanish shotguns and the pistol his great-great uncle used at Shiloh—thought how he turned on the radio loud enough to drown out not the result of his procedure but the noise of preparation, to make it seem routine when he inserted the cartridge and released the safety and, with grace, because he always had been an athlete, moving with deliberation that nonetheless felt practiced, raised it to his mouth and licked the barrel and squeezed.

His marriage had collapsed not out of restlessness or boredom but of its own weight. He met Janet in graduate school, and they married and moved to Manhattan in 1972. They found an apartment on Riverside Drive and, three years later, bought at the insider's price. He placed their bed against the window and, rising, saw New Jersey, the Palisades jutting above the tame rush of the river. They went to Chinese restaurants and late-night double features and The Frick Collection and the Guggenheim. He worked in what had been the maid's room, a cubicle glutted with books. They would be faithful forever, until death did them part; they needed nothing in their lives but each other forever and ever; they were a sufficiency together and incomplete apart. He would remember those phrases: the litany of love breathed into his neck, his ear, on pillows, in the shower stall.

"I believe there are three things," she said. "Three concentric circles, if you like. Sex, consciousness, and history. Sex and history are polar opposites, and when you fuse them you get consciousness. That's what I've been working on." Janet said this, not joking, with consequential earnestness, tracing—with her fingernail—the concentric circles on his thigh. "This one is consciousness," she said. "And here's history. And then a little higher, here, it's the dialectic—sex."

Increasingly he thought it comic—her scrutiny of self. Their marriage consisted of talk. Janet believed in intense, continual articulation; she accused him of dropping off to sleep or changing the subject or refusing to give her the credit of an answer. She said he listened harder to the radio than to her, and her opinion of his work mattered less to him, apparently, than the opinion of that illiterate high-heeled groupie from the publicity department, or those darling children he taught at The New School. He said that wasn't true, she was his toughest critic. What's that supposed to mean? she asked, and he said what I said.

Increasingly he gave readings in cities a plane trip away, and it was easy afterward to take what he thought of as solace. There were ambitious girls in graduate programs, with novels of their own. They read him their first chapters and wanted his response; they kept the work-in-progress in boxes by their beds. He took a Visiting Professor job in a writing program in Baltimore, and then one in Syracuse, and then a position at Princeton in order to commute. When he returned at night Janet met him at the door; she couldn't sleep without him, she had been waiting up.

"I missed you," he would say.

"I missed you."

"What did you do all day?"

"Do?"

"I mean, did you have fun? Did anything happen to tell me about?"

"Nothing important," she said.

He took off his raincoat. "Mail? Calls? *Un*important?"

"To you." Her sketchbook lay open, face down.

"When this job is over," he said, "let's take a vacation. Somewhere hot."

"When this job is over you'll get another."

"Not right away."

"Right away."

He could find no answer. She said this with a voice
so expressionless as to seem feigned. They embraced.

In September he went to his high-school reunion.
There was to be a cocktail party and, the invitation
promised, frolicsome remembrance of things past. There
was a questionnaire entitled: "Twenty-fifth Reunion Test:
what Vegetable do you think you were and what
have you become? Will you bring your Spouse or Significant Other? Name? Can you (check one) still do the
quadratic equation? Five laps around the track? Remember Smitty's Dog?"

He had not intended to go. The questionnaire
evoked that self-congratulatory coyness that had marked
his high-school years—the sense of inherited merit and
car pools with chauffeurs. He had been a member of
the second most popular clique. The world divided, said
Janet, into those for whom high school meant the best
years of their lives, and those for whom it represented
the worst. Robert disagreed. For him it meant a staging
process, a wash of expectation through which girls
moved wearing cashmere, and he conjugated Latin verbs
and jostled in the lunch line or the locker room.

The class secretary called. "We haven't heard from
you," she said.

"I know. I'm sorry."

"They're coming from all over." Her voice was reedy, soft; he tried to remember her face. "Two from California, one from Oregon, and three from Atlanta."

"Congratulations."

"You're coming, aren't you? Author, author . . ."

"I'll try."

"We've got the highest percentage," she said, "of any reunion class in the last eleven years. If I can get seven more people we'll have the highest percentage ever."

So he had promised to come. It was not a promise he felt obliged to keep. That Saturday morning dawned brightly, however, and he was restless, headache prone; he had no other plans. He drove approach roads to the campus knowing when to brake and where to turn, with the kind of body knowledge that outlasted time. The school was slate-roofed, turreted, with iron entrance gates. The classroom buildings were fieldstone, and the library and auditorium and gym and dining halls were brick.

He had been successful at school. The caption to his yearbook photo read BORN TO SUCCESS HE SEEMS. Yet he carried with him, dormant, the seeds of that first forced growth—the conviction of showiness, merely, that his was a talent more rumored than real, and his adult gesturing still adolescent strut.

Arriving, he first saw his teachers. They had not changed. The Japanese mathematics teacher was as sprightly as when she tried to teach him calculus; the physics teacher had retained a horseman's swagger to his walk. They formed a welcoming committee. "Bobby Potter," they exclaimed. "How are you? Welcome back!"

The woman who taught French, whose breath was tinged with caraway, stepped forward, offering her cheek, and said, *"Je t'embrasse."*

"J'entre dans la salle de classe," he pronounced. They laughed.

His history teacher, bearded now and using a cane, labored up. They had been his elders, always, and therefore exempt from the arbitration of time. Behind them in the quadrangle a herd of strangers clustered to long trestle tables where there were hors d'oeuvres and a bar.

Helen Applebaum Morris embraced him. They had played strip poker in eleventh grade; he read the name at her neck. She said she had three children, was about to send her eldest off to college; he's six foot two, she said, he looks at me, this bruiser, and says, Mom, I'm hungry, wash this shirt. Can you believe it, Bob?

Then he was surrounded. Those he sat next to in eighth grade, those he played basketball with, those he sang with in *Iolanthe* when they made a chorus of peers— they gathered near him, chortling, pointing to their name tags, lifting glasses, and swallowing shrimp. Jim from California had flown in that afternoon. He mentioned Burt Bacharach's name: yesterday Burt Bacharach had been playing tennis on the adjacent court. Jim from Colorado arrived from Italy. He was into Buddhism, very deeply into Buddhism, and there was a guru near Montecatini he planned to study with. Those baths, those healing waters—he pursed his lips and narrowed his eyes and softly kissed the air. He spoke the guru's name. Then he handed Robert a card. "If you're ever in Boulder," he said.

Peter from Seattle loved it there. You get used to

the weather, he said, there's no more rainfall than New York, it's just it comes more steadily. He was a labor lawyer. Now he went canoeing every weekend, and sometimes after work, and the salmon jumped straight for his freezer. They had a second drink. Black women in uniform tended the bar. Eric, a Gestalt therapist, lived in Baltimore. He introduced his wife; she was pert and freckle-faced. She knew one of Robert's books. They had met at Esalen while doing primal scream.

The secretary approached. A redhead grown gray, she wore a jockey's cap, backward. She handed him his namecard. "Bobby Potter. Welcome back."

"How do you attach this thing?"

She showed him, peeling tape. A wind came, threatening rain. "I knew it," Eric said. "I could smell the rain, I always can. Ask Janey about it, ask her if I'm ever wrong."

"Yes," said Janey. "Often. But he's right about the rain."

They laughed together happily, as if this perception were shared.

Then they moved into the auditorium for slides. They shouted out their classmates' names, applauding. The token Negro had been photographed most frequently. He was shown with the basketball, the football, a protractor, his arms around his teammates, with a carnation in his buttonhole, and sporting a beret. There were pictures of the senior year drama production, *Caesar and Cleopatra*. The boy who played Apollodorus had died in a car crash; there was a moment of silence when his photograph appeared. Caesar wrote homoerotic verse and lived in Los Angeles now.

Ralph Atcheson who played the ukulele was cajoled to play again. He happened to have brought it with him, just in case. They all said how much fun this was, how they should keep in touch. They pressed business cards on Robert and wrote in their home phones; they said they couldn't wait to read the story he would write about this day. "You travel," Helen said. "Come see me in Washington soon."

The class secretary read off the results of the questionnaire. The most frequently named vegetable was eggplant, the most frequently named animal the koala bear. Sixty-two members of the graduating class of 1962 were present; forty had responded to the data sheet. It was not too late, the secretary said; she pointed to a corner table piled with questionnaires. "If you've been inspired by this inspiring occasion," she said, "please tell us how you feel."

Robert coughed. He blew his nose. At a certain point, he told himself, foreknowledge is as actual as event.

The last Sunday of September, he left Jimmy at what used to be their home. Janet, entertaining, was not pleased to see him. "My former husband," she said. She introduced Robert to the Kappelmans and Cravens and to a man named Magid. Robert said, "I can't stay," and she accepted this. "I've got to get back," he told the Cravens, who smiled.

Janet wore white. She inclined her cheek to Jimmy, embracing him, and said, "There, there."

"Thank you, Daddy."

"See you next week."

"Did you have fun?" she asked, offering her profile to Magid. The image of youthful maternity, she bent to Jimmy, concerned.

He nodded.

"Good," she said. "Has he fed you?"

"Bread and water," Robert said. "And eel soup for breakfast this morning."

Magid had a wrestler's thick neck. His hair was close-cropped, graying, and he sported tasseled loafers and brown tweeds. Robert appealed to him, leaving. "It's a wonder the kid eats at all."

"Nonsense," said Janet. "I asked if he'd had lunch."

"I did," said Jimmy. "I ate."

He hated the end of the visit, their ritual bickering. It happened this way, always, an aggrieved politeness edging up to argument. But he could not bring himself to leave Jimmy in the lobby; he made a point each Sunday of arriving at the door.

They had gone, the day before, to the Yankee doubleheader. Robert had had visions of camaraderie, of hot dogs and heroics and the two of them hoarse with shouting, the game a thriller till the final pitch. At the entrance to the stadium, he bought them both programs and hats. They hurried up the ramp. Jimmy brought along his mitt, in case of a foul pop. Their seats were good; he explained to Jimmy why this was the house that Ruth built. There were records and percentages he remembered with no trouble—names like Miller Huggins and Joe McCarthy and Tommy Henrich and Lou Gehrig. He knew about Lefty Gomez and Red Ruffing, even if he had not seen them pitch; he had seen Allie Reynolds on TV, Vic Raschi, and Joe Page.

"I started coming here," he said, "after DiMaggio retired. Then of course there were the Mantle years."

"When was that, Daddy?"

"The fifties," he said. "And the early sixties too.

We called them the Bronx Bombers. Men like Gil
McDougald. Yogi Berra. Casey Stengel."

"I've heard of him," Jimmy said.

"And 'the crow.' Frankie Crosetti." Robert looked
in vain for Frankie "The Crow" Crosetti in the coach-
ing box. "And Phil Rizzuto. That guy on TV. Hank
Bauer. They used to be my idols."

"Can I have a hot dog?"

"You may."

They admired how the vendor snapped his dollar
bills together, and the way he balanced, teetering, to
hold out a hot dog and roll. The men around them
wore windbreakers and carried radio sets. There was
much shrill laughter in the box across the aisle. He
pointed to the bullpen and its plaques. "That's where
they honor the great ones," he said. "That's better, even,
than getting your number retired . . ."

"This hot dog's cold," Jimmy said.

The afternoon was raw. The beer was flat, and
Jimmy did not want a sip; he picked up and pounded
his glove. Robert did not know the names of the latest
Yankee stalwarts; nothing, it seemed, was at stake. They
discussed the designated hitter rule. The men across
the aisle were drinking gin.

"It's too cold," Jimmy said.

"We'll get another."

"No. I mean, just sitting here."

"It's only the sixth inning," Robert said. "Maybe
the sun will come out."

"It won't. It's boring."

Men dropped flies. They struck out repeatedly. In
the last half of the seventh inning, Jimmy said, "I want
to go."

"Let's stay till it's over."

"Just *this* game, OK?"

"All right," Robert said. "We can go."

He gathered his papers and cup. There were pea-nut shells at his feet, and sandwich leavings, and a dis-carded scarf. The batter bunted on a third strike pitch. The ball went foul. A woman to his left threw back her head, revealing a mouth full of silver. A traffic helicop-ter banked and wheeled.

His skill was a surveyor's skill, his habit that of witness. He could identify snippets of speech, the overheard fragment, the volitional veiled glance. He knew, in a room, who was sleeping with whom, or wanted to; his talent was control. Reviewers praised his tact, his chilly noticing eye. They did so, however, in terms as measured as his own—and this had come to worry Robert; his work had been at best a moderate success. Like Roland's pal in the palace, he said, he was waiting for the call. The call would be a clarion; it would come from a reverberating distant horn; it would crack the very sinews of his throat. "Moderation in all things" was the advice a doctor gives, and an insurance agent. It did not work for art. He dreamed of a great sum-mons, an immoderate subject, the panic that is Pan's penetrating entry, a cry. Meantime, he built his small books. They were shapely and succinct. He was neither stupid nor lazy, and he wanted once to write a story or a novel that was larger than its author, that would dem-onstrate craft anchored, not adrift. With increasing bit-terness, he doubted that he would.

On his way back he stopped in Weston for a drink. His friends the Hartogs had purchased a farm—a white sprawl of buildings with lawn tractors and the neighbor's hay in what was once a barn. They had made a sauna of the chicken house. Robert arrived at four-thirty. The afternoon was hot. Pieter Hartog was recovering from hepatitis; he told Robert it had been the strangest thing. One day he was feeling fine, smoking, boozing: business as usual. And the next day he had liver trouble, hating the taste of bourbon, nauseated by smoke. He supposed it was a clam. He would like to claim the needle, or something fashionably short of AIDS—but it must have been a clam. Pieter laughed. You know how mussels can be full of grime and shit, he said, how one sandy mussel can ruin the broth—well, that must have been what did it in his case. And he didn't find it funny even now. One of the first things that goes when you're sick—Pieter took his arm, avuncular—is a sense of humor. You keep just about everything else. You notice the nurses, for instance. But you fail to find things funny that had been uproarious before.

It hadn't been that simple for Leslie either, Pieter said; she took it on the chin. She probably thought he was banging some junkie, some infectious number at the office. They were going to the Yucatán next week. Uxmal and Chichén-Itzá, those would be the tickets: a tequila sunrise for breakfast and a margarita at lunch. He could have shown her Cancún. He would have taken her to Cozumel, or Puerto Vallarta, but they're on the beaten track and mostly she wants to get off.

Tommy Hartog was back for the weekend, from his boarding school in Montana. "Wears his old man out," said Pieter. "Wish I'd had that arm . . ."

"If you'd care to catch, sir?" Tommy asked.

"I'd like that," Robert said.

The men had rum and tonics on the porch. Tommy

swung on a suspended tractor tire; the tree it was tied to was dead. After some time he approached with three mitts. He threw the ball and caught it in one hand, repeatedly.

"Batter up," said Pieter. "I'll get the fungo bat."

They ascended to the meadow. A fire siren sounded to the west.

His mitt was stiff. He pounded it, remembering those hours spent with neat's-foot oil and rags, the saddle soap and liniment and sweat-absorbent leather that meant Saturday mornings, or summer, or practice after school. He had played second base. Tommy threw the hardball, and he caught it in the webbing of his glove. Then he threw to Pieter, and Pieter to Tommy, and Tommy tagged imaginary runners and threw them out at the plate. As Robert's sureness returned, and he put some force behind the throw, Pieter seemed to flag. He complained about the sun. Tommy, however, grew bright in the declining light, and his throw snapped into Robert's pocket with a satisfying *whomp*. Robert fired back. The boy caught the return throw, returned it, and soon the two of them exclusively played catch.

He was sweating now, elated, at the outer limit of his arm. He shagged flies and gauged the bounce of grounders with an accuracy that surprised him. Pieter, watching, picking his teeth with whip grass, cheered. They retreated the length of the meadow, and the man and boy were intent now, competitors. Then something happened to him that had not happened in years: a release in action, a sudden setting free, a grace that caused him to run faster and throw harder and catch the baseball more securely than he could run, throw or

catch. He was winded soon but continued; his hair grew
wet with sweat. Then Tommy laid down his glove.
Robert called, "I've had enough," and theatrically spread-
eagled, falling backward in the grass. There was a white
slice of moon. The following weekend, he promised
himself, he would see his son.

In October he drove to Vermont. He had been
invited to the second annual "Apple Harvest Festival"
reading Monday night. Robert could foresee it all: the
praise, his counterfeited modesty, the question period,
the deserted hall his host would tell him was an impressive turnout for this place. They would pay enough
to cover his expenses in Newfane, and he would spend
the night before the reading with the woman married
to his editor; she had called him ten days earlier to say
she would be free.

There was much weekend traffic heading south.
There were many DETOUR and NO SHOULDER signs.
Melissa had arrived before him at the inn. She was
drinking sherry in the lounge.

"I'm sorry," Robert said.

"Don't be." She stood.

"Leaf-peepers. I hate them," he said. "We're leaf-
peepers also, of course."

There was no one at the desk. She kissed him on
the cheek. "Hello."

"Hello."

"I'm starting to unwind," she said. "It took all
afternoon."

"Have you registered?"

"Yes." She gave him that half-grimace of complicity he had first noticed six months before. You should

see the bathroom, baby. Copper. They've got a copper
sink."

He smiled. He looked around him at the inn, the
empty vestibule, the tiles and beaming and plaster that
represented "rustic charm"; he had been more weary
than he knew. There were magazines on a table: *Country Living, Art in America, Vanity Fair, Yankee, Newsweek, Vogue.*

"I'm glad we're here," he said.

"Happy anniversary."

He checked his watch, the date.

"One hundred days," she said. "Since the last time
we promised not to meet this way again." She lifted
the glass to her lips and tongued the sherry. "Your
health."

They ate at a lodge down the road. Melissa wore
a white silk dress, a strand of pearls; her hair was coiled.
The whole effect—the rouge, the rings, the cigarette
holder—seemed an incongruity: a woman on a mountain slope but wearing three-inch heels. The food was
pretentious. They drank two bottles of wine. The waiter
blandished them, flourishing the saltshaker and pep-
permill and ashtrays as though these were objects of
value. He kissed his fingertips and then the air; he ig-
nited the duck and said, "Aaah!" He asked, repeatedly,
if everything were to their satisfaction; Robert nodded.

"Is something wrong?" she asked.

"No. Why?"

"You've been, oh, distant. Somewhere else. I
haven't seen you since the snails."

"I'm here."

"Yes."

"You look lovely."

"Thank you," said Melissa. "But that isn't what I meant."

He brought himself back to attention. "What did you mean?"

"Just that you seem preoccupied." She buttered bread. "Is something wrong about tonight?"

"No. You're the one with commitments, remember?"

"My sociable hermit," she said.

Her form of flattery was to repeat his own previous opinion; he had used the phrase "sociable hermit" the last time they met. He was not by nature convivial; his work required this. He suffered fools gladly, he told her, as long as they bought books.

"It killed the cat," she said. "I know. I don't mean to crowd you."

"You're not. If I knew what was bothering me . . ."

The waiter wheeled the dessert cart to their table. There were lemon mousse and chocolate mousse and strawberry tarts and cakes and the house specialty, a charlotte Malakoff. Robert ordered charlotte Malakoff. As he tasted the first forkful, the candle on their table guttered out.

She also had been busy: her schedule was insane. She crisscrossed New England, she said, leaving Tim and Sally with the housekeeper at home. She was working her way up the Corporate Ladder, but it felt like Child-Life Swings. Had he ever noticed the way they space the rungs? The bottom rungs of a Child-Life ladder are spaced close together, easy to climb; as you get higher, however, the spaces are farther apart. So you keep small children off the top where falling's risky;

she had made it, this year, to middle management of the Division of Design.

At the table next to them a man announced, "I'm living in Ottawa now. My father's in New York. I see him every month."

Her dress had ridden up along the thigh. He dropped his hand there and squeezed. It felt like a revision of his furtive gropings when in school: the knees' articulation slick in pantyhose.

"Let's go," Melissa said. "If it's all right with you."

"All right." He put down his fork.

"This coffee's rotten."

He folded his napkin, then rolled it. She continued her complaint. He, Robert, couldn't know what it meant to marry young and sleep with a beautiful boy until he turned away from you and chose his own beautiful boys. He was off in Hollywood, making deals, making it with tennis players in the clubhouse shower; she had accused him of that. She had driven him into the closet, then out of the closet and to the West Coast. His paperback line was shoddy, failing, he wasn't there for the kids. . . .

Someone opened a door in the hall; wind entered. He paid. They moved outside. Their breath was white smoke, visible, and Melissa shivered. "What happened to summer?" she asked.

"You know what they say"—he tried the old joke—"about weather in Vermont. It's nine months of winter and three of poor sledding."

She laughed. She took his arm. A sadness that he could not name was with him, however, and would not be dispelled. It clung to him as she did when they went back to their room, took off their clothes and went to bed. It was a compound of time passing, drunkenness, dissatisfaction, flesh. It took him in its mouth and opened its long legs to him and sang his name in darkness and whimpered in the sheets. It was ardent, acrobatic, and it whispered that it could not let him leave. It said he was married to silence, wedded to failure forever. It breathed beside him through the night and woke and showered and had coffee and croissants and grape jelly from the vine behind the inn. Melissa too was with him, but she drove back to her husband in White Plains.

PALINURUS

When the novelist George Chapman asked Enoch for a favor, Enoch said, of course. He had been doing so for years and saw no reason to stop. It was a pattern between them. When Chapman required money, Enoch wrote the check; when Chapman needed a place to retreat to, he used Enoch's house in Vermont. In smaller ways also—the phone calls at two in the morning, the jerry can of gas when Chapman's car ran dry, the protective caution with which he fielded questions (from interviewers, ex-wives, creditors) as to the writer's whereabouts—Enoch made himself of use. "My buddy," Chapman called him. "My sidekick. My rod and my staff."

This last allusion was typical. Chapman knew the Bible and liked thinking he had servants; he was too busy, he claimed, to clean up "that mess, my life." It was other people's business to pick up the pieces and balance accounts. He focused wholly on work.

The nicknames were typical also. Chapman liked to label things and make them over by naming. "Any fool," he said, "can call a spade a spade. The artist calls it 'hoe.'" For the two years he wrote *Virgil,* he referred to Enoch as "my pal Palinurus"—that faithful foredoomed helmsman who was sacrificed at sea. *"Te petens Palinure,"* he would mumble, squinting, as if the horizon were water. Chapman himself did not swim. *Virgil,* with its homespun folksy wisdom, its startling transformation of Dido into rock star and Aeneas to her bodyguard, was made into a movie; Chapman coauthored the script.

While at work on the story "Quixote at Home," he insisted on calling the younger man "Sancho." "My faithful retainer," he said. In fact Enoch was tall and thin, whereas Chapman in his forties acquired a pronounced potbelly. But the truth behind appearances, the novelist would say, "is what we're after, isn't it; that's why I dream for a living. It explains my mournful countenance, the nightmares, the bad teeth."

"Bad teeth?" Enoch asked. "I didn't know your teeth were bad."

"Pitted. Carious. Noisome." Chapman lit his pipe. "Like your hair, pal. Falling out."

"Have you seen a dentist?"

"Every week."

They kept track of each other. Chapman needed acolytes, and Enoch gladly served. With the notion of

a memoir or critical biography, he took notes. He kept
a journal labeled C and recorded his reactions to the
novelist during, then after, a visit. He organized their
correspondence in much the same manner, by year. He
had a dozen folders and he kept them by his desk.

Enoch felt in the presence of greatness. If some of
it rubbed off on him, so much the better, he thought;
if not, the mere proximity sufficed. Chapman flattered
him in person, and this could be more gratifying than
praise behind the back. Over time Enoch acquired some
of his mentor's habits—the love of sour pickles and
Stilton, the bottles of beer before sleep. To have heard
the conversation, to have read the drafts of manuscript,
to have suggested changes and to see those changes
made: such would be his reward. He remembered
Yeats's phrase about how hard it is, when your own
work has come to nothing, to "be secret and exult."
"Of all things known," Yeats wrote, "that is most difficult."

Enoch was a writer too. At forty-four he was the
author of two novels and a monograph on Conrad. This
last remained in print. His career had little of the reach
and bright trajectory of Chapman's, nor the success.
He taught.

He was an only child. His father died when he was
young, his mother died on April 7, 1988. He had been
teaching at Middlebury College—his marriage a failure,
his wife remaining with her carpenter in Thetford, his
sons Ricky and Allan being raised by a stranger, with
chickens. If there were any comfort in his mother's rapid
illness, it was how he kept from her his own impending
divorce. Dying, she had asked him if he were as happy

in his marriage as she had been in hers. This was the one lie Enoch could remember telling; he stroked her thin hair, the irradiated stubble, smoothing the skin at her temples. He told her, softly, yes.

She had not believed him, he knew. Earlier, she would have pressed and questioned him—eliciting from his hesitation, the half-evasive half-inventions and the way he changed the subject—that Rita had moved up the valley and was not coming home. But, dying, his mother was tired; the pain made her aloof. She wanted her boy to be settled; she settled for Enoch's white lie.

"What I want from you," said Chapman, "is something you should think about."

It was midnight; they were drinking. They were sitting on the porch.

"What I want is a favor."

"All right."

"I've got this mess of manuscript." He waved his arm inclusively at the porch rail, the elm stump, the cars in the yard. "Those books. All those cardboard boxes. You should be my executor."

"Your what?"

"In case something happens. In case you outlive me, you bastard."

"Well, since you put it that way"—Enoch rocked back again, tilting, savoring the warm night breeze—"since you put it with such, such *delicacy*. The actuarial tables . . ."

"I'm not kidding," Chapman said.

Then Enoch stopped rocking and, sober, said yes, it would be an honor. It would not, he hoped, come to pass.

His ice cubes had melted. He turned to his guest.
It had been a difficult spring. "Have you been working?" Chapman asked, and he had no answer. What
Enoch read was stale and flat; what he wrote was un-
profitable.

In the protective darkness, rocking, he continued
his complaint. Even the boys annoyed him. Their jostling, daylong rumble, the racketing clatter and fuss from
their room, the hours he spent managing the house (Rita
off at Country Things, selling quilts and draping hoops
with sweaters and meeting her carpenter for coffee, he
came to learn, and hanging the SORRY, WE'RE CLOSED
sign in the window while she opened her legs to him
on the camp bed by the delivery entrance), the weekly
round of shopping, cooking, the flutter in his thighs
when he spent more than minutes rototilling what would
not be a garden—all this aggrieved him. He smoked.
He weathered May, then June. For the final two weeks
of his marriage, as if in opposition, the sun shone every day.

"I used to think," said Chapman, "that we carried
it all with us. All that baggage in our heads. Old lovers,
our parents, the taste of applesauce, our fourth grade
teacher's maiden aunt's lisp"—he raised his glass—"the
watermark in stationery, telephone calls, old books. But
we don't. We lose it, it passes. All that's lovely passes."

"Have another?" Enoch asked.

There were constellations, but he could not name
their names.

The writer shook his head. "It's time to quit. To
get some sleep."

"I'm glad you came, George. Really."

Chapman was solicitous, and this did seem strange.

"She picked the hell of a time to leave you, didn't she? Rita, I mean."

"We left each other."

"Yes?"

They slept till noon. The grass required mowing, but Enoch could not face it. He sat on the porch instead, rocking, drinking coffee. Chapman was to give a reading in Detroit, then Salt Lake City, then Denver. His novel *Spindrift* had appeared; the first printing had sold out. "A magic, sprawling book," the advertisements proclaimed. "This is vintage Chapman: a literary event!"

Enoch drove him to Burlington Airport, and they shook hands formally. They would see each other soon, they promised, they would go fishing together.

"So we go off headlong, hurtling to eternity," Chapman said. He did not appear to be joking. He wore his cowboy hat. He carried his typewriter with him, as always, and his black leather suitcase, its handles reinforced by string. The last view Enoch had of him was distant, at the Northwest gate; he was standing by the counter, threadbare, plump, smoking an unlit pipe, raising his hand—not waving it—in the hieratic gesture of farewell.

When he died in Denver it was, somehow, not a shock. The car that hit him went out of control; the driver collapsed and plowed into the taxi station by the Brown Palace Hotel. The driver, Clarence Hovey, died on impact too. The coroner reported this. The writer had been pinioned (facing the other direction, lighting his pipe, protecting it) and crushed—though Chapman's companion and publicist, Ms. Margot Zimmerman, escaped unharmed. It was, she told the newspapers, a bolt from the blue, a total devastation; they had been going to lunch.

Enoch attended the funeral. Avoiding the airport, he drove. Chapman had been born and raised outside of Philadelphia; he was buried in the graveyard where his parents had a plot. A sister was buried there also. The day grew hot. On August 22, he would have been fifty years old. There were mourners Enoch recognized, and many that he failed to; the coffin stayed shut. To his surprised relief, when he introduced himself to Chapman's lawyer, the man knew his name. "You're the executor, right?" he said. "The literary executor. He asked me to include you."

"When?"

"Include you in the will, I mean. Last month."

So Chapman must have made the choice *before* his trip to Enoch's house and their drunken discussion on the front porch. How like him, Enoch thought—to come to a decision and then ask as if for a favor what in fact was prearranged. He must have known, of course, that his host would accept. He might have taken for granted that the offer would be flattering: *"Te petens Palinure."*

On the way home he fought sleep. He drove his Subaru station wagon—silver, rusting, six years old. Its backseat disgorged candy and Walkman batteries and Kleenex and socks. He would have left it with Rita, but she had the carpenter's truck. The carpenter's house was passive solar; it backed into a hill. Its windows were unpainted and green with hanging plants. Enoch wanted to be able to collect his sons in something they would recognize; therefore he kept the car.

The Subaru provided him with the illusion of family; parked, it still could seem as if Ricky and Allan might come bounding from the IGA or Fox Village Movie House or renovated Grange Hall where they went for child-care on the mornings that he taught. Those final months, he had done all the driving. Rita had had it, she said. She was tired of being the home-maker, the perfect provider, the one with MOM'S TAXI stuck to the bumper; let Enoch make arrangements for a change. Now she was staying put. Now his muffler needed fixing, and the tailgate rattled, and he had to hold the steering wheel to keep from veering left.

A year passed. He took a leave of absence from teaching; with his mother's legacy, he could afford two years. He grew a beard. His old sense of entitlement had faded; he could not bring himself to fight for cus-tody, acclaim. The divorce went through uncontested; he saw little of his sons. He buried himself in Chap-man's papers—the unfinished drafts, the sketches, the letters and journals and libretti and eleven versions of a play.

There had been a flurry of sympathy after the ac-cident; admirers wrote to condole. There were tele-phone calls and visits from doctoral candidates working on *Virgil* or the early novels or the three books of short stories. Rumor reached him also. Chapman was a sui-cide; he had been dying of AIDS. Margot Zimmerman was his new mistress; her husband had driven the car. He had left a million dollars or, alternatively, a million-dollar debt. He had known he was going to die; he had had premonitions all that week.

There was an article in *People*; there were tele-vision interviews and a speculative essay in *The New*

Republic, comparing Chapman's fate to that of his great predecessors: D. H. Lawrence, Thomas Wolfe. A piece in the *TriQuarterly* compared him to both Hart and Stephen Crane. There was talk about a musical based on *Sharon's Speedboat*—the last, unfinished play. *Spindrift* ascended the best-seller list, remaining there ten weeks. There were letters sent, in care of Chapman's publisher, asking Enoch for a photograph or lock of hair or clothing scrap or page of manuscript, and it was at times unclear to him if they meant Chapman's manuscript or his, Enoch's, own.

Jonathan Alton called often. Six years before, they had been introduced by Chapman in New York. The party was in honor of the publication of *Virgil,* and there were many people drinking white wine and Perrier. Chapman appeared amused; he stoked his pipe. "This guy's writing my biography," he said. "Imagine that."

Alton was a sallow man with a ridge of scar tissue under his chin; he had been Chapman's colleague when they taught together at Rochester. Then Chapman got famous and quit. "I couldn't wait," he said to Enoch later. "I had to write best sellers to get out of bloody Rochester, *comprende?*"

Alton, however, remained. At the funeral, wearing a black three-piece suit and bow tie, he commiserated with Enoch as if they were old friends. Repeatedly, he blew his nose. "It's up to us now, isn't it?" he said. "It's really up to us."

"What is?"

"We've got to see it through."

The biographer proved indefatigable. He wanted

clarification on the whereabouts of manuscripts, the various drafts and their dates. His interest in detail (where had Chapman been on June 27, 1979; what was he wearing and what did he say when the divorce from Caroline, his second wife, was settled; who had been at the party, then gone fishing in the Chesapeake in 1980?) seemed to Enoch pointless—or at least beside the point. At the funeral he'd copied out, then fretted over the accurate spelling of names inscribed in the Memorial Book. He'd noted the starting time of the service, its duration, and who had tears in their eyes. It took him longer to research a text than Chapman had taken to write it; by 1989, he began on 1981. It was fortunate for Alton, Enoch thought, that his subject's production had—abruptly, irrevocably—ceased.

The calls grew plaintive, urgent. Alton made them, he would say, in order to keep Enoch up to date. "You're the executor. You ought to know." With the disconcerting habit of assuming their shared purpose, his letters outlined the book's progress. "I've blocked in Chapter IV. I can't seem to settle it, though. I'm having trouble with 'Homer,' the tone of his decision to locate the last scene in Darien. How much of this is unconscious association, and how much a bad joke? What do you think? I feel I've lost my bearings—there's just so much to do!"

On the anniversary of Chapman's death, Alton mourned: "My office is a shambles. The fifth chapter's killing me. I mean this literally. I wonder if you'd write a letter to my Chairman, stating you know me, and that you acknowledge the importance of this project. Only if you're comfortable saying it, of course."

Two weeks later things were worse. "In a manner of speaking," wrote Alton, "we're in the same boat, you and I. We've lost our captain, we're adrift." Enoch had an image—fleeting, fading—of a wave, the whelming rush of Chapman that had swept them off their feet.

The biographer's great fear was that he worked too slowly. Someone else would "scoop" him or might "steal a march." There were only so many publishers, only so much interest in a writer's life, and what would happen if some fast-talking journalist, say, some Chapman groupie got a contract; what would happen in that case to his chances of promotion, his own scholarly career? "The trouble is," said Alton, "George died before he authorized me. You know the way he used to be: the more the merrier."

"I didn't know that. No."

"Of course. It's just the way he was. You're lucky you got it in writing."

Still, Enoch felt a kind of kinship with the man. That dogged persistence, the systematic snail-paced accretion of data, the reverential caution with which the biographer verified fact—all this felt familiar. They spelled the same ghost. He could have predicted the call.

"How are you, Enoch?"

"Holding on." The day was waning brightly. "I was thinking of you."

"Oh? What were you thinking?"

"Nothing much. I just had the feeling you'd call."

"Did you get my article? The one from *Toho-Bohu?*"

"Yes."

"Do you dream about him every night?" Alton coughed. "There's so much wreckage in his wake."

"Do you ever think of—what was his name? That driver?"

"Hovey. Clarence Hovey. All the time."

* * *

Clarence Hovey is sixty-six years old. He drives a 1987 Oldsmobile Cutlass Supreme. It is black, with red interior trim. He is a retired C.P.A. who keeps his hand in doing tax returns and with the occasional consulting job; his doctors tell him he should ease up a little, relax. He has diabetes and must regulate his diet; he can't be at his desk all day or out in the woods by himself. He doesn't mind it, truth be told; he intends to take up carpentry and has improved his golf. This morning he puts on his golfing cardigan, his yellow pants, and turns on the TV to catch the local weather: sunny, chance of evening showers, seasonably warm. He drops candy in his pocket and puts on his Broncos cap. He plans to wash the car, then drive out to the Fairview Club to see what's up, what's doing, who's making up a foursome and could use a fourth. He turns off the TV while they describe a fire in Aurora, a "blaze of suspicious origin" with at least one woman dead. He has lived in Denver thirty years and watched the place get fancy, watched it through hard times and good and now hard times again. When he drives up to the Soft Cloth Wash, his is the third car in line; he wants the Red Star Special: undercarriage and hot wax. He's on his ninth wash—tenth one free—and the attendant takes six dollars, punches his card, says "Fine day."

He shuts off the radio. The aerial retracts. He puts the car in neutral, checks the windows, settles back. He feels the jolt beneath him when the track engages, watches soapy water drench his windshield, then his windows, then the slap of cloth like kelp on his hood, roof, windows, doors. Lights blink at him: first red and then amber, then green. He rests his right hand lightly on the steering wheel. It always makes him sleepy: the blue nylon brush advancing, the rollers, the jets of hot air. He shuts his eyes an instant within this charmed enclosure. It is, Clarence supposes, as good for the car as a bath for the body—an easy, mechanical passage out of darkness into light. When he emerges, blinking, the attendants wave him forward. He puts the car in drive again with something approaching reluctance; he cracks the window open half an inch. They perform their complicated dance with rags and take the red indicator clothespin off his windshield wiper, smiling, and pat him on the driver's door and disappear. He nods. He taps the horn.

It is 11:37. He feels fine. On impulse—because it would have been faster to circle than negotiate downtown—he follows the flow of traffic (thinking of his daughter's daughter, six years old and cute as a button, sending him that tape of her first piano recital, "Twinkle, twinkle, little star," and the audience applauding, and then she pipes up, "Grandpa, wish you could be here. When are you coming to visit?") and glides beneath the buildings' shade, and slowing down because he has to (a delivery van, a taxi stand by the Brown Palace, a lady in a Mustang changing lanes), Clarence sees the true dark rise before him, the tossing spume behind his eyes, the black beyond, and feels the sudden relinquishment, floating release, and reaches for what even as he touches it he knows he is too late to suck, the candy to counter the insulin shock, and turns toward the taxis and a fat man with a pipe.

"What I want to know," asked Chapman, "is how long you're planning to stay."

"Where?"

"In this house. This little palace with a porch."

"A man's home is his palace," Enoch said.

"You're spoiling yourself, *tonto*." Chapman gave his high, staccato laugh. "You're doing it for egotism— holding on for safety's sake."

" 'The artist at risk,' correct? I've heard that line before."

"What I mean is," Chapman said, "you've con- structed this elaborate system of domesticity. You're minding the store when they've taken the store, mind- ing the barn though the horses are out. You're pre- tending you've got chickens when they've flown the coop."

"Last call. Ten minutes. The bar closes down."

"I'm trying to tell you," he said, "mortality's the subject. It's the only issue worthy of our serious atten- tion. Death. And what you're doing, Enoch, is practic- ing avoidance; you're getting up and getting dressed and trundling off to work each day as if you were im- mortal, as if we wouldn't die."

Margot Zimmerman called too. She was putting back the pieces of her life. She felt that she knew Enoch like the brother that she never had, she very much looked forward to meeting him someday. She would like to tell him her side of the story; a note was in the mail. She had been working for George's publisher in sub rights, not publicity; the reporters got it wrong. She had first met Chapman in the office in New York. It didn't matter now. What mattered was the way he told her thank you when she asked if he'd like coffee; his face lit up, his whole expression changed. He was a famous author, fourteen years her senior, but you could tell from how he took the cup that she was the one bearing gifts. It wasn't the standard old man on the make, the artist in town for the night. He paid *attention,* let her know (not saying it, just smiling, staring, just burying his nose in what she brought him—coffee, two sugars, no cream) that he was needy, grateful, and that his need and gratitude were not just for the coffee but the fact of its existence: yes, and hers.

"You understand," she finished, "why I wasn't at the funeral. I simply couldn't face it. I think about him every day, I wake up feeling haunted. But it's water under the bridge. My husband has been wonderful. We're leaving for Switzerland tomorrow on what I suppose you'd call a second honeymoon." Her voice was breathy in his ear. "I wanted you to have the last thing George was working on that day in the hotel. It's the start of the sequel to *Spindrift.* The very beginning, I think."

Her letter arrived the next day. The envelope was white. It contained no language of her own, but only the note she had promised. The paper had been folded into eighths. He recognized the handwriting, the yellow foolscap Chapman liked, the wide margins, dark blue ink.

"Though holding the tiller, I fell. Three nights I clutched it, tossing, from Detroit to Salt Lake City to this mile-high wind-swept plain. And I did not for I could not die at sea; Apollo forbade it, foretold I would land. That part of our shared craft I took will leave you with no helmsman, although you man the helm. I did not quit you willingly; I did not shut my eyes. The rock-rimmed shore draws near. This is the fate of all who value failure, who think

it more distinguished than the easeful thing, success. Savages attacked me as I set foot on Italy, weighed down by these wet clothes. They are my winding sheets. Hero, if you love me, throw dirt upon this corpse."

"What you have to understand," Rita told him, leaving, "is not to be so serious. You used to take things lightly, Enoch. Look on the light side for once."

"You sound like a commercial."

"No."

"The good life," Enoch said. "Come on over for a thirty-second spot. This afternoon we'll do a promo for Bud Light."

"All this darkness in you. It wasn't there before."

"My mother never died before. My wife never left me before."

"I'm sorry, I really am sorry. You know that."

"Yes."

"But it's not what I'm talking about. I mean this anger, all of a sudden."

"Don't talk about it," Enoch said. "There's nothing left to say."

"The problem Chapman poses," Alton wrote, is how best to utilize what he in conversation would frequently refer to as 'free-floating myth.' By this he meant that mythic referents are everywhere about us and that to consider them too curiously is to kill the cat. At any rate that was his answer when I asked him, on the afternoon of April 7, 1983, why he had chosen the flight from Troy as the governing principle of *Virgil*, but then referred to *The Aeneid* in language at best inexact. Some decry his scholarship, others his rush into print. Few will deny, however, that the tale-telling energy so marked in Chapman's early prose derives its impetus in part from his reading of the classics when recovering, at fifteen, from a broken back. His fall from the ladder had at least this second consequence: immobilized, he read. What passionate escape for a young man in bed! What compensatory excess in the flights of fancy in that darkened upstairs bedroom in the house on Granger Street! School, for young George Chapman, was a chance to read.

"This was the lifelong wound and its accompanying bow. This was his forge, his crucible. Uncle Harald from Millerton Falls had attended college (the first member of the Chapman family to do so) and he gave George the Harvard Classics that summer, twenty-seven dog-eared volumes that were an introduction to what the writer later called his 'brave old world.' So it is possible to think of Aeneas as the young man propped on pillows, staring out the window and fantasizing escape, while his father in the living room drunkenly describes the plight of the worker at United Steel. It is possible to think of Dido as the girl on the street corner, waiting for a bus. At any rate some such reverie prefigures what became the fevered, fertile inventiveness of the work; Chapman himself described it as an 'adolescent's damp dream.'

"He was not wholly serious. He called all 'voyage' novels derivative of Gilgamesh, and said Palinurus's tiller is the ancients' oar. Such leaps of the imagination, it may be argued, characterize the autodidact no less than the invalid; they need not make too large a claim nor lay a heavy burden on the scholar's expertise. 'Do not understand me too quickly,' was one of Chapman's

mottos, pinned above his work desk in the second
Cambridge apartment. We have tried."

Enoch poured a beer and cut a wedge of cheese.
He carried his meal to the porch. It was his accus-
tomed place: a prow jutting out over grass. Clouds were
building westerly, and their shadows on Red Mountain
moved like water. The logging roads and power lines
looked, from his vantage in the valley, like rocks on a
far shore.

It grew dark. He held out a piece of Stilton, but
there was only air. Whatever had so trammeled him
had slipped its moorings, drifted loose. Whatever kept
him in its thrall had lasted one full year.

He shut his eyes and pictured—corporeal, this final time—his dead friend in the chair. Chapman was
declaiming, reciting W. E. Henley's "Invictus." He
wanted to warn Enoch of the dangers inhering in pride.
His teeth were brown. " 'I am the master of my fate,' "
he intoned, " 'the captain of my soul.' What unbeliev-
able nonsense. 'Head bloody but unbowed.' What you
have to understand is the reason they believed him—
old, crippled, crazy Henley—is because of meter. It's
because his amazing sentimentality was expressed in
rhyme."

Translucent, Chapman rocked. " 'I am the captain
of my soul,' " he said again. "Ridiculous. That's probably what the third mate on the Exxon tanker thought
when he ran aground and spilled oil in Alaska and
wrecked the fisheries. While his master slept it off be-
lowdecks, the boozy captain, Full Speed Astern! When
your work has come to nothing, be noisy about it, pal."
His voice grew distant, as if conferring release. "The

prince of wanderers, whale-roaded, the casual familiar . . ."

Enoch ate. In the morning he would drive to
Thetford and go swimming with his sons. They have
learned to dive. Rita would be canning; she stands there
wreathed in steam. She would be wearing the apron he
gave her, and the carpenter would enter from his
workroom, forearms white with sawdust. The carpenter would put his hands on Rita's hips and say, "It smells
of berries, here," and shavings from his overalls would
flutter to the floor. They hold each other, leaning, in
the fragrant steam.

"What I want from you," said Chapman, "is to act
as my executor."

"And what does that mean, really?"

"Nothing. Keeping track."

"I'm not sure I'm so good at that."

"I trust you," Chapman said.

" 'For counting overmuch on a calm world, Palinurus, you must lie naked on some unknown shore.' "

The moon appeared. It would be a proper burial.
They stretched.

THE
BRASS
RING

VASTATION—that was the word in his head. He had used it once before, when young, and his father's friend complained. "You mean *de*vastation, don't you? Why don't you write what you mean?"

"But it's a word."

"Vastation?"

"Yes. It's what Catholics say, I think, when they can't locate God. When they can't find Him anywhere. It's the absolute absence of God."

"Except you're Jewish," said Meyer Rosen. "Jews have no right to that word."

"It's in the language, isn't it? The dictionary." Frederick Hasenclever raised his voice. "You don't *have* to be a Catholic to use a dictionary."

"*I* don't use one when I'm reading." Meyer Rosen nodded. "Devastation's what you mean. That's why you don't sell many copies of your books."

They were standing in the living room of the Rosen apartment, by the jade plant and the Käthe Kollwitz, across from the self-portrait by Kokoschka. Kokoschka's gaze was baleful; his eyes appeared half-closed. It was hot. The party was in honor of Frederick's father's sixtieth birthday, and his relatives were eating shrimp and drinking Campari and soda and white wine and exclaiming at the view of the East River from this height—how traffic on the Triboro was crawling, how the skyline changed each year, how well he, Fred, was looking, without that awful beard he wore for his book jacket picture, and did he want to look like a rabbi, and how was he liking New Hampshire, what courses did he teach?

There were aunts and cousins and business partners and his younger brother, Arnold; there was cold roast beef and turkey and beef salad and pâté. "The thing I'm proudest of," his father said—when it came time to offer a toast—"is friendship. Is my family and friends. Is the memory of my beloved wife Lilo, and how wonderful you were to us last year." Briefly he faltered, halted. "Is how much a friend my sons remain to me, and matter to each other, and I don't say I've deserved it but will try. Your friendship, Meyer and Ilse, who made this occasion, everyone"—he raised his glass—"there's nothing you could ask I wouldn't give you. Gladly. The suit off my back."

"That's because it's worn out," Rosen called. He was the host; the guests laughed. He was an investment banker, with a collection of Nolde watercolors in the

bedroom; he and Hans Hasenclever had been friends
since their shared childhood in Berlin. He wore a blue
monogrammed shirt and a dark blue foulard and was
taking a proprietary interest in young Freddy's progress; he wanted to know the marketing strategies for
this new novel; just because you use the word "vastation" doesn't mean you shouldn't sell . . .

"I thought you said," said Frederick, "that *was* the
reason."

"One of them. The other is the sales force, the
way they choose to market."

"It does my heart good," said his father, nearing,
"to see the two of you like this. Conferring together,
the business man and the artist. It meant so much to
your mother"—he squeezed Frederick's cheek—"that
we should stay in touch. That's what they mean by *present*. To see you here this way."

"I have to leave, Dad. Soon. First thing in the
morning, I teach."

"You hear that?" Rosen chortled. "All those shiksa
horse-girls in the hills. Our Freddy is spreading the word.
Our Freddy is filling their heads. Go with God," he
said. "And then may God help you. 'Vastation.' "

For twenty-five years he did teach, moving to
Northeastern and Amherst and finally Columbia. His
father died. Arnold moved to the West Coast. Meyer
Rosen, too, was dead—though Fred heard this only
secondhand and somehow imagined the old man, a fat-
ter, less placid Bernard Baruch dispensing strict opinion still from the park bench by the river. He smoked
cigars, then a pipe. He married one of his students—
an Episcopalian from St. Paul, whose paper on Fitzger-

ald had been suffused, he wrote on the margin, with
an insider's insight. Sarah came to his office next morning. "Why did you say that?" she asked. "What exactly
did you mean?" She fingered the fringe of her skirt.

Their marriage was childless; it lasted three years.
She left him for a contractor from Minneapolis with
whom she had gone sailing and played hockey as a girl.
Colin had been waiting; he was her one true beau.
Frederick, by contrast, with his "Jewish bonanzas of
mouth-love," was simply not her scene. She had been
reading *The Time of Her Time*. If she left now, Sarah
told him, she could go with no hard feelings or regrets.
She read Werner Erhard, too. She knew it would be
painful, but they could let bygones be bygones, and
there's no time like the present to start with the rest
of your life.

Two years later he married again—this time a di-
vorcee with three children of her own. Lavinia owned
a fabric import firm and an apartment on Park Avenue
into which he barely fit, with his additional records and
bulky red Selectric, and his books. She liked the fact
he worked at home and could answer the phone; she
loved the way he got on with the kids. And he did
enjoy the ritual of making lunch and helping with
homework and meeting them for ice cream and then
coffee and then cocktails while Lavinia was traveling;
he stayed while she made buying trips to Bangkok and
Bombay. Once he joined her, and his gleaming lac-
quered wife seemed scarcely less foreign to Frederick
than the sari-swathed hostess at the Ashoka Hotel. He
was, he realized piercingly, alone and far from home;
he had flown across the world to join a woman in New
Delhi of whose history he was as innocent as the woman

handing him his key. When they divorced, in 1982, it was uncontested; he was fifty and bearded again and issueless, the author of six books.

His reputation, if small, felt nonetheless secure; he had twice been nominated for the American Book Award. He contributed to literary quarterlies and joined symposia and, having received grants himself, dispensed them for the National Endowment for the Arts or the Bush Foundation; it was a pleasure, he would say, to give other folks' money away. He lived on Claremont Avenue, in a Columbia-owned apartment, and watched with what he thought of as dispassion while his students grew famous and rich. Their pictures were in magazines, often—*People, Newsweek, Esquire, Time*—and he himself would sometimes be mentioned as having put the seal of his approval on their prose. He went to movies based on their books, or for which they wrote the screenplays, and their publishers sent him the glossy promotional packets that heralded success. They stared at him—the girls, the gifted boys—from supermarket racks. His own work appeared without fanfare, and sometimes he remembered Rosen's bluff conviction that the market could be rigged.

As he settled more and more into middle age (his morning bagel in the toaster oven, his decaffeinated blend from Zabar's, his baldness no longer a sorrow), Hasenclever asked himself if he had missed some turning, or failed to face some challenge; his most recent novel was titled *The Brass Ring*. The book was about a German-Jewish refugee who changes his last name in order to succeed. He does so, in the advertising business, but then discovers that his lack of honesty has barred him from promotion; the owner of the agency is an old German Jew. The two of them engage in discussions, wrote the reviewer for *The Nation,* "bordering on the Talmudic. These authenticity *mavens* have a sideline in TV. What seems at stake in Hasenclever's work is the quiddity of things, the suchness of gesture as act. And his elusive hero is not quite the protagonist, nor even the old mogul Lehrman. We sense a shadowy third figure—the one who grabs the ring, the carousel horseman with prayer shawl and *payes,* the groping compassionate self . . ."

Was there mockery in this? What in heaven's name, he asked himself, did the reviewer mean by "quiddity of things"? What shadowy "elusive hero" could he have created, and what sort of "devotional author"—a tag from the review in *Newsday*—has no faith in God? That a writer is his own worst critic may be conventional wisdom, but it is nonetheless wrong. Hasenclever knew himself; he was fifty-six years old, farsighted, and there was nothing to see.

In New York for an audition, Arnold came down with the flu. It was January 3. He had flown in from Seattle and felt "punk" all through the flight, as if the pressure in the cabin were calibrated wrong; he went straight to the hotel. He took aspirin, drank scotch. When he tried to stand, his feet hurt so badly he could not stay on his feet. He tried to dominate the pain and distract himself by walking in the hall. Then he kept his feet above his head. He stood on his head; he took cold and scalding baths. His knees felt as though they were crushed. He took a taxi to the Emergency Room of the nearest hospital and was barely conscious by the time he arrived. They saved his life. He pieced all this together, later, lying in Intensive Care unable to breathe, speak or move. He had what was variously described as acute idiopathic polyneuritis and Landry's ascending paralysis and Guillain-Barré syndrome. He could move his eyelids; that was all. He conveyed his needs by blinking while the nurse held up a chart. It could take him half an hour to spell "Right elbow," for instance, or "Rub foot."

The prognosis was uncertain; those who did not die at once had a chance of full recovery. The recuperation period could last up to two years. After three weeks of Intensive Care, he was transferred to the Institute for Rehabilitation Medicine, the "Rusk." He would improve. Hasenclever learned the news from Arnold's third wife; her voice was reedy, high. Ginger was calling from Phoenix; she and Arnold had been separated for six months. She was living with a systems analyst for an engineering firm in Phoenix; he gave her a sense of security that Arnold never gave. "He wants to see you," Ginger said. "He's ready for company now."

"Yes."

"I called. I was up there just last weekend."

"I'm sorry. I was out of town."

"Don't worry. He's insured."

"Will he know me?" Hasenclever coiled the cord. "Why didn't I know this before?"

"He has trouble focusing. He didn't want to worry you. He's lost a lot of weight."

"Is there something I can do for him? Bring, I mean?"

"Chocolate. You mustn't be shocked."

He tried to imagine a catheter, a tracheostomy, a view dictated by the pillow's placement at the neck.

"And now he's being wonderful. He's got his sweet tooth back." Her voice changed pitch, increased. "His eyes, Fred, it's astonishing. They positively *shine*."

The cord was black.

"He wanted me to let you know. He didn't want a visit when it was so terrible. He's getting better now."

"Of course."

"I was named as the person to contact, but you're the next of kin."

He pressed his nose. He closed one eye and saw only the flat of his hand. They had played tennis together. They ate and gesticulated and collected each other at airports with a shared assumption of mobility so common as to go unnoticed until gone.

It had had, to begin with, the flavor of dream. There was a night nurse whose right arm he focused on: the puckering flesh at the elbow, the bracelets and wrist. Arnold saw the glucose bottle, its transparent teat. He did not know the date or time or, absolutely, where he lay; he had seven doctors. They announced their number to him, as if there were safety in numbers and he would be reassured. At first he watched them with relief; they could help him, he was certain, they knew what was wrong and the procedures by which he could and would be cured. They succeeded each other, conferring; they stood at the foot of his bed.

Often there were students also—deferential, intense, wielding clipboards. They turned him cautiously. They raised his feet and rotated his arm and sponged him down and asked him, if he understood, to signify by blinking. He blinked. This was an involuntary mechanism as well as voluntary, however, and sometimes when he blinked they asked him to please blink again while they consulted the chart. The danger of not blinking is that you go blind.

His tongue felt huge. It filled his mouth. Had he been able to spit he would have spit; there was spittle on his tongue. He practiced swallowing. There were motel beds that jiggled for a quarter; they were called Magic Fingers, and the bed would hum and purr. He supposed it was for sex. He had never tried out Magic Fingers with a partner, but he shoved three quarters in once somewhere in Iowa and jiggled on the green chenille bedspread, feeling like a salesman. That was how his body felt in this unmoving bed, as if not merely a finger or forearm or foot had fallen asleep but all of him, the bone beneath his stretched skin protuberant, the blood too thin to clot. He closed his eyes. He would get better, they assured him, it was only a question of how much and when; you look at the big picture, that's the point. The point is you're recuperating and you're young and healthy, look at those stroke victims, for example, I wouldn't want to name names. Alfred Anderson had no left side to speak of and would not regain it; Porfirio in the bed beside him was a double amputee. Count your lucky stars. That was what the nurses said: count your lucky stars, your blessings, plan for the future, think how much worse off you could be. So he tried to imagine how he could be worse and what much worse would be.

Faces neared him: mouths like fish, making sucking motions at the air—chins with powder or pockmarks or hair. It was as if he held a camera, held it steady on the shoulder or a tripod, focusing on what swam into his vision indiscriminately—the venal, over-scrupulous, the saccharine, concerned. "Your face looks like a monkey's ass"—he spelled this to an X-ray technician, or thought he did, or wanted to: the pouches of her cheeks, the plucked line of her eyebrows and the parallelepiped of birthmarks at her neck. They were not unkind, were kindly; they meant well. They arrived and asked him, "How ya' doin', Arnie? How's the boy?" When he still was unable to speak, they sent in a psychiatrist. "This is a stressful period for you," the man pronounced. "It's difficult, we understand that, a time for anxiety, right? I know you can't discuss it yet, but sometime you'll want to discuss it. Remember I'm ready to listen, OK? OK." The man patted his sheet. He rose, limitlessly satisfied, and promised, "I'll be back."

For some time where he lay he entertained himself: he could have spoken if he chose. This was a charade he played. He did not choose. He had lost everything but memory, an infant at forty-eight, beginning. Elected silence, he blinked at the medical students: I'm an actor, I'm playing a monk. They studied their clipboards and coughed.

Room 504 had five beds. A nurse was lifting Arnold's leg. She lowered it and covered it with sheets. His face was bright. He needed a shave. The flush on his cheeks made it appear as if he had been exercising or out in the sun. He turned his head. He could do that. "Well, well," he said. "Look who's here. About time, schmuck." His voice was a rough whisper. There was a tube in his throat; another tube curved down toward his mouth.

"I'm Susan," said the nurse. "We haven't met."

"I'm his brother, Frederick. Hello."

"This is a good time," she said. "I was just finishing."

"Bye-bye," said Arnold. He said it audibly. "See you tomorrow."

"Same time, same station. If you don't stand me up."

"I wouldn't do that."

"One day you will," Susan said. "I'll be coming here to work and you'll be in the Bahamas."

"I'd take you with me, darling."

"They all say that." She took an armful of linen from a chair by the bed. She blew a kiss and moved away. Hasenclever sat.

"She's wonderful," said Arnold. "Everyone's been wonderful."

He loosened his tie. "That's impressive."

"Wonderful. They had to turn me every six hours. Maybe more often—I lose track of time. But I never lost the knowledge of how wonderful they were." His eyes glistened; he did seem grateful. "Tell me everything," he said.

"I brought you chocolate. Ginger told me to fatten you up."

"For the kill," said Arnold. "That must be what she means."

He slipped two Toblerone bars out of his jacket pocket. His brother had blue eyes.

"That's wonderful," said Arnold. "Perfect."

"Would you like some?"

"No. Not now." Infinitesimally, he shifted his head. "Put it in the drawer over there."

Then there was silence between them. Hasenclever heard a television behind a curtain in the room.

Someone muttered, sleeping; a wheelchair hummed past. Arnold demonstrated the workings of the tube beside his mouth. He sucked and spat at it, and the television turned on. He made sucking motions, and the channel switched. So did the volume and contrast control. Then he spat decisively and the machine went blank.

"Tell me when you're tired. I don't want to tire you out."

"Five minutes."

"As long as you want."

"I knew I wouldn't get the part. There's nothing for me in New York. *Gornisht.* I don't even know why I came."

The blue intensity of Arnold's gaze had slackened. His speech slurred. Hasenclever said, "I'm going now," and he did not object. "Come back," he said. "You can watch me work my automatic reader. It turns the page. It does everything but tell me what to read."

"Take care of yourself."

"Yes."

"Not to worry." He patted the bed. "You'll be doing Errol Flynn remakes. You'll be turning cartwheels . . ."

Arnold made no answer. Hasenclever left. Two women in wheelchairs had come face to face by the first nurses' station; they could not negotiate the turn. They backed away from each other, then forward, like bumper cars at Playland or a county fair. A travel poster for Biarritz hung in the waiting room, as did a poster of *Sesame Street*'s Big Bird. He pressed the elevator button repeatedly, waiting. By the Gift Shoppe he breathed freely and waved at the policeman. A one-armed violin player, his bow held in his mouth, took money in a hat.

*   *   *

One evening the writer had cocktails with a colleague. Her husband was a doctor; medical books lined
the shelf. While she went to replenish the cheese and
nuts, he pulled a volume at random—turning to the
index, then Chapter 56. Barry G. W. Arnason observed in a footnote, on page 1110: "Other commonly
encountered designations for this entity in the English
and American literature include idiopathic polyneuritis, acute febrile polyneuritis, infective polyneuritis,
postinfectious polyneuritis, acute toxic polyneuritis, acute
polyneuritis with facial diplegia, acute infectious neu-
ronitis, polyneuritis, mononeuronitis, radiculoneuritis,
polyradiculoneuritis, myeloradiculoneuritis, myelorad-
iculitis, Guillain-Barré syndrome, Guillain-Barré-Strohl
syndrome, and Landry Guillain-Barré syndrome."

Frederic went often to the Rusk. Wanting air, he
told the cab to let him off on Thirty-fourth street and
Second Avenue. Then he walked. Weekend fathers
stood in line for that day's double feature, or—as spring
progressed—bought hot dogs and pretzels at a Sa-
brett's. Inside, the elevator might disgorge a bald black
legless woman laughing. "The phone," the woman told
him. "I got to use the *phone.*" On the second floor a
man with a walker would enter; he made a *Brrr* sound
repeatedly, spraying. Porfirio cried out in Spanish,
sleeping; he beat at the bed with his fists. A green cart
made delivery of what looked like fruit.

Arnold gained weight. He covered his mouth while
he ate. He could eat salami, but he had trouble with
crackers. He could open jars and cans, and he cut out
coupons and stirred Jell-O in physical therapy; he drank
from a wineglass because of the stem. He had periodic
spasms of exhaustion—but his progress was surprising,

week by month. He had purely focused on working his way back to health. Frederick admired this resolve.

Still, there did seem something fretful about the way he exercised and ate, as if his comfort and well-being were of universal interest. He hoped to pass unnoticed in the street. But he also expected to be made much of, fussed over; he wanted to be left alone and also wanted pampering. He was happy, hearing music—Gershwin, early Mozart, the Goldberg Variations. Frederick purchased a Walkman, and brought tapes. Arnold sat in the wheelchair leafing through books: the autobiography of Alec Guinness, photographs of Burma or by Margaret Bourke-White. He studied faces intently but seemed unwilling to read. His eyes were weak, he said. The animal exuberance about him, once, had gone.

"My artistic children," their father like to say. "My writer and my actor. Thanks heaven you won't starve." Arnold liked performing, even in high school, and studied jazz dancing and how to stage fights. He had been a gymnast—tight, springy muscled, strong on the parallel bars. Frederick, the studious brother, had not known what to make of this dervish—Arnold on the diving board or parapet, while he did not like diving and feared heights. Laurence Olivier, according to Arnold, said an actor requires physical strength; it is the first tool of the trade.

He went to Juilliard and LAMDA and joined repertory companies in Chicago, San Francisco, and Seattle; he never did play Romeo or Hamlet, and now he was missing Macbeth. That was how he measured age; he hadn't given up quite yet on Prospero or Lear. Not that he played Shakespeare much, but Shakespeare

wrote a part for every age of actor; you could measure
your life by his parts. Meantime, Arnold worked. He
did the odd commercial and the sidekick in a series
that ran for eighteen episodes; *Billy and the D.A.* had
been the name of the show. Once Hasenclever, late at
night, saw him on TV. His brother was being a drunk.
He said "Melancholy baby," often to the pianist; he
rolled his eyes and tugged at his collar and slurred, "Play
me one for the road. One more time."

The maimed were everywhere about the Rusk,
pitching themselves at the traffic or bravely up on
skateboards or sunning in wheelchairs in doorways. He
saw his brother routinely; the policemen in the lobby
knew Hasenclever's name. Arnold improved. Visiting
hours were late, and often there were others in the
room—though not often there for him. Arnold's
neighbors came from Puerto Rico and had large families. Their daughters played canasta every day. Porfirio
who had no legs was excellent at cards; he had worked
as a croupier.

At times the men met in the hall. "Are they
crowding you?" asked Frederick. His brother shook his
head. "The first thing you get rid of is the need for
privacy. That goes so quickly you wouldn't believe it."

"What next?"

"Pride."

"You should be proud of yourself."

Arnold smiled. He used a wheelchair now that he
could guide by buttons. "It's slow."

" 'Slow but steady wins the race.' "

He ceased smiling. The play of attitude across his
face seemed somehow volitional, as if he prepared

himself to frown, then frowned. The elevator opened. A woman on a hospital bed lifted her right hand. She did not move her head. The linoleum was marbled, mottled: red and black.

"You're getting better."

"Yes."

"Remember what Dad used to say? *'Wenn man eine Operation durchgemacht hat, dann braucht man eine bischene Erholung.'*"

"I don't remember, no."

"After an operation, it takes time to recover."

"Now tell me how much I've grown," Arnold said. "Since the last time you visited, tell me how grown-up I seem."

"I'm sorry."

"Don't be."

"Are you in pain?"

He shook his head. When they first brought him to his bed, he fell asleep in comfort; when he woke the pain was gone. He had felt nothing else, except in the "procedures"—the nasogastric tube replacement, lumbar puncture, EMG. What he felt was shock, drugged puzzlement, a disembodied floating that was like relief.

"How long will they keep you?"

"Here?"

"Yes."

"I've got to figure out," said Arnold, "where to go to next. And when I stop improving, that's when I get sprung."

A black orderly with an anchor on his forearm cuffed the wheelchair. "Hey," he said. "How goes it?"

"It goes."

Hasenclever rolled his wrist so he could check his watch: six-sixteen.

"It's boring," Arnold said. "You can't imagine how boring this is. I can beat an egg by now. And I'm sanding wood. They change the sandpaper each week, so it takes more strength. I position checkers on a checkerboard."

"Do you swim?"

"A little. Mostly in the pool I practice how to walk. And then there's the tilt table. They've got me at ninety degrees."

The note of pride and the exacting accuracy were familiar; he seemed truly on the mend. The Puerto Ricans laughed. They crowded to the elevator, bearing pineapples. "I'll take you," Frederick said. "If you want a place to stay when you get out of here, you come with me."

Arnold turned his wheelchair. His room was the fourth on the right. "It's kind of you."

The writer stood. He adjusted his sleeve. Each gesture felt adroit to him, the coordination fluent to the point of mockery. "I mean it. You can stay."

Deracination, he told his students, is the commonplace condition of contemporary man. It is the rule, not exception, in our mobile time. How many of us live where our parents' parents lived and have no need to improvise an answer to the question "Where do you come from, where's home?" The executive and migrant worker are alike in this. Voluntary exile is a subtle, sapping thing. The tree dissevered from the root can take a transplant, possibly, but the root system must be handled with some care.

By April, using crutches, Arnold managed stairs. There were none in the apartment. There were hallway runners, however, and the doorsill to the bathroom was pronounced. Hasenclever studied the rooms closely to see how his brother might fit. He prepared what used to be the maid's room and was now a storage closet. The apartment faced a corner: south and east.

Experts from the hospital arrived on May 15—in order to evaluate facilities, they said. A brother and sister, Koreans, they came from the suburbs of Seoul. "This is a most nice apartment," they chorused, shedding coats. He tried to examine the space with their eyes, to see what they, measuring, saw. They told him that the patient would be ambulatory but would require handle insets in the shower stall. Arnold could arrange his transfer from the wheelchair with a transfer board; he had practiced getting into and out of cars. They had a sample kitchen in the first floor of the Institute, as well as a model living room and bedroom and dinette and bath.

The rollaway bed was too low. It should be set on blocks. The passage to the kitchen would be difficult to manage, and Hasenclever should remember that the patient would have difficulty lifting food from the refrigerator shelf. This would not continue. His provisions should be stored—the juice half-poured, the cereal measured, the berries within easy reach—on the bottom shelf. "The juice half-poured?" he questioned them, and they nodded, smiling; we mean half a glass.

Frederick agreed. His guests accepted tea. Only while they measured the kitchen table's height did he start to say that such precaution seemed excessive; Arnold had a life elsewhere, and would leave. But as they left him, bowing, nodding, it came clear to him the stay would be indefinite. He would be his brother's keeper, he told the Koreans. They laughed.

* * *

He was working on a book about Brazil. "Brazil" became a country of the mind. It was a nation ruled by a provisional junta, but the junta did want unity, so there was perfect union—if provisional, if fleeting—in city and in country, for the elderly and youthful, male and female, rich and poor. Such distinctions fell away. The artisan—the man in a wineshop, fresh from his potter's wheel or lathe, come to dispute at noon—might also be a senator or scholar or a priest. Here flourished just such a union of the political, artistic and religious life as Yeats dreamed in *A Vision* might have obtained in Byzance. Yet you can't go back to Constantinople—so Hasenclever's hero sang. We've changed its name. We call it, now, Brazil.

I thought they call it Istanbul, said his antagonist; on my map that's how it's spelled. The traveler flourished his atlas, explaining. Here's the White Sea, Vastation, and here the Despond Slough. Leander swam the Hellespont, using something like the breast stroke, to gain his promised land. O ye of little faith, said Hasenclever's hero; though you close your eyes it is not night, that you fail to hear a waterfall does not render the waterfall silent. The citizens of our republic listen for a music that is not a marching band.

I admire such a passion, said the girl. Indeed, it feels exciting—here she squeezed his hand—but I don't know how to swim yet and don't trust the vasty deep. She ran her fingertips lingeringly down the skin graft on his forearm where the numbers had been burned. Trust it, says the artisan, and pours unwatered wine.

He bought balloons and streamers. He festooned the entrance foyer, as if for a child's birthday, criss-crossing crepe at the center. It formed a canopy. The colors were pastel: yellow, orange, white, and green. He cut the letters WELCOME out of colored paper, draping the sign from the crepe. He bought noisemakers and leis and conical paper hats and Taittinger champagne. He bought more cheese and salami than they could possibly eat.

Hasenclever worked in what he recognized as a frenzy of avoidance, rolling back the rugs. He diced onions and hard-boiled eggs for caviar; he put two bottles of the Taittinger on ice. He cut lemon into wedges, placed the caviar and sour cream in bowls, unwrapped the melba toast. When Arnold arrived he was waiting. The buzzer announced him. He went to the door. An attendant stood behind the wheelchair. They both were wearing raincoats, and Arnold had a lap rug also. Its pattern was tartan, its colors green and black. His cheeks were red. He had been recently shaved. There were indentations at his temples; his lower lip slanted, his eyes seemed half-shut.

"We made it," the attendant said. "I'm Bob."

"You made it," the writer repeated, and Arnold said, "Hello."

The balloons were an embarrassment. The crepe was in the way. He wheeled toward the WELCOME sign and stopped before it, staring.

Bob said he was heading out and Arnie was a trouper and ought to take it slow. You ought to seen him leaving—all those nurses kissing him, that candy he left at the desk. Hasenclever gave him twenty dollars, and Bob straightened his cap and withdrew.

The chandelier was on a rheostat. He increased the light.

"You know what Susan asked me? 'How many

assholes have you met—twenty, twenty-five?' " Arnold's voice was low. "I said I used to meet that many every morning, I must have known ten thousand in my life. And she said, 'Guess what, every one of those assholes can walk.' "

He shook himself out of his coat. Frederick retrieved it. "Are you hungry?"

"No."

"Let's go into the living room," he said.

The carpet that he thought of as too thin was an encumbrance. He steered his brother to the coffee table, angling widely past the couch. Then Arnold transferred to the couch. He rearranged his feet. Arnold was crying, he saw, had been crying since arrival, making sounds in his throat as if a bone were caught there. Hasenclever bent above him, but he shook his head. He fled to get the caviar, the salami and champagne. In the kitchen, too, time telescoped. He saw his parents everywhere. Lilo stood in the kitchen, complaining about the fashion in which Hans cracked eggs; he was spilling the egg yolk over the bowl rim and careless of the shell. "It's good for the digestion," Hans proclaimed. "You don't want too much egg yolk. You use too much salt."

Repeatedly the writer asked himself if he had failed them, how he failed; what was Arnold doing somewhere else and therefore unprotected? Could he have protected him; could it have been helped? A baby passes by a stove and reaches for the kettle and is scarred for life; a second's hesitation at the crossroads and the train keeps coming and the driver dies. Lavinia's children were grown. They sent him birthday cards. Between them, the brothers had married five times. He made his way back to the living room, balancing the tray. Arnold had recovered. A blue balloon by the window inched past the sill, then fell.

Yet Hasenclever had been spared; his life was a constant such sparing. Others died. They crossed the street or crossed a supermarket's second aisle or a line they had been warned against by someone with a cross-hatched scope who lay in a duck blind or tower. They were blown up while waiting for tickets or buying magazines.

His parents' generation died in Bergen-Belsen or Dachau. They died in Auschwitz and Sachsenhausen and Munich and Berlin. His generation died of myocardial infarction or lung cancer or on New Year's Eve in Saugatuck and Valentine's Day in Nashville, skidding; they died behind the wheels of Corvairs, Rivieras, Datsuns, convertibles, jeeps. They died by their own hands. They placed their heads in ovens or jumped at an onrushing subway train or jumped from the Golden Gate Bridge. They died by misadventure with the toaster; they crashed in airplanes and buses and Boston Whalers and on the jetty at low tide. They used cyanide carelessly, attempting to fumigate bees. They misused the shotgun or leaf mulcher or linseed oil or heroin or ladder or the station wagon on ice.

Meyer Rosen joined the party. He approved of the champagne. Hasenclever opened the champagne, not popping the cork but releasing it. Then he poured. "Go with God," said Rosen. "Didn't I tell you to travel? You need a dictionary, though. *'Entschuldigen Sie mich, mein Herr, wie kommt man zum Post'*? Excuse me, sir, where is the post office?" Ginger was doing the rhumba, or perhaps the tango; he could not be certain, since she practiced in the hall.

Their mother brought a dish of mussels with a separate bowl for broth; the broth had parsley floating in it, and a fleck of parsley appeared on her thumbnail. He remembered how she diced the scallions and the garlic and the parsley, the feel of the cutting board afterward sluiced down with lemon, the buttery brine in their cups. He could taste and see and feel and smell and even hear them; they were a tactile presence, a part of him inalienably, the marrow of his bone and pith of his eyebrow and muscle, ligature, and teeth.

EVERYTHING

The long, looping syntax of things, the way they wind together then unwind, the feel of the light in your mouth, the sound you make while touching it, the slant of the sunshine precisely the angle it arrived at yesterday, only not *now,* not through the same set of trees or at the equivalent instant, not this minute of the watch he fails to wear—yet keeping watch—not needing radium strapped to a wrist, the reminder (as if anyone needed reminding how time itself is circular and deadly not least because dull, the measure of man's metronomic regularity—this man's, at any rate, who soon enough would be patted and fed and prepared) of our dutiful segmenting declension, the habit of a hierarchy, compassed degrees: fifty-nine to sixty, twelve subordinate to one—and the sun where it was once and would be routinely, as if fifty-nine and sixty are and should be parallel, as if it matters, is of consequence, the sun and dial and generation rising but to fall, his brothers dead or dying or coopted or corrupt, his actual cousin doing just fine, thank you, a C.P.A. south of Glens Falls; it's not what we'd planned for, this split-level, says Georgy—Martin cannot help it, thinks of him as Georgy still, would introduce him even now as Georgy, even at seventy-eight, if ever they might meet once more or furnish introductions—but Georgy worked for General Electric in Fort Edward, and retired there, and the likelihood of such a meeting now again is slim; it's not so bad, he used to say, good benefits, time off for good behavior, he liked to go hunting and sailing, they have this camp on Lake George (and Bindy, George's second wife, never failed to make a joke of it, a point that she points out by laughing, lifting her arms, her chin, the single dimple on her right cheek creasing, George bought this place before we married so they named the lake here after him, they're sweet to put it on the map and put up all those signposts so even after too many Manhattans we can't lose our way. How many, he asked, is too many; she lifted her hands to him then, two, six, who's counting, you can find us in the dark), and long ago he, Martin, had done so and sat on the rock outcrop while his cousin snored within, and watched the slate-gray water beneath its mist-sleeve, rising, thinking how the Indians had split that surface earlier, deer swimming in front of them, startled, the inlet not too wide to ford—imagining what deer must feel, wet panic, the waterlogged forelegs unable to leap, the long, snouting hollow birch behind it implacably, hissing, no camouflage in water where your head remains outstretched like his own above the rocker pillow, pinioned, and then the bow-and-hatchet man, the shadow, the uplifted arm, the stench of mortality nearing—he shut his eyes and saw not his housekeeper but Bindy, pulling her negligee over her knees, crossing her hands there, smoking, flicking the ash at the water, asking him is something wrong, is there something we or anyone can do?

He told her, or tries to, about regularity, our brothers corrupted as three-day drowned game: you can make the same turn ninety times, coming out of the same driveway; you could make it nine hundred, nine thousand times, can make it till the brake pads fail while sun slants through the frost rime that you failed to bother wiping, till the road goes slick and a pickup with a driver fiddling with the radio, his right hand at the dial and left hand just touching the wheel, his sleep this past night troubled, his daughter not back until three (and though he'd waited in the living room, watching football from the coast, nodding off, dozing with the long day done and what the hell's the point, it's now or later, sooner or never, giving her time and rope and falling asleep at the two-minute break, waking as she tiptoed past, the screen a blue haze only, ready to tell her the things that she does, the way she worries him, her mother too—yet something in the way she walks, some aspect of her high-hipped gait, the care she takes to let him sleep, the way she pushes the knob in gently, and the blue glare contracting till blank, the streetlamp light in her disarrayed hair, some attribute of beauty that he has not seen in her before and knows will not remain, will tarnish from this newly minted precious thing, this coinage called womanhood—something of that stayed his hand and held his tongue and kept him in the armchair while she tiptoed up the stairs), and therefore he broods now, dialing, inattentive, and does not notice the car nosing out, the intersection that had been a driveway entrance only, threatless, abandoned or at least unoccupied, the way what was habitual now shifts. And if that is the case for a driveway, how much more true of highways and the crossroads of a nation, the inside lane on I-80 by Moline when diesel rigs explode—the air is wet, he drops his head as if to dive, as if the wind were liquid, he can hear as clearly as if clicking stones across that inlet, as if Bindy spelled it out, I'm dying of boredom, of your good cousin, of life beside that snuffling hulk and Hudson Falls and Glens Falls and Fort Edward and the Library Committee, stripping with a single gesture, arms out, and diving splay-footed into the lake, the length of her swirling, submerged; I dare you, Bindy offers, what's wrong with it anyhow, why not, he's sleeping, and anyhow he'll never know, and anyhow he wouldn't mind, and what did you come here for otherwise, why?—the start of the visit, the knee raised, the instep, the startled beginning again.

"Martin, it's too cold out here."

He straightened.

"You have to come in."

He blinked. He licked his teeth—the uppers, left to right.

"They'll be coming for the photographs in half an hour. That nice man from the interview. You were sleeping. You messed up your hair."

Mrs. Thompson's voice, he thought, might have been gentle once. Now it sounded like mosquitoes in his ear.

"We've got to get you ready. We'd better come in from the porch."

Is there a word, he asked himself, for many mosquitoes at the same time? Are they a cluster, gaggle, pride; would mosquitoes be a swarm?

"Up we go now, Martin. Easy does it. Up."

Strange, he thought, that she should call him Martin whereas he, her employer, her elder, spoke of her as Mrs. Thompson—did not think of her as Kate. She had been his housekeeper for eleven years.

"*That's* better. In we go."

The maple leaves cascaded where he watched. There had been an early snow. The birch were finished, and the beech, and the oak tree at the driveway's edge stood sere and bare and brown. He must remember, later, to check the variorum on "bare ruin'd choirs"; what did "choirs" mean, and what sort of church allowed birds? "Where late the sweet birds sang," made sense, but "choirs" was a puzzle, music merely; he'd puzzle it out.

And she was right, his chittering chorus, his shrew: it had been growing cold. He lifted his arms, rolled his neck. She collected his blanket and mug. She steered him to the door. The newel-post and railings needed paint. His rocker, weightless, abandoned, rocked. "What time is it?" he asked.

"Three-thirty. Almost four. That nice young man's coming at four."

If it had been a woman, she would have been less eager—more protective, more solicitous, more watchful of his privacy. If it had been a pretty woman—and

most journalists have flair, at least, and television women
have a scrubbed gleam about them, and the young girls
writing now are not, he knows, uneager—then heaven
help the visitor. Mrs. Thompson would be dusting. Mrs.
Thompson would be fluffing up the pillows and making
significant noises and pointing to her watch. The last
one, she'd thrown out. The girl had brought all Martin's books for him to sign—a selection anyway, a baker's goodly dozen—and she told him they were
wonderful and meant everything to her, and always had,
and sat beside him on the couch with no bra and pert
little nipples and so much perfume he had sneezed, her
red hair flicking his shoulder as he bent to write. "You're
cold," said Mrs. Thompson. "You must be tired, Martin. Maybe we can send them with suitable inscriptions
when he's feeling better."

"But I drove here all the way from Portsmouth,"
said the girl.

"Then you can drive right back. Just leave me your
address and postage."

"I'm all right now," he said. "I'm fine. Why don't
you bring us a drink?"

Sniffing, she had gone to make the tea, and he had
had ten minutes and reached for the redhead and she
drew back from him, shocked—pretending shock, he
was certain, playing hard to get, playing for time. "We
don't have much of it," he said, and fell on her bare
legs, and squeezed. He was a strong man still, and heavy,
and she lay beneath him, rigid, while he told her of
King David and Abishag the Shunammite and how the
old king needed warming and what he would require.
"Don't," she said. "Please don't." That was one of the
things he required, the wriggling protestation, the heart

beating under his fist, and it would have worked, was working, her hair in his right hand, her knee at his left, when Mrs. Thompson came back in—to ask, she told him later, if their guest took milk and sugar—and cried, "Oh no, oh not again," and the girl jackknifed beneath him and stood and that was that. Mrs. Thompson had bundled her out. Then she had bundled him up. Then she had bundled him into the daybed in the library. Prepositions are as various as women, he had written, their minute alterations of language—"up, out, into, in, around"—their manipulative meaning like the skeined tune and tone of the skin.

Martin Peterson, the novelist, had been "promising" and then was "accomplished" and now was "distinguished"; this year marked half a century since his first book appeared. There were citations, celebrations, a *Festchrift* from his publisher, a renewed campaign to win the Nobel Prize. It wasn't his idea. He didn't have much hope. He had earned what he won and given good weight and been translated into more languages—he lost count at seventeen—than a normal man might speak. Once, in Singapore, he had taken an airport taxi and complimented the driver on his excellent command of English. "I speak nineteen languages," the driver had announced. He remarked this without undue pride. It turned out he spoke English and eighteen Malay dialects; inflection is what matters, the taxi driver said.

Martin and his third wife stayed in the Raffles Hotel. The manager received them. He was waiting on the steps. There are too few serious people these days, he said; the businessmen all stay in something

recent, something modern; they have not even heard
of Somerset Maugham and don't even know why
they should. We are honored that you're with us, sir,
he said.

He had traveled with Margit, the year before she
left. She had had enough, she said, of his needy preen-
ing; she needed a life of her own. She wanted to have
children with a husband, not a husband too arrested to
have children in his life. "Your phrases turn less nicely
than your ankles," he had said. "You should save your
mouth for what it's good at." But that evening, in the
Raffles, she was pure compliance. He could remember
the hooded look she gave him as she stepped into the
shower long after he forgot the details of divorce; he
could remember the small of her back, but not the name
of the lawyer or who settled for what; he remembered
the rum and the fish and the long-fluked fan and palm
trees in the courtyard and the pool. She had been more
beautiful than anyone, but her small hands were not
beautiful; he rinsed them free of soap.

And it was like this often now, a half-remembered
turn of phrase, the echo of another's work he thought
of as his own—the detail that, enlarging, fills the frame.
He remembered someone's teeth and someone else's
laughter, this one's habit of clearing his throat, that
necklace on a bureau—its rumpled glinting, the purple
scarf, the gold watch and mother-of-pearl cuff links from
his father, the fragment from the Greek anthology he
used as an epigraph once. " 'In my nineteenth year,' "
he recited, " 'the darkness drew me down. And ah the
sweet sun!' "

Then there was the epitaph for a sailor lost at sea.
" 'This gravestone lies if it says that it marks the place

of my burial.' " That was all. That was it in its entirety. He remembered, for instance, a diner—the blue Formica counter, the white coffee mug and sugar doughnut and the napkin dispenser and ashtray and saltshaker in a perfect parallelogram when he rearranged the mug—remembered how the waitress had strawberry marks on her forearm, how she knew the customer beside him and was saying, "What I think is, if she doesn't want to rollerskate that's fine; why pay for all them lessons and them broken teeth, why make her do something she's too scared to do?"—remembered how the man at his right smiled, nodding, dipping his cruller in milk—but could not for the life of him imagine why he had gone to the diner or what he was doing there or when.

Bindy would be dead perhaps and certainly not swimming. George would weigh two hundred pounds. He had used them in his book about the love affair with that Peruvian who married someone else and rented out canoes. While Mrs. Thompson readied him—the washcloth at his neck, his mouth, the brush, the shirt button, the cuffs—he remembered his heart's darling, the lilt of her laughter, the falling of her arms.

At four o'clock the car arrived. He could hear it in the driveway, then the engine closing down. The boy had sandy hair. He wore blue jeans and a leather vest and a blue shirt with white collar—like a stockbroker slumming or a doctor on vacation. Hauling stiff black boxes and cameras and shoulder bags and a tripod, he made several trips from the car. Martin watched this from the couch. He moved confidently, easily; his boots were cowboy boots. He was whistling, adept at the work. Mrs. Thompson, too, enjoyed it; she held the screen door open while he carried in the lights.

Then she introduced him. "Martin, you remember Peter."

"No."

The boy advanced. "It's good to see you, sir." He held out his hand.

"We've met?"

"Last Thursday, sir, remember? And you invited me back."

"I don't remember. No."

"Well anyway, I'm here," the boy said breezily, and started connecting the lights.

"What's he here for?" Martin asked.

" 'The usual.' To bother you. That's what you said last week."

Mrs. Thompson giggled. "I told you he has brass. He asked me if you want to look like Frost or Hemingway this time. He says he can do either."

"Get me a podium," the writer said. "Give me a president first."

"Excuse me, sir?" said Peter—rolling the hooked rug away, setting the tripod in place.

"Get me a podium, and then I'll look like Frost." It came to him, however, that the boy would have worn diapers at the Kennedy inaugural—or maybe was not even born. "All right." He glared at Mrs. Thompson where she held the electrical cord. "How long does this vaudeville take?"

"It's important, Martin. It's the cover photograph."

"One word is worth a thousand pictures. You know I say that, always." He never had said this before. He was feeling ornery, did not like how his housekeeper had organized the session, how she and the boy were in league.

"I couldn't agree with you more." The boy was being charming. "I did read your trilogy, sir, as you suggested last Thursday. It's wonderful. I loved it."

He doubted this. "What was their name?"

"Sir?"

"The woman in the second book—the one who gets pregnant—what's she called?"

"Ariel, of course," said Mrs. Thompson. "Everyone knows that."

"He didn't."

"Ariel," the boy said. "I love what you did with her. Smile."

So then they settled into what he did know and could do, and Martin sat there smiling and then serious, looking straight ahead, then left, then right, then down and at his books. He allowed himself to drift. The way the light falls glancingly across an upraised palm, his father's love of marmalade, the thick-cut bitter taste of it on toast, wisteria by the garage, systole and diastole, this improbable adherence to the surface of the earth, so that falling one falls down and dying by water drifts up; his mother's ring embedded in the flesh behind the knuckle, her tennis racket in its press, his dream of Margit early on, the way she would enfold him, so passionate, so pleasing, the smell of brie on biscuits and the taste of shrimp—we do not leave this easily, not cease the circuit's spasm, the pain at the knee when one kneels, the tang of apples in the autumn, woodsmoke, ceremony, hillocks, the horn, the split-leaf maple flaming, dog snuffling at a groundhog's hole, that gathering tightness prior to sex. He shut his eyes, then opened them. The shuddering release, the phone left unanswered, and doorbell, the taste of prosciutto on melon, rain on a tent flap, the first sight of the Parthenon, or Stonehenge, or the World Trade Center, the second subject of the first movement of the Schubert Quintet in C major—the feel of her hand in his, gripping, convulsive, her bed a harbor where he beached: he blinked. There are bills to pay and objects to acquire and the long diurnal round of meals and sleep and argument and manners and disease; there is music, oxygen, barbed and chicken wire. What seemed unimportant becomes important, critical; he would rectify the slave trade, violated borders and dispossessed peoples and forced labor camps and drug addiction and penury and sickness and starvation in the four dark corners of the earth.

"I'm afraid he's not himself. I told you he gets tired."

"Fifteen more minutes," said Peter. "That's all I need." He changed film.

"Are you awake?" she asked. Martin made no answer. Mrs. Thompson neared him, looming. "Would you like tea?"

He let his mouth hang down.

"Since the operation," she confided. "He just hasn't been himself."

"How long ago was that?" asked the photographer. He was back behind the tripod. He was adjusting the lights.

"It's not the operation, really. That was a success. It's what happened to him afterward."

"What happened," Martin said, "is he allowed his

housekeeper to talk too much. Yes, tea."

She colored; she patted her hair. She made for the kitchen, retreating.

"I did read those novels," Peter said. "Her husband's name was Sam. Her sister was called Marjorie. You dedicated them to someone called Yvonne."

"Yvonne." That had been his first wife. She died, he learned, last month. She came to Martin nightly and he covered her with kisses: he woke rigid, drenched in sweat. The smell of her stayed on his hands. He hesitated to wash. He needed her far more than he had recognized, or told her, more than he had known. This lack of knowledge on her part tormented him. He told her nightly, as she faded, while he woke. She rose from the pillow. Her arms were damp, her ribs pronounced. He needed her to scold him for survival. She would be a crone, she had warned him, one of those women with no extra flesh and breakable needle-point bones. What are needle-point bones? he would ask—incurious, needing only to keep her in conversation. Her hand had been translucent, lifting.

He pictured her in Mexico and Point Barrow and Versailles; she had told him of these places and the way they made her feel. He followed her. He admired her street slang in Cuernavaca, the brilliant glance of her big-irised eyes. She squeezed herself against him while he slept. She could describe the ice rime on a field of snow at Christmas, or the "honey bucket" they used for plumbing in Alaska. She returned. Always she appeared before him, legs scissoring his, an intervening presence where he walked. She wanted competence, space for herself; she wanted the vistas of Point Barrow in midwinter, with only a seal at the edge of her

vision and maybe one conical cloud. She could last forever on one box of crackers and a pound of tea; she
needed him, wanting him tonguing her collarbone and
there, darling, there in the small of my back.

He had picked a four-leaf clover for her by the
barn. He bent and, in a single motion, collected and
offered it up. She had never found a four-leaf clover
and was gratified. A white-tailed deer leaped past them,
bounding for the tamaracks. "It's perfect," said Yvonne.
Once when they were thirsty on the beach a man approached them, saying, "I've got a headache. I shouldn't
drink this. Here"—and offered them a bottle of white
wine. Once while they were making love a bee settled
on her arching neck; by the time he reached to brush
it off, she had been stung. He reconstructed that. Of
such stuff were his memories made.

By the time the tea would cool sufficiently to drink,
she had arrived. He could not keep her out. Yvonne
lay on the beach or stood by the car or studied a cluster of leaves. Her shadow fell across the picket fence.
She inhabited the bathroom mirror or the faucet or the
butter dish; she left her fingerprints. He wanted to
powder the room. There was a dust that fingerprint
experts used, and usage would show everywhere; there
would be thumbprints on the walls and floors and cab-
inets and towels. Her palm would be emblazoned on
the icebox door. It adhered to his knee and arm and
shoulders. Her flesh had flaked minutely and drifted by
the sink.

"What I like about it," Peter said, "is how you make
them history. Historical convergence is what I noticed
there."

He roused. He licked his teeth.

"That's what you were saying, right? In the interview, I mean, last Thursday. About the way the past gets present, since the present is 'no country for old men.' And if I understand you, that's why we're always young. How we stay in touch with history."

"Something like that," Martin said.

"What you said was—I checked the transcript—'It doesn't help the body but it mightily comforts the mind.' "

Mrs. Thompson brought them tea. "Are we finished?"—he turned toward her, querulous. "How long does this go on?"

"Do you need?"—she tilted her head to the hall.

"Yes."

"Excuse us," she told Peter. "We're off to the little boys' room."

He remembered going with his sisters and his father for the Christmas tree. They would make a journey of it, jostling for position; they would drape a dropcloth in the open flatbed of the truck. "You want that tree to rest easy, don't you?" their father would ask. "You wouldn't want it to scratch." He and his sisters would nod. They could have cut a tree behind the house or from the fence line by the overpass—but they went every year to Ned Fellers's farm.

Ned Fellers knew the family, he liked to say, since back before the Flood. He had a yellow moustache. His hair was white, and what colored his moustache was nicotine; his teeth were brown. He had difficulty seeing when they pulled into the driveway. Dogs surrounded them. He would fumble with the door latch, then step into the mild December air as if it were true winter, shivery, wearing gloves; he carried a hatchet and saws. Ned would invite them in for tea, but he and his sisters would fidget so their father said, maybe later when we've cut the thing, all right? "I'll put the kettle on," said Ned. "You don't want to keep them waiting."

Then they would trek to the ridge. It was important not to spot the tree too soon. He never could distinguish between Scotch and white pine, Fletcher fir or Douglas or balsam or spruce. Fellers planted stands of each, and their father would always say, well, what do we want this tree to be, what kind this year, how big? In the corner of his eye Martin saw the one he wanted, knowing by its contour just how perfectly the tree would fit, how the others would agree, would say his choice was beautiful, this is the perfect one. Sometimes, however, the perfect one would prove on closer scrutiny to have an imperfection—a bend in the trunk, a clutch of missing branches where it had been crowded by the next pine in the row.

At some point while they wandered their father would say, this is far enough in, we don't want to drag it a mile. Then they would double back, assessing and discussing and finally determining—at that point where impatience took over, where desire overmastered caution—which tree to cut. They would take turns with the saw. They each could take five strokes. He had been the youngest, and therefore he went first. Their father took the original cut, establishing the point where Martin continued, and the angle, and he would guide his hand.

When the season was over they took out the tree. This too was ritual. There would be days after New

Year's when the needles fell in clusters to the carpet
underneath, and their mother said, we don't want to
burn down the house. Wouldn't you say, Martin, it's
getting to be time? At length he would agree. He and
his sisters would dismantle all they'd hung judiciously,
taking hours to arrange: the balls, the ornaments, the
popcorn and gingerbread men. Their father cut the
strings with which he had steadied the tree. It tilted.
They carried it out of the house.

Birds eat the dying needles, Ned Fellers had explained: you stand a pine tree in the snow and if there's
nothing else around a sparrow can live off the sap. It's
nice to know a tree keeps being useful once it's cut.
Martin picked off what tinsel he could. They carried it
toward the brush pile by the fence.

Then, in the weak slanting light, the lawn came
alive with silver—strands of tinsel that blew free. They
lodged in the flagstone paving. They worked their way
to the fence. They lifted in the breeze and winked at
him, as if the whole garden were precious, dew lasting
all the bright day. His mother told him to pick up that
trash, but he left the tinsel alone.

What he meant to tell the boy was not convergence, *confluence,* was how time is a trickle that feels
like a river to swimmers, and then it trickles out. Man
cannot step in the same stream twice. Except he, Martin, was doing just that, was chewing the past like a
cud. While Peter packed and was dismissed and said
he'd send the proofs along, or maybe bring them
by if Mr. Peterson felt up to it, he tried to formulate a
phrase about the son as father, Peter and Peterson,
the way they mirrored each other, child and man,

how orthograph and autograph and author graphically
linked.

But it made no sense, made nonsense, and he was
too tired. He wanted his dinner in peace. This was the
time of day he loved, the lengthening shadows, the low
brilliant light. Mrs. Thompson would turn on the television news. They were blowing up the tankers in the
Gulf. They were hoping that prosperity would trickle
down. They were knaves and fools in Washington, and
all the more lamentable for meaning what they said.

It came to Martin, suddenly, there had been pi-
geons in Hagia Sofia; they roosted in the eaves and
swooped and ululated and shat with impunity there. So
that kind of church did host birds. Those particular bare
ruined choirs made a museum now. Margit had worn
her slate-blue suit, and they stayed in the Pera Palas.
He remembered the barman—brown, compact, wiping
the counter carefully—saying with great satisfaction,
"Brandy, I have." Their shared history, he saw, could
be plotted by hotels—the grand relics of the grander
past where Martin felt at home. She gripped the bed-
post rattlingly and rose on her knees in the bed. They
had reached Istanbul the night before some sacred feast,
and streets were clogged with sheep. All night he heard
the sounds of bleating, the muezzin at his window. In
the morning there had been no sheep, and the gutters
ran with blood.

The housekeeper brought him his scotch. She had
added water, and no ice. "He's a pleasant fellow," he
said to Mrs. Thompson, placatory. "You were right."
There were floaters in his eyes. The window framed a
photograph. The meadow appeared to sprout snow. He
thought of those two-dollar paperweights you shake to

make a squall. A hut on a hillside would find itself buried, a green tree go white. The deer would look like reindeer till the flakes settled again. Yet the shift in seasons altered nothing else; the glass would not grow cold as it registered winter, the hunter did not shiver or take off his coat with the thaw. Such systems were protected, a synthetic storm.

Then the telephone began. They called about the prize—the Pulitzer? the National Book Critics Circle?—and wanted to know his opinion of this year's recipient. "Never heard of it," he said. "But Mr. Peterson," they protested, "you're in the jacket copy. You're credited with having sponsored this novel when nobody would publish it."

"Nonsense."

"So you feel justice has been served?"

"Don't quote me," Martin said.

"You *don't* feel justice has been served?"

"*Servus.*" He hung up.

They called about the reading in his honor at the Library of Congress, and if he could attend. Mrs. Thompson told them he would try. The documentary about him was being shown that Saturday; they called for his opinion. He told them he was pleased, extremely pleased; in every particular, really, it improved on the original. The house they showed, for instance, was so much more appropriate than the one he had really been born in. He loved it all, them all.

Mrs. Thompson brought his dinner. She was a jolly old soul. He tasted what she set before him, but it had no taste. He invited her to join him. She would eat no lean. She used remote control to turn on the

TV. There were girls in bikinis, on water skis, and a ship's captain with gold braid on his uniform. There were happy couples promenading, and a black man with a trumpet.

"What are we eating?" he asked.

"Grilled cheese," she said. "And tuna."

"Is there celery?"

"Pickles."

A blonde, glistening with the pleasure of a swim, emerged to smile at the new member of the crew. She shook her hair, exuding packaged animality. Then there was an advertisement for Maxipads, and one for cereal, and one that took him some time to decipher: a brunette looking out of a window, getting dressed, descending to a car which snouted up into the alley where she lived. Men stared at her, and then the driver glided off, and Martin asked, "What are we watching?"

"Nothing. An advertisement."

"Tomorrow I'm planning to work."

She looked at him.

"I don't suppose you take dictation."

"No."

"What was her name—the one who did? The one who took dictation?"

"Irene. She'll be here tomorrow, Martin. Tomorrow's the morning she comes."

"That's good." He ate a pickle. "That'll be fine."

"You have a pile of mail."

"I'm writing tomorrow. Not letters." He shifted his potato chips. He did not want them near the pickle juice.

"Your women," Mrs. Thompson said. "The ones who take such care of you, who always have—Irene,

for instance. You forgot she takes dictation." She pressed
a button; the TV went blank.

"I wouldn't forget *you*."

She sniffed. "And there's the night nurse coming
soon. Mrs. Mirabelli."

He was the messenger again, the emissary, the one
with the white flag. "It's only that I want to work."

"Go right ahead," she said. "Don't let me interrupt
you. I'll finish the dishes. You work."

So then he settled down to write, the language
inching up the shale like water in a tidal pool, filling
slowly where he sat, the voice in the well of the throat,
the story of his second wife, the story of apprentice-
ship, the way she hurtled home from market, so gladly,
so dark-eyed, her arms full of fruit—the hard first spate
of study, night classes, the old men telling stories, the
cordwood he cut (and remembered walking, years ago,
past men with retrievers and hunting gear. They were
drinking by a duck-blind, wearing orange caps. There
were half a dozen of them, bearded, overweight. One
of them wore waders. He hailed Martin, asking, "Hey
buddy, which way's town?" Another said, "What town
is it?" as if this were a joke. They laughed and slapped
each other's backs. They burbled hilariously, repeating,
"You call that a *town*?" Teal beat overhead. They
wheeled and shot and stumbled, while the dogs tore in
circles. He continued, feeling what he felt again now:
himself the target, leaving . . .), then sound enlarging
into shape, a paragraph, a page, a chapter, library, Al-
exandria in flames—contending, however, contending
with water. He dove.

The scotch was unblended, Glenlivet. He swallowed cautiously, sipping. But ah, the sudden soaring lilt of it, those words by which he lived, the astonishing regalia of his titles on the shelf: and how had he come to this pass? There had been some injury, some consequential rupture, some way in which he lost what he had worked so long to find—the sheaf of script with which he started in his nineteenth year, the notebooks, the letters, the light on the page that the pond at midday, refracting, might cast, and endurance—his mother, his father, the pattering trill of gossip, rain on the windows on Sunday, the decanters on the sideboard and the lilac by the door, his wives, his friends and professors and sisters and critics and associates and place of my burial and editor at Scribner's, all death-undone, so many, their strange eventful history, the raindrop that falls farthest on the pane . . .

What was difficult to tell was if he dreamed or wrote them, those men and women huddled in the corners of the room. He had been in such rooms, often. He was unimpressed. He had described them enough. They edged toward the canapes and eyed each other joylessly and spoke of book contracts and paperback sales and foreign sales and auction floors, the ways of the publishing world. It had been his trade. He made a living from books. But it was strange to Martin still that art should be a business, that there was profit in it as well as certain loss. The ballyhoo, the overpraise, the cultivated jockeying, venality, the fool's gold blurbed as real—or, conversely, true talent ignored—this subsided near him, lately, and went dim. There was a stuffed polar bear in the Explorers Club. There was a boy on the porch. He could not hear what they were saying—who was in, who out, who promoted, who bypassed,

who wielded the tin gavel in which parliament of fowls.
He did not try to hear. "The parliament," for instance:
had he written that, or meant to; was it a short story
or the tipped cap to Chaucer—the bard he'd named his
Newfoundland in honor of, beloved, one hundred fifty
pounds of panting slavish sweetness, the noble black
head, the pink tongue? So when he thought of Chaucer
now he thought not so much of pilgrimage or Canter-
bury as a pet. He was writing his memoirs. He completed the third volume while they lounged about the
pool.

Martin had discomfort but no pain. He shifted in
his seat. The light was fading, westerly; he watched.
The point of entry is the center of a circle. The circles
are concentric, and at the pond's perimeter they double back, contracting.

"Have we been being gloomy?"

"No."

"Your nose." She gave him her handkerchief. He
used it. "That's better."

"How are your children?" He lifted his head.
"They'll be coming east for Christmas, am I right?"

"Why, yes, they will." She studied him. He would
not cry. "How nice of you to remember."

"And little Kate? The youngest? Jane's daughter,
isn't it?"

"She's wonderful." Now Mrs. Thompson grew expansive. "She's a hellion, that one. She whistles through
her teeth. She's got her front teeth missing, and she
points her finger there and gives me this enormous smile
and says, 'Gammer, my gap!' "

He shook his head to clear it. "I want to go back
to the porch."

She checked her watch. They compromised. "Just for a little?"

"A little."

"Don't you love the weather, though? Don't you wish it was always like this?"

"I do," he admitted. She opened the door. She helped him through. The rocker had his blanket. "I'll sit here just a little."

"Tomorrow we do letters," Mrs. Thompson said.

Correspondence: he mocked it, it bored him, was boring, was pat, no more than a comes-around goes-around tag line remaining with him nevertheless to come around and go around and fail to fade, no matter how he sat quiescent, how the swallows flashed fluttering by, and now the bats—recurrence: this momentary certainty that everything suspended falls, that motion accretes inertia, inertia motion, and all things inflated collapse—from the balloon, the tire, from the bullfrog's calling, the rubbery pneumatic flesh of its throat distended to croak, then convulsing, *glut glut,* from the way his own flesh grew tumescent, emitted, collapsed, from the way the economy inflated, the black band of blood pressure circling an arm—everything examples it, the trees are an instruction, rain, the hospital bill, the credit system, the heat engendered by decay, and everything is circular that once argued causality, the arc, the sudden shattering (that time he was thrown from a horse, that time he missed the second step on the staircase descended habitually, these months, that time the maroon Dodge pickup with the tailgate rusted out, the right front fender painted green, boxing gloves slung from its mirror, swerved to avoid him and skidded and went down the embankment by the driveway where he'd braked; when he got out and went to help and clambered down the frozen slope he head Sinatra crooning "Autumn in New York" on the truck radio; it's nothing, the man said, my daughter, that sumbitch, the ice, just give me a hand with this winch—the jolt or rearrangement, Bindy near him at a party, presenting cheese, whispering, how could you do it, how, why to me, why last night you bastard, what did you mean?— the way the veil of what we call propriety is rendered transparent by need, the surface of the pond by trout, the air by dum-dum bullets, so when will I see you? I need to discuss it, we have to . . .), remembering that, time he waited on the tree stand three days into the season and a man and woman walked into the clearing underneath, holding hands, he dark-haired, she blond, she wearing leather boots and silver fur and with no coy preliminary or any of the actions of seduction leaned against a maple trunk and raised her coat and raised the dress while her lover dropped his pants, she wearing nothing underneath, he jockey shorts, then entered her, her long legs taut, the two of them absorbed beneath him, not looking up, not around, not saying anything while Martin watched with what even then he recognized as an aroused dispassion this buck and mating shudder and slap of flesh on flesh, all of it so quickly done that he barely saw what he was seeing before they straightened, steadied each other, replaced their clothing with a negligent attentiveness and, holding hands, walked off; it is diversion, all of it, a way to pass the time, to move from fifty-nine to sixty, twelve to one, not serious the looping components of subject and object, clause upon clause—and if even such diversion might depend or signify, might produce a child or marriage or gonorrhea or divorce, her ass as pert beneath him as the white-tailed deer, retreating (the silver box, the apple tree, the trusty oak, *sans* teeth, the days of courting . . .), then why not break the pattern, smile at this night nurse who's taking his pulse, Mrs. Thompson departing, materialized, and what he did not manage but might again, again.